"Thank you for y

Savannah's lips were s
better than this particular slice of humble pie, but
she got the words out.

He shook his head. "The kids can help you inside.
If you need anything—not that I'm assuming you
will—" he held up his hands "—but if you do,
holler."

He strode across the grass, leaving Savannah staring
after him. His walk was powerful, his upper body
swaying slightly, his arms swinging. Everything
about Elias Parker spoke of hard work and
capability.

But he wasn't to be trusted. No man was. Elias
offered help one moment, but in the next, let her
know he was certain she would fail. Girard had
asked her to marry him, but at the last moment, he'd
fled rather than go through with the wedding.

Even her father wasn't reliable, never home for
more than a week at a time, always traveling, always
putting business first.

No, a woman shouldn't put her trust in a man. She
was better off on her own.

It might be lonely, but it was better than a broken
heart.

Erica Vetsch is a transplanted Kansan now residing in Minnesota. She loves history and romance and is blessed to be able to combine the two by writing historical romances. Whenever she's not immersed in fictional worlds, she's the company bookkeeper for the family lumber business, mother of two, wife to a man who is her total opposite and soul mate, and an avid museum patron.

Books by Erica Vetsch

Love Inspired Historical

ERICA VETSCH

His Prairie Sweetheart

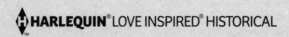
HARLEQUIN® LOVE INSPIRED® HISTORICAL

Recycling programs for this product may not exist in your area.

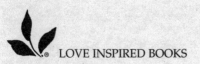

LOVE INSPIRED BOOKS

ISBN-13: 978-0-373-28361-3

His Prairie Sweetheart

www.Harlequin.com

Printed in U.S.A.

Be merciful to me, O God, be merciful to me,
for in You my soul takes refuge;
in the shadow of Your wings I will take refuge,
till the storms of destruction pass by.
—*Psalms* 57:1

Many thanks to Berit Oviatt and Jody Rosedahl for help with the Norwegian translations (any mistakes are solely mine), to Allie Pleiter, harpist extraordinaire, for help with the care and feeding of harps, and to my husband, Peter, for taking me to Vesterheim to research Norwegians in America.

Chapter One

Raleigh, North Carolina
August 1887

The humiliation. That's what the gossips of Raleigh were calling it. Rehashing it with delighted horror in the tearooms and front parlors of the city.

Savannah Cox kept her chin level and marched down the church steps, careful to slant her parasol to keep the August sun off her face…and if she was honest, to block out the looks. She put on her most remote expression, a reflection of the cold numbness that surrounded her broken heart. Agony at the core, a shell of ice around the pain, and proper manners covering all.

After all, a lady's pain was like her petticoat; she must never let it show.

Three weeks ago she'd ascended these same steps arrayed in bridal white, eager and naive, surrounded by bridesmaids and anticipation. Shame squeezed tighter than her corset. Would it always hurt this much? Would she forever walk in the ignominy of being a jilted bride?

Perhaps, but she wouldn't do her walking here.

Savannah climbed into the family carriage, ignoring

her younger sisters' chatter. Aunt Georgette patted her neck and temples with a lace hankie. "Poor Savannah. You're being so brave. I'm just glad your dear mother isn't here to see…" She tapered off with more fluttering and patting.

Next to Aunt Georgette her sister, Aunt Carolina— broad, mannish and practical to her marrow—crossed her arms. "Nonsense, Georgette. Think for one moment what you're saying. You're glad Bettina is dead? Savannah will survive this, and the sooner everyone stops feeling sorry for her, the sooner things can return to normal. I, for one, think she made an expedient escape. If Girard Brandeis was so callow as to bow out at the eleventh hour without so much as an explanation, then he doesn't deserve our Savannah. Now, let's talk about something else."

Savannah stiffened. This was her chance. She'd dreaded introducing the subject, but she was running out of time. Inhaling a breath for bravery, she blurted out, "I wanted you all to know I've accepted a teaching position in Minnesota, and I'm leaving Raleigh the day after tomorrow."

Her sisters stopped nattering, Aunt Georgette dropped her hankie and a spark of something—was it admiration?—lit Aunt Carolina's eyes.

The coach lurched as the driver slapped the lines and the horses took off, harness jingling, wheels whirring.

"You've what?" Aunt Georgette found her voice first.

Savannah spoke with more conviction than she felt. "I said I will be teaching school this fall. In Minnesota. I leave on Tuesday."

Aunt Georgette blinked, and her face crumpled. "This is tragic. Think of the scandal. Savannah Cox, of the Raleigh Coxes, running off into the night to nurse her broken heart. Whatever will I say at the garden club, or the Aid Society, or at Priscilla Guthrie's soiree next Friday?"

"I imagine," Aunt Carolina drawled, "you'll say whatever gains you the most attention, and that you'll say it dramatically and with great frequency. Now sit back and be quiet. I suggest we wait until we're at home before we get further explanations."

Savannah shot Aunt Carolina a grateful glance, but she knew a reckoning was in her future. Father might be the titular head of the family, but not much happened without his sister Carolina's blessing. What if she forbade Savannah to leave? Did Savannah have the courage to defy her? What if she encouraged her to go? Did she have the courage to follow through on her plans?

Houses flashed by, and the horses' hooves clopped on the cobblestones. Aunt Georgette dabbed herself, her brows beetling, her lips moving as if rehearsing what she wanted to say. Savannah's sisters, Charlotte and Virginia, whispered behind their fans.

Church had been a nightmare, the first service since...*the humiliation*. Savannah hadn't heard a word the preacher said, had only mouthed along to the hymns and stared straight ahead the entire time, feeling the eyes on her, the speculations swirling.

Oh, Girard. Why? What was wrong with me that you had to run rather than marry me? What did I lack? Did you ever really love me? How did this happen? All the same questions ran round and round in her head like a waterwheel, tumbling and splashing and getting nowhere.

When they arrived at the house, mounting the steps to the three-story Italianate mansion the Cox family called home, Savannah headed straight for the room they jokingly called "headquarters"—Aunt Carolina's sitting room.

One of the servants had closed the tall shutters against the sun, and the tile floor and soft colors made the room the coolest in the house. August in Raleigh was brutal. Because of the wedding, they'd put off their annual trip to the coast, and Savannah missed the cooling sea breezes.

Right now she was supposed to be on her honeymoon, a month-long sailing trip up the coast to New York City. She shoved that thought from her mind.

Aunt Carolina glided into the room—she never walked anywhere—and rang the brass bell on the desk. The maid came in, followed by fluttering, scuttling Aunt Georgette.

"Clarice, bring some lemonade." Aunt Carolina took the pins from her cartwheel hat and eased it from her piled iron-gray curls. "I'm perishing in this heat. And tell the cook luncheon will be late." She eased her comfortable bulk onto the settee and tugged off her lace gloves. "Sit, child, and start at the beginning."

Savannah removed her own hat. She'd known a confrontation would be coming, but now that the moment was here, she wondered if she should just take it all back, pretend she'd never said it, claim temporary weakness of the mind. Aunt Carolina skewered her with a "get on with it" stare. Savannah swallowed and wondered where to start.

"She's distraught, that's what." Georgette fussed with her fan. "She can't be held responsible for anything she says or does when she's in such extremis. Poor thing. I mean, the *humiliation.*"

The mention of that word steeled Savannah's resolve. This was why she had to leave. She was smothering

under a blanket of pity. Words popped into her head…
or maybe poured out of her heart.

"I am not distraught. Nor do I have a nervous condition, though I might develop one if people don't leave
me alone." Savannah dropped into a chair. "Aunt Carolina, I answered an advertisement I saw in the newspaper. You remember that client of Daddy's who came to
dinner, the one from Saint Paul? He had a copy of the
Pioneer Press with him, and the moment I saw that clas-
sified advertisement, I knew I should apply. I have to get
out of Raleigh, at least for a little while. If I don't, I'll
forever be known as the girl who got left at the altar."
She clenched her hands in her lap, pressing against her
legs through all the layers of fabric and hoopskirts to
still the trembling in her muscles.

Clarice entered with a tray of glasses. Ice tinkled in
the pale yellow liquid as she poured. Savannah loosened
her fingers to accept hers, careful to hold it securely
given the condensation already forming on the outside
of the glass. She sipped the tangy sweetness, letting the
cool lemonade ease the tightness in her throat.

"You've never taught school a day in your life. What
makes you think you can now?" Aunt Carolina asked
over the rim of her own glass. "And why Minnesota?
If you want to teach, why can't you find a school in At-
lanta or Richmond or Charlotte? We have family and
friends in those cities with whom you could stay. You
wouldn't be so alone that way."

"I graduated from normal school. I have a teaching
certificate. I'm sure teaching a few children won't be
beyond my capabilities. And I chose Minnesota because I want to get away and start fresh. If I stay with
friends or family, I'll still have to endure their questions

and pity. I want to go where nobody knows me, nobody knows what happened."

"Have you discussed this with your father?"

"How can I? He left the day after the wedding on his business trip and hasn't been back since. Anyway, he'd only tell you to handle it, the way he does everything that isn't work related." She tried to keep the bitterness from her voice, but at Aunt Carolina's frown, Savannah knew she hadn't succeeded.

"If you only want to get away for a while," Aunt Georgette interjected, "why don't you go up to New York City? Your father offered to pay for the trip... Anyway, I think you should stay here with your family, where we can support you and look after you. I'm sure the scandal will die down eventually."

"I don't want to go back to New York. I'm supposed to be there right now with—" Savannah broke off, not wanting to say his name aloud, her heart once more sinking under a wave of pain and disillusion.

Aunt Georgette subsided.

"I can understand that." Aunt Carolina drained her glass and set it on the side table. "However, Minnesota seems extreme. Where in Minnesota is this school, anyway? In Saint Paul?"

Savannah shook her head. "It's in the western part of the state. A small town called Snowflake. It's a small school, too. Less than a dozen students." At the moment, that sounded blissful.

Aunt Carolina stared at her hard. That was the trouble with Aunt Carolina. She could hear all the things you weren't saying and detect all the things you were trying to hide.

Finally, when Savannah was sure she was going to

veto the entire proceeding, her aunt's lips relaxed, and she blinked slowly.

"All right. I give my blessing, but it comes with a warning, too." Her eyes narrowed. "You are trying to outrun your embarrassment, and I can understand that, but you're also trying to outrun your self-doubt and hurt. You need to learn that while you can remove yourself from the circumstances, the feelings are going to go with you. You can't run from what's inside yourself, and it's foolish to try. Until you deal with your feelings, they're going to own you, whether here in Raleigh, in New York City or in the wilds of western Minnesota."

But the feelings were too painful to address. If Savannah opened the door to them, they would swarm out and engulf her. What Aunt Carolina said might well be true, but for now, Savannah's only hope for recovery lay in keeping her feelings locked up tight and escaping to a place where she could start anew.

"Why do I have to be here? I didn't hire her." In fact, this was the last place he wanted to be. Elias Parker hitched his gun belt on his hip and tipped his chair back to rest against the front of the jail. He reached down and ruffled Captain's fur. The collie rewarded him with a nudge from his wet nose and a swipe of his rough tongue.

"You're here because I need your help. Because I have to go to Saint Paul to appear before the State Board of Education and don't know how long I will be gone." Elias's brother, Tyler, straightened the lapels on his checked suit and adjusted the angle of his bowler hat.

Propping his boots on the hitching rail, Elias pushed his hat forward and crossed his arms. "Why are you dressed like a snake-oil salesman? You look like you just fell off a Baltimore bus."

"And you look like you just fell off a wanted poster. I'm trying to make a good impression on the new teacher." Tyler checked his watch. "The stage is late."

"The stage is late eleven times out of ten." Elias scanned the street from under his hat brim. As the town sheriff, it was his job to keep an eye on things and anticipate trouble—something not too difficult in a sleepy farm town like Snowflake. "Tell me her name again."

"Miss Savannah Cox." Tyler said it as if he was reading copperplate writing with lots of loops and whorls.

"And she's from the Carolinas somewhere?" Elias grimaced. "Why'd you go and hire somebody from so far away?"

"Small matter of 'nobody else applied.' After the last two fiascos, I promised myself I'd find the perfect applicant, but Miss Cox was the only one who answered the advertisement." Tyler fussed with his collar.

"Better to hire nobody at all than have another black mark on your record." Or have a prissy girl arrive in town, flirting and leading you on one minute, and then decamping without a backward glance the next.

"The children can't afford to lose another year of schooling while we wait for a better applicant. I'm counting on you to look after Miss Cox. I can't be here often. I have an entire county to supervise. You'll be right here all the time."

"It's not like I don't have my own work to do, you know." Which usually meant sweeping out the jail and making sure all the stores were locked up for the night. Snowflake was as quiet as a church on a Tuesday morning. Which wasn't a bad thing because it gave Elias time to help his folks out on the farm. And evidently, time to babysit the schoolteacher. "How old is this woman, anyway?"

"I don't know, but she had such a refined way of writing, and used such fine stationery, I assumed she was middle-aged or better. She sounded very mature in her application letter."

Elias scratched his chin, feeling the rasp of whiskers he hadn't bothered to shave that morning. A "mature" female teacher might set some of his anxiety to rest.

"Here comes the stage." Tyler straightened and slipped his watch back into his vest pocket. He rubbed his hands together and scrubbed the toes of his shoes on the backs of his pant legs as if he were preparing to meet royalty.

The coach rocked into town and pulled to a stop across from the jail. Elias let his boots drop to the boardwalk and levered himself out of his chair, righting his hat and bracing himself to meet the new teacher. "Stay here, Cap." He motioned to the dog, which subsided into a hairy heap beside the chair.

Elias formed a mental picture of the new teacher based on Tyler's assessment. She'd probably be a dried-up old stick with a prunes-and-prisms mouth and no sense of humor. She could pose for the illustration in the dictionary beside the word *spinster*. She most likely carried a ruler and couldn't wait to smack a kid's hand for the slightest infraction. Elias foresaw a long winter ahead if Tyler made him look after her for the entire term. Then again, she'd probably take one glance at the living conditions and bare-bones schoolhouse and scamper back to where she came from.

He rounded the coach just as Tyler opened the stage door, and Elias braced himself to greet an old crone. Instead, a slender gloved hand appeared, and a dainty gray buttoned boot, followed by yards of light blue skirts. A decorative—if impractical—hat emerged, and then she stood on the dusty street.

Elias sucked in a breath and held it. Surely this wasn't the teacher? He peered over her shoulder, expecting another woman to be perched on the seat, but no one else occupied the coach. He looked back at the young lady.

She was perfection.

Miss Savannah Cox.

In copperplate. With loops. And whorls.

His breath escaped slowly as every thought of crabby spinsters scattered like buckshot. If his teachers had looked anything like her, he might've enjoyed school a bit more. Come to think of it, he might be tempted to enroll again.

If she was a day over twenty, he'd eat his spurs. Fair skin that surely felt like rose petals, full pink lips, and those eyes…blue as Big Stone Lake, and about as deep.

But her crowning glory…that hair. Elias had seen some yellow hair before—this was the land of the Scandinavian immigrant, after all—but *yellow* didn't seem the right word to describe hers. Gold? Wheaten? Honey? Flaxen? They all fell short.

"Are you Mr. Parker?" She said it "Pah-kah" in a Southern drawl as slow and sweet as dripping sorghum syrup. Elias stepped forward, but halted when he realized she was speaking to his brother.

"I'm Tyler Parker, the school superintendent. Welcome to Snowflake, Miss Cox." He swept his bowler off his head and smoothed his hair like a boy in Sunday school. "We're so pleased to have you here."

Elias tucked his thumbs into his gun belt and leaned against a porch post, aiming to strike an I-am-not-bowled-over-by-a-pretty-face posture, even though she'd knocked him for six. As he strove for some aplomb, his mind raced. He'd never seen anyone less suited to teach the Snowflake school. If Tyler had any sense at all, he'd thank her kindly, buy her a return ticket and send her on her way. The poor girl would perish here before the first snowfall.

If she lasted that long. She might turn out to be just like Britta, who had stayed just long enough to break Elias's heart.

Miss Cox squinted up at the bold sunshine and turned to retrieve her belongings from the stage. She withdrew a parasol and snapped it open. Elias blinked. The parasol exactly matched her dress, must've been created just for her outfit. He'd never seen the like. Where did she think she was, New York City?

Poor Tyler. He'd picked a winner this time. She was pretty to look at, but about as practical as a silver spoon when you needed a snow shovel.

She stared at the buildings lining Main Street, at Tyler who rocked on his toes and rubbed his hands together again, then finally at Elias, sizing him up from his boots to his hatband. His thoughts must've been evident on his face, because even though he touched his hat brim and gave a nod, her chin went up and she seemed to freeze. Lips tight, she looked around once more, as if hoping for city streets and fancy houses to appear. She didn't glance his way again.

Elias shook his head. What was she expecting? A royal welcome? Brass bands and banners? What had his brother saddled him with for the next nine months? She looked tighter wound than a reel of barbed wire.

"Please—" Tyler took her elbow "—come up here out of the sun. You must be tired after your long journey. This is my brother, Elias. He's the town sheriff, but for today, he's tasked with seeing you safely ensconced in your new dwellings. He'll take care of the baggage." Tyler ushered her onto the boardwalk, making clearing motions ahead of them though there was nobody around besides the stage driver. Treating her as if she were a fragile pasque flower. That might be fine for Tyler, but she'd get no such coddling from Elias. She'd chosen to come to western Minnesota, and she'd have to learn to stand on her own two feet out here. Or go back where she came from. They needed a teacher, all right, but not one like this.

"Hey, Sheriff." Keenan hopped down from the high stagecoach seat and coiled his whip, threading it up his arm and onto his shoulder. "Good traveling weather, but we could use some rain." He spit into the street under the horses' bellies. "That's some looker I brung ya, huh?" His version of a whisper rattled the windows of the stage office, and Miss Cox's already straight spine stiffened. If she put that nose any higher in the air, she'd drown in a rainstorm.

"Just get up there and throw down her bag." Elias adjusted his hat. "I'm supposed to be the teamster today, getting her where she needs to go."

"Her bag? You mean *bags*. They're in the boot." Keenan swaggered toward the canvas and strapping covering the rear compartment and began setting valises and trunks and bags on the porch.

Four, five, six, seven. "All of these?" She had more baggage than an empress.

"And one inside the coach, too." Keenan shook his head. "She put up quite a fuss about being careful with that one. Must have all her china in it or something. She brought near everything else she must own. Maybe she's planning on staying in the territory. It could be she hopes to snag her a husband while she's here and set up housekeeping. Way she looks, I reckon they'll be lining up. Won't matter if she can't cook a lick nor sew nor garden. A fellow might marry her just to have something that pretty to look at every day."

Wonderful. This just kept getting better and better. Maybe she *had* come out here hoping for a husband. There were more men than women in western Minnesota, and a woman of marrying age got snapped up pretty quickly. Pity the poor sap who wound up with her, though. A man needed a helpmeet out here, a woman who could tend the house and garden and children, and help in the barn and fields if the need arose. Miss Cox hardly looked the type to pick up a pitchfork or hoe a row of potatoes. More likely to know how to pour tea and do needlepoint.

Elias gathered several of the bags and brought them to the steps. He staggered, just to get his point across to Tyler. Who needed all this stuff?

"Ah, good. You can load Miss Cox's things in the buckboard." Tyler slanted Elias a "behave yourself" older-brother glance, forbidding him any comment on the exotic import standing in the shade of the porch. "I will check in with you as often as I am able, Miss Cox, but Elias will make himself available to assist you in any way he can, should the need arise."

"Sheriff Parker." She held out her gloved hand, and Elias let her bags thump to the porch before taking her fingers for a brief clasp. "I'll try not to be too much trouble, I'm sure."

Ahm shu-wah.

Elias swallowed, steeling himself not to be swayed from his position by nice manners. He'd been down that road, much to his regret, and he had no desire to repeat his folly.

She turned to Tyler. "Mr. Parker, is this all there is of the town?" She looked both directions along Main Street. Actually, it was the only street. Twenty or so buildings, none of them grand, lined the thoroughfare.

Tyler cleared his throat. "Um, yes, for the time being. But we're always growing. Snowflake is mostly a farming community, but we're hoping to draw more commerce to town. Having a good quality school will go a long way in enticing family-owned businesses to our little settlement."

"I see." Her faintly bewildered tone said she didn't see at all. She'd probably never lived anywhere with fewer than a thousand people within shouting distance.

"The buckboard's over here." Tyler ushered her up the street. "We'll have you at your lodgings soon."

Together, they walked toward the buckboard, and Elias, left with the baggage, forced himself not to stare at the graceful sway of her walk and the way her dress trailed and draped in layers and ruffles. He'd never seen a getup quite like that. She looked as if she should be at some garden club or tea party...not that he had any notion what women wore to tea parties, but her outfit had to be more suited to a social engagement than to traveling across the prairie.

"And which building is the school?" She had to look up at his brother, who wasn't all that tall. Elias had a feeling he'd dwarf her, since he was half a head taller than Tyler.

"Oh, the school is north of town a ways. They built it there because that's where the greatest concentration of children is. We're almost up to a dozen students now." Tyler smiled and held out his hand to help her into the buckboard. "I do apologize that I am unable to make the rest of the trip with you. I'm heading east on the stage for some meetings in the capitol. I'll return as soon as I can, but you'll be in good hands with my brother."

Elias stowed bags and boxes on the backseat and floorboards. Miss Cox sat in the front seat like a little plaster statue, eyes forward, hands throttling her parasol handle, rigid as a new fence. He was just about to climb aboard when a shout shattered the sultry afternoon air.

"Sheriff, don't forget this one." Keenan stomped over, grappling with the odd-shaped box he'd removed from inside the stage.

"Oh, my." Miss Cox fluttered like a bird. "I can't believe I forgot. I must be more tired than I thought."

Elias scratched his head. Where was he supposed to fit that monstrosity? If he'd have known she was bringing enough stuff to supply an army, he'd have brought his pa's farm wagon.

"Please, be careful. That's fragile."

He sighed and wedged the bulky parcel in so it wouldn't jostle, then climbed aboard and gathered the reins. Looking over at the jailhouse porch, he whistled. Cap shot up and bounded across the street. Elias scooted over and patted the seat between himself and Miss Cox.

Captain needed no second command. He leaped aboard and planted his furry rump on the hard bench. His tongue lolled and dripped dog spit, and he gave Miss Cox a friendly sniff.

She recoiled, eyes wide. "Get back!" She shrank further, looking ready to bolt.

"Whoa, easy, ma'am. He won't hurt you." Elias cuffed Captain on the shoulder. "He's gentle. You act like you've never been around a dog before."

Swallowing, she righted her hat and sat more upright,

pressing against the far armrest so hard he thought it might break. "I haven't, especially not one so…big."

Captain grinned, showing a lot of teeth, his heavy tail pounding Elias's leg.

"Are you sure he won't bite?" Her voice trembled, and a little arrow of guilt pierced Elias. Not enough to overcome his scorn at such irrational fear, of course.

"Unless you're a bank robber, or a horse thief, or a stubborn sheep, he'll keep his fangs to himself. Cap's a first-rate sheepherder and police dog, aren't you, boy?" The big collie tried to lick Elias's face, and he laughed, shoving him back.

Tyler frowned, fussing with his tie as he stood by the buckboard. "Perhaps you should leave him here."

"Nope. I told Pa I'd drop him off at the farm after I ran your errand for you."

"But Miss Cox—"

"Miss Cox will be fine. She'll have to get used to a lot worse than sharing a seat with a friendly dog if she's going to survive out here."

He chirruped to the sorrel mare, and the buckboard lurched, leaving Tyler behind. They soon reached the outskirts of town and headed north.

Miss Cox leaned forward to talk around Captain, who had his snoot in the air, sucking in the breeze created by their forward motion. "Where are we going? I thought we were heading to my lodgings."

Elias frowned. Did she think he was taking her on a sightseeing tour of the county first? "This is the quickest way to the Halvorsons'."

"The Halvorsons'?" Her parasol caught the breeze and jerked upward. She fought it down. "Is it always so windy here?"

"This isn't windy." She thought *this* was windy?

"The Halvorsons are the folks you're boarding with. Didn't Tyler tell you?"

The dog leaned against her, and she pushed him away. "Boarding with a family? No, he didn't mention that. I thought I'd have a room at a boardinghouse or hotel."

"Got no boardinghouse nor hotel. Is that gonna be a problem? The stage hasn't left yet if you want to go back." He tried not to sound too hopeful.

Miss Cox pressed her lips together and shook her head. Even under the shade of her umbrella, her hair glowed in swoops and curls, all pinned up under a hat that had nothing to do with deflecting the elements. What she needed was a decent sunbonnet or wide-brimmed straw.

"How much farther is it?" She sounded tired, and Elias's conscience bit him again. After all, she'd come a long way. It wasn't her fault that she was unsuitable.

Or that she stirred up memories of Britta.

"Schoolhouse is two miles out of town on the north road. The Halvorson place is the closest farm to the school."

"And how far apart are the house and the school?"

He shrugged. "If you take the road, it's about a mile and a quarter around, but if you cut across the fields, it's about half a mile, I guess."

"A mile and a quarter. I suppose by buggy that won't be too bad."

Elias laughed. "Doubt anybody will fetch you in a buggy. Or a wagon, either. You'll walk, same as the Halvorson kids. The students who live farther than a couple of miles will ride ponies. There's a livestock shed and corral at the school." He slapped the lines again, urging the mare into a faster trot. "There's the schoolhouse. School starts on Monday, but I guess you know that."

The clapboard building shone white in the sunshine, sporting a fresh coat of paint. Elias had been part of the work crew that had seen to the new paint job early last spring before planting time. The money for the new school building—a vast improvement on the old sod-and-log structure they'd had before—had come from a bequest, and Tyler had hoped it would be an enticement in hiring. So far, it had sat empty far more than it had been in use.

Just short of the school, Elias turned at the crossroads to head west. "The Halvorson place is over there. We'll be there soon."

"Could we stop at the school first? I'd like to see inside."

She didn't look particularly eager, but maybe she was just forestalling having to meet more strangers.

"Sure, if you want. Tyler gave me the key to give to you." He turned the mare and headed toward the schoolhouse, wishing it was Tyler showing her around. It was his brother's job, after all.

From the corner of his eye, he studied her again, frilly dress, lacy gloves, fancy shoes, remote touch-me-not expression. He'd give this "ice princess" a week before she hightailed it back to where she came from.

Chapter Two

The beastly dog leaned on Savannah again, and she gently elbowed him upright. Her dress would be covered in dog hair soon. His hot, moist breath puffed against her cheek, and his tongue lolled, dripping saliva.

But his brown eyes were friendly. Friendlier than his master's. From the moment she'd stepped off the stage, she could feel the sheriff's disapproval—which puzzled her. He didn't even know her. Why should he take such an instant dislike?

The buckboard jerked to a halt in front of the tiny white building, and the sheriff jumped down, rocking the conveyance, forcing her to clutch the seat.

Thankfully, the dog followed him instead of breathing his doggy breath in her face anymore. "Thank you for stopping, Mr. Parker."

"Call me Elias."

Mr. Parker—Elias—sauntered around the horse to help her down. Savannah could feel him sizing her up… and to judge by the skeptical tilt to his brows, finding her wanting. She knew she wasn't at her sparkling best, travel-worn and tossed into what felt like a foreign land. Her self-confidence had sunk to an all-time low ebb with Girard's defection, and the sheriff was doing nothing to bolster it. She felt strange and a bit weepy, which wasn't like her at all before her broken engagement, but now seemed to be her constant state.

Elias, on the other hand, exuded confidence. Tall, muscular and in familiar surroundings. Dark hair, gray eyes and, when he bothered to smile, deep creases in his cheeks. He'd probably never suffered a setback in his entire life.

"The school's been closed up since last Christmas, when the teacher left town." Elias tromped up the steps and opened the door. The hinges let out a terrific squeal. "It's going to need a good cleaning before Monday."

Savannah furled her parasol and stepped past him into the building's foyer. A beadboard wall greeted her, with doorways on either side that led into the classroom. A crock stood in the corner, and several shelves with hooks ran along the walls. To the right of the entry door hung a rope, held to the wall by large metal loops. It ran up through a hole in the ceiling.

"School bell. Don't ring it now, or folks will come running, thinking there's an emergency." Elias tipped his hat back on his head and tucked his hands into his pockets. "Schoolroom's through there." He indicated the doorway with his chin.

Great blocks of light fell through the western windows onto the hardwood floor. Three rows of desks took up most of the space. Not patent metal and wood desks but rough-hewn benches and long, slant-top desks with a single shelf beneath, clearly locally made.

On a slight platform sat a teacher's desk and chalkboard, and behind the last row of desks, a small iron stove. Portraits of Presidents Washington and Lincoln graced the spaces between the windows, and an American flag hung proudly in the corner.

The air smelled stale, and dust covered everything and danced in the air. Savannah's trailing skirt left a track as she made her way to the front of the room. Aware of Elias watching her, she sought for something intelligent to say. Nothing came to mind. She was too fuzzy-headed with fatigue.

The dog trotted up the aisle as if he owned the place, his nails clicking on the floor. He sniffed around the desks and sneezed. Savannah didn't know much about dogs, but she did know they should stay *outside*. She kept a wary eye on him as she placed her hand on the back of the teacher's chair. From here she was supposed to rule this little kingdom.

The crisis of confidence that she'd carried around since Girard had jilted her welled up and threatened to paralyze her. What had she been thinking to come so far from home?

"You might want to check out the list of rules for teachers. They're posted by the blackboard." Elias said it casually, but she sensed a challenge in his tone. Was she imagining things, or was she overlaying her insecurities onto him?

Scanning the paper tacked to the wall, she wilted inside. Clean the lamps, haul water, haul coal, scrub the floors and windows once a week, check the privies, clean the livestock shed, be circumspect in her behavior, attend church regularly, start the fire by seven each morning in cold weather so the room will be warm by eight. Savannah blinked. She'd never scrubbed a floor in her life, much less mucked out a stable or hauled coal.

This whole thing was a mistake. What had she been thinking? She wasn't suited for any of this. The sinking feeling she'd been fighting for days grew in her middle. Fiercely, she battled it down. Somehow, some way she needed to regain her belief in herself. If she couldn't do that, what future did she have anywhere?

"Tyler wanted me to give you this." Elias spoke from just behind her, startling her. She whirled as he pulled a paper out of his back pocket. He walked to the desk, leaned over and blew, sending dust puffing into the air, then spread the sheet on the blotter. She followed him, trying to still her beating heart.

Her contract.

"You can fill it out now if you want." He slid an ink-well and pen toward her. "Or you can read it over, think about it and weigh up if you really want to sign it. The stage will be back on Tuesday if you decide to leave."

She frowned. "Why do you seem so eager for me to run away?" The man didn't even know her. She might be a bit daunted, but he didn't have to assume she was a failure before she even got started.

He parked his hip on the corner of the desk. "Maybe because I've been down this road before. The two teachers before you skedaddled the minute things got tough. The first one was a man—a city boy, I'll grant you, but even he wasn't tough enough to stick it out through one of our winters. The other was a girl." Elias paused and rubbed the back of his neck. "She only stayed for a couple of months, and when she left, she didn't even resign or say goodbye. Just hopped on the stage one morning and took off." With a shrug, he paced a few steps down the aisle and then turned to look at Savannah once more. "She caused a lot of hurt…among the students and their families, I mean.

"And here you come, fresh from the South, a slip of a girl with a fancy paper that says she's a teacher, but precious little else to recommend her for this job." He took off his hat and swept his fingers through his hair. "I hate to see the parents and kids get all excited, only to have you walk away in a week or a month because life out here is harsher than you thought. Not to mention that my brother has a lot riding on you. Better you call it quits now than disappoint everyone."

"What makes you think I will disappoint everyone?" She spoke through her tiredness and the tightness in her throat. "I graduated first in my class from normal school, and though I've never lived in Minnesota, I assume other women do? If they can, so can I."

He threw his head back and laughed, the strong column of his throat rising from his open-necked shirt. "Miss Cox, I doubt you share anything other than gender with the women around here. They're hardy Norwegian stock, hard workers, practical and used to getting by without much luxury. From the way you dress and the amount of baggage you brought, I surmise you've never been within a stone's throw of milking a cow or plucking a chicken or hoeing a garden."

"Well, it's a good thing I'm not being hired to do any of those things." She snatched the pen, dipped it in the inkwell and signed her name before her courage could wilt entirely under his criticism. "I will teach school and follow the rules, and if I need help, I'm sure I can find someone who won't be as grudging and skeptical as you are." She snapped the pen down on the desk, snatched up her parasol and marched toward the door.

She'd show him.

Savannah wanted to slam the schoolhouse door, but her aunt's training in the fine art of being a lady came to her rescue in time. She climbed aboard the buckboard, snapped open her parasol against the ruthless sun and searched her reticule for her fan. Flicking it open, she cooled her hot cheeks.

He strolled down the steps, his shaggy canine on his heels, and took his seat with a long-suffering sigh, as if humoring a toddler in a tantrum.

Which made Savannah want to bite a nail in half. Sheriff Elias Parker would know the meaning of the word *determination* before this school year ended.

"Do all your fans and parasols match your dresses? Is that what's in all these bags and boxes?"

That's what he wanted to talk about? "Some of them match. I can't see why it's a concern of yours." She regretted her sharp tone at once, but then again, he'd made no bones about how he felt about her qualifications. He seemed to think he could sum her up just by looking at her, so why couldn't she do the same?

He fell silent.

When they finally approached a cluster of small buildings, Savannah found herself praying Elias would drive right by. A tiny abode, the size of the summer kitchen of Savannah's house in Raleigh, sat in a dusty yard, and though it had a peaked, wooden roof and log walls, part of it appeared to be built right into a small hillside. Surely this wasn't one of those horrid sod houses or dugouts of which she'd heard? Chickens pecked along a fence, and a row of laundry hung out on a line for all the world to see.

The sun bounced off the whitewashed cabin, nearly blinding her. At least the paint made it look clean and tidy. But it was so small. How many people lived here?

Too close for Savannah's comfort, a pair of pigs rooted in a sty next to a sturdy-looking barn. The barnyard smells rising up in the summer sunshine had her flapping her fan. How did anyone stand it, especially in this heat? Not a tree broke the horizon for as far as she could see, though fields of corn and wheat rustled in the breeze. What she wouldn't give for some decent shade and a glass of iced lemonade.

A woman emerged from the house, wiping her hands on her apron. She had her blond braids wrapped around her head like a halo, and her smile was sweet.

But her calico dress was faded and drooping, and she wore...wooden clogs on her feet. Savannah glanced at her traveling costume, the fine sateen cloth, the ivory lace and her kid gloves. She'd thought it serviceable enough when she donned it at the hotel that morning, but now she understood what Elias had meant about her parasol and fan matching her dress.

"God kveld, Elias. Er at den nye læreren?" The woman greeted Elias and bobbed her head, smiling at Savannah.

"Ja, dette er hun." Elias hefted a couple of her bags from the back. *"Hennes navn er* Miss Cox.*"*

Two children, both fair and sun-browned, tumbled out of the house. They skidded to a stop when they spied Savannah. Surely they would be her students, as they were both school-aged. Perhaps ten and twelve? The girl found her voice first, firing a rapid question at Elias. He replied, and Savannah understood not a single word.

"Pardon me."

Elias turned, and she motioned him over. Setting her bags in the dirt, he went to her side. "What?"

Lowering her head and her voice, she whispered, "It's rude to speak in another language and leave someone out of the conversation. Why aren't you using English?"

From this close, she could see the blue flecks in his gray eyes and the beginnings of a beard shadowing his slim cheeks. When he leaned in, she smelled sunshine and cotton. "We're speaking Norwegian because the Halvorsons don't speak English."

A strange trickling feeling started in her chest—probably what was left of her courage draining out. "Are you jesting?"

"Nope."

"I'm to board with a family that speaks no English."

"They're the closest family to the schoolhouse." His shrug made her want to scream. She'd traveled across the country, leaving everything she knew, and he was going to dump her with a family that didn't even speak English?

Then the little girl edged over, eyes sparkling, freckles spattering her nose. She reached up gently, as if sensing Savannah's fear, and took her hand. *"Du er pen. Mitt navn er Rut. Du vil dele rommet mitt."*

Savannah looked to Elias.

"She says she thinks you're pretty, that her name is Rut, and that you will be sharing her room." He continued to unload the bags. "This fellow is Lars, Rut's brother, and this is their mother, Agneta Halvorson."

Savannah remembered her manners, slipped from the buckboard and went to Mrs. Halvorson. "I'm pleased to meet you. Thank you for welcoming me into your home." She took the older woman's work-worn hand in hers.

Elias translated for her, and Agneta beamed, motioning for them to come inside. As Savannah entered the small house, the smell of something rich and meaty greeted her. Her stomach gurgled, and she put her palm to her middle, her cheeks heating. But Agneta just laughed, a delightful sound like bells. She spoke to Elias, pointing to a steep stair in the corner. Lars and

Elias staggered up with Savannah's baggage, and Rut's eyes widened as they went out for another trip.

Agneta put her hand on Savannah's shoulder and directed her to sit at the table. She did as she was bidden, surveying the room. The walls had been painted pale blue on the upper half and a rusty red-brown on the lower. Small-paned windows let in a little light, but the room was dim. A large fireplace and hearth of a construction she'd never seen before took up one corner, and a long table with benches sat before it. Two small cabinets hung from the walls, painted with flowers and scrolls, and a large sideboard with fine carvings took up one wall. In the corner, with a sheet curtain hanging around it to separate it from the rest of the room, sat a bed covered in a pretty quilt.

Rut sat across from Savannah and propped her chin on her palm, staring.

Through it all, Agneta chattered away as if Savannah could understand every word. Savannah tugged off her fingerless lace gloves, folded them with her fan and tucked them into her handbag. Her parasol leaned against her leg, and she caught Rut eyeing it. Mother and daughter exchanged a few words and Rut nodded. She popped up and went to Savannah, holding out her hand, then pointing to Savannah's hat, bag and parasol.

"Oh, you want to take them?" Relieved at understanding at least one thing, Savannah reached up and removed her hatpin, easing her fascinator-style hat from her hair. "I must look a mess, what with traveling and the ride from town." She smoothed her hair up from the base of her neck, wishing she was at home so she could sink into the claw-footed tub and wash away the dirt and tiredness.

Elias and Lars clattered down the steps, and Lars

went outside right away, leaving the door open. He dropped to his knees and Captain bounded up, licking his face and tumbling him backward into the dirt. From the sound of his laughter, the boy didn't mind.

"There's just the one case left. But there's no more room upstairs." Elias put his hands on his hips. "What's in that thing, anyway? Oh, wait, I forgot. It's none of my business." He shrugged. "I'll bring it in, but it will have to stay down here."

When he'd brought the case in, he set it near the bottom of the stairs. "I have to be going. I promised my pa I'd stop by his place. He owns the next farm to the north of here, about a mile or so."

Strange that she had to force herself not to grab hold of his arm and beg him not to leave her. Savannah barely knew him, and they hadn't exactly been cordial to one another. And yet she wanted him to stay.

Perhaps she was seeing things that weren't there, perhaps it was her tiredness putting thoughts into her head, but she thought she glimpsed a triumphant, challenging gleam in his eyes, as if he was daring her to beg him to take her back to town.

She gathered the last bits of her dignity, put on her remotest expression—the one that her sister Charlotte called her "queen look"—and said, "Goodbye, Mr. Parker."

"I'm telling you, Pa, you never saw such a proud bit of goods as that new teacher. Tyler must be out of his mind. And he's laid it on me to look after her while he's courting the bigwigs in Saint Paul." Elias unbuckled harness straps as he talked.

Pa leaned on his pitchfork. "She can't be that bad. She has the qualifications to be a teacher, doesn't she?"

"Oh, she's probably got some paper that says she passed her classes." Elias led the mare to the watering trough. "But that doesn't mean she's ready to take on the Snowflake School. She's too young, too Southern and too pretty."

Pa's eyebrows rose. "Since when did being pretty mean you couldn't teach school?"

"Since Miss Savannah Cox hit town. I'm telling you, Pa, she won't last a week. You should've seen her, nose in the air, frills and ruffles and a skirt that trailed the ground, parasol and fan and fancy hat. I'm sure she doesn't own a decent pair of boots or a coat. It probably never gets below freezing where she lives. She had enough baggage to stock a general store. And she's tiny, too. Just a little bit of a thing. How's she going to tote the coal and water and break a path through the snow across the fields come January?" He turned the mare into the corral and forked some hay over the fence before following his father to the house.

"Evening, *Mor*." Elias kissed his mother on the cheek. "That smells good."

"It's *agurksalat* and *kjøttboller*. Vash your hands." She dished up the cucumber salad and meatballs, setting the dishes on the table. "Tell me about da new teacher."

Over dinner, Elias did, repeating everything he'd told his father and nearly everything he'd thought about Savannah.

By the time he was finished, his mother was looking at him in that way she had that said she was disappointed in him, that he'd done something wrong.

"You say she vas cold and distant? You say she looked like da 'ice princess'?" Ma began clearing plates. "And how many times haff you left your home and family and traveled a long vay to a place vere you do not know da language or da customs or da climate? This new teacher must be frightened and lonely, and you are telling me you did not make her feel *velcommen*?" His mother shook her head, her gray eyes sad.

A hot, shameful prickle touched Elias's skin. His ma must've felt that way when she'd left her native Norway to come to America. Lonely and strange, not speaking the language, not knowing the customs. What a dunderhead he must've looked, enjoying Savannah's discomfort, driving away from the Halvorsons' so sure in his mind that he had been wasting his time. Well, he *was* sure that he'd been wasting his time, that she wouldn't last long in the job, but he could've been nicer about it.

"I just don't want a repeat of last year, that's all." He scrubbed his palms on his thighs under the table. "The kids deserve better than that."

His parents shared a long look. Surely neither of them had known how he felt about Britta, about the plans he'd been making to court her? The plans that had been shattered when she'd left without saying goodbye.

Pa picked up his newspaper and dug his spectacles from his overalls pocket. "Your ma's right. And anyway, who says the new teacher can't adapt? Your ma didn't know a lick of English when we met, but that didn't stop us from communicating." He winked over the top of his paper, and Ma blushed, as she always did. "Tyler must have faith in this Miss Cox to do the job. It's up to us in the community to make sure she feels welcome and to help her in any way we can. Just because one or two teachers didn't last doesn't mean this one won't."

Ma looked Elias hard in the eyes. "Tomorrow you vill be nice to da new teacher. You vill go to da school where she vill be cleaning it for Monday, and you vill invite her to our house for dinner after church on Sunday, *ja*?"

"*Ja, Mor.*"

Elias accepted the slice of apple pie she handed him. He would be nice, he would look after the new teacher until Tyler returned to take over the job and he would pass along his parents' invitation, but he would also stay aloof. He couldn't risk getting too close to an outsider who wouldn't last past the first frost.

Chapter Three

The Halvorsons rose before the sun, and Savannah rose with them. Her muscles ached from the bouncy stage ride and the night spent tossing on a rope-strung, straw-tick bed for the first time in her life.

How she missed her feather and kapok mattress and her down pillows. She missed her sisters' chatter as they dressed. And she missed the familiar house sounds of the servants carrying tea trays and tapping on doors. Most of all, she missed sleeping in on a Saturday morning.

Rubbing her neck, she strained to see in the dim light of the loft. A single, small-paned window at the end of the room showed the grayish-pink light of the coming dawn. Mrs. Halvorson called up the stairs again.

The loft was divided into two rooms, not by a wall, but by a curtain of pillow ticking material strung on a wire. On the far side lay Lars's portion of the upstairs space, a fact Savannah had been conscious of as she tossed and turned last night.

Rut rolled out of her side of the bed and plucked her dress off a peg. She glanced over her shoulder with a quick smile, said something Savannah couldn't understand and began dressing. Savannah slipped from beneath the quilt, ducking to avoid hitting her head on the steeply sloped roof. She wrapped herself in the shawl she'd laid close to hand the night before, and searched through her luggage until she found the valise she thought contained her most serviceable skirts and blouses.

Rut tapped Savannah's shoulder, raised her eyebrows and pointed to the buttons up the back of her dress. *"Vennligst?"*

"Oh, of course." Savannah began to do them up for the little girl. Through the curtain that divided the room came rustling and bumping, followed by clattering down the steep staircase.

Rut soon followed, leaving Savannah some privacy in which to dress and fix her hair. She found herself banging her elbows on the roof, barking her shins on the many boxes and bags, and struggling in the cramped space to find what she needed. She would have to bring some organization to her possessions if she was really going to spend the school year here.

She paused. Of course she was going to spend the school year here. She'd signed a contract, given her word. And besides, admitting defeat before she even started wasn't her way. Why, Aunt Carolina would never let her live it down if she quit this soon.

Shaking out a tan-and-blue-plaid blouse with a minimum of lace, she paired it with a businesslike brown skirt. The severe lines of the front fall and the spare draping and gathering to the bustle would surely be suitable for a schoolteacher. Digging farther, she found the box containing her new, high-topped black boots, the most serviceable footgear she'd ever purchased. Almost no heel, sturdy laces and dull black leather. Savan-

nah wrinkled her nose as she stuck her boot-clad foot
out and surveyed the results. Her sisters would laugh.

Fully dressed, she eased down the precipitous staircase into the kitchen. Mrs. Halvorson stood at the cupboard slicing bread, her back to Savannah. There was
no sign of the children, and Savannah didn't know how
to ask where they'd gone. How was she ever going to
survive here when she couldn't talk to anyone?

Except Elias Parker, who thought she should be sent
back where she came from before "big, bad Minnesota"
did her in. Savannah grimaced and pushed Elias to the
back of her mind.

"God morgen."

Mrs. Halvorson's greeting pulled Savannah out of her
thoughts, and after a pause, she replied, "Good morning, Mrs. Halvorson."

The woman beamed and pointed to herself. "Agneta."

"Good morning, Agneta. Please, call me—" she put
her hand on her chest "—Savannah."

"Sa-vah-nah."

"Yes."

Agneta reached into the sideboard and handed her
some cutlery, then motioned to the table. Grateful for
a job to do, Savannah set the table, taking the stone-
ware plates from the shelf where she'd seen Agneta put
them after washing up last night. As she found tin cups,
Agneta beamed and nodded. Again this morning she
had her braids crisscrossed atop her head, giving her a
girlish appearance. Her apron covered most of her dress
and had been embroidered with cheerful yellow-and-
red flowers along the hem.

Just as Savannah placed the last cup, Lars and Rut
came in. Lars carried a small pail of milk, which he
handed to his mother before washing up at the basin

beside the door. Agneta took the milk, poured some through a piece of cheesecloth into a pitcher, then the rest into a pair of shallow pans on the sideboard. Per Halvorson came in and opened the door that went into the dugout portion of the dwelling. A dank, cool, earthy smell rolled out, and Agneta carried the pans inside.

The children tugged out the bench and sat at the table. Savannah took the place she'd occupied the night before, and when everyone was seated, Per bowed his head. Though she couldn't understand the words, Savannah was grateful. At least she had been placed with a family that prayed together.

A small wave of homesickness crept into her heart. This morning, Aunt Carolina, Aunt Georgette and Savannah's sisters would be sitting on the back veranda sharing breakfast. The girls would be home from the Minton Ladies' Academy for the weekend. The day would include shopping and tea downtown, perhaps a few calls upon friends. The evening would hold a symphony concert, or a stroll through the city gardens, or buggy rides with some of the young men in their set.

"Sa-vah-nah?"

She looked up. Agneta held a plate of thinly sliced meat for her.

"Oh, I beg your pardon." She took a piece of the meat and passed the plate to Rut. Bread followed.

Sandwiches for breakfast? She had to expect that, along with the language, the customs and food would be different. With a slight shrug and a mental note to do everything she could to blend in to her new surroundings, Savannah buttered her bread and slid the meat between the two slices.

Rut giggled and Lars stared.

Savannah stopped, her food inches from her lips. "What?"

Agneta scolded the children, who had the grace to look abashed. They fell to eating, and Savannah noticed that they placed their meat atop the bread and ate it with a fork. Open-faced sandwiches.

Heat prickled her skin, and she slid her top piece of bread aside and picked up her fork. Painfully aware that she'd made some social gaffe, she found her appetite had fled.

The Halvorsons spoke little during meals, and as soon as they'd finished eating, they sprang up. Agneta pointed to Rut and Lars, then a large basket beside the door. She showed Savannah the contents: a scrub brush, soap, rags…cleaning supplies. Agneta waved in the direction of the school, made a wiping motion with one of the rags and pointed to Savannah and the children.

"Oh, thank you." Savannah had wondered about how to get the school clean and ready for Monday. Evidently, Agneta had thought ahead.

They went by road instead of cutting across the fields, which were high with corn and wheat. Lars brought along a small bucket of water, and Savannah couldn't think why, since she had noticed a pump right by the school. Rut and Savannah carried the basket between them, and Rut chattered the entire time, as if Savannah could understand her perfectly. Evidently, she thought total immersion into the language was the best way to teach Savannah Norwegian.

The belfry appeared first over the waving corn, then the white school building. A horse and buckboard stood out front, and someone sat on the steps. A loud bark erupted and a furry streak shot toward them, bounding and wagging and wiggling.

The collie, Captain. Lars set his bucket down, dropped to his knees and embraced the dog.

Elias rose from the porch, long and lean, his hat pushed back, revealing his dark hair. "Morning."

Savannah and Rut arrived together, and they set the basket on the ground. Rut clattered up the steps and took Elias's hand, swinging on it as she gazed up with bright eyes. He winked at her.

"Thought I'd come and make sure there isn't anything that needs fixing, broken boards or loose hinges." He motioned to a small toolbox he'd brought. "With the place sitting empty for so many months, there's bound to be some issues."

Savannah nodded, unsure if she was glad or annoyed. With him here at least he could translate for the children, but it felt almost as if he didn't think she was even up to the task of sweeping out the school without his supervision.

Entering the school, she was again hit with the smells of dust and stale air. She moved to the closest window and tugged on the sash. It didn't budge. Glancing over her shoulder to make sure no one was watching, she looked for a lock, but there didn't seem to be one. Savannah braced herself, pressing the heels of her hands against the frame, and pushed again. With a groan, the window came up an inch and stuck.

"Here, let me help you with that." Before she could move out of his way, Elias stood behind her, his arms coming up on either side. He raised the window with ridiculous ease, but all Savannah could think was that he smelled like shaving soap.

She wanted to bolt. One of the things she had loved about Girard was the smell of his shaving soap. Her chest ached and her breath snagged as she closed her eyes against the now familiar pain of his desertion.

"Are you all right?" Elias asked.

Her eyes popped open and warmth flooded her cheeks. "Um…yes. Just…" She stopped, unwilling to reveal that much about herself. "I was debating where to start on the cleaning. I think I'll work from the top down. Cobwebs first." She glanced at the dusty webs along the ceiling and in the corners, trying to gather her composure. When would she stop feeling so raw? When would the hurt ease?

Girard, you've left me in a shambles. Even though I wouldn't have you back if you came gift-wrapped with a guarantee, I can't help feeling the loss, the hole you created in my life, in my heart.

Elias said, "I'll open the rest of the windows, then you should come out with me to see how to work the pump. You're going to need plenty of water for scrubbing today."

"I know how to pump water." Indignation colored her tone. Her foundations were crumbling enough without him assuming she was an idiot.

"I imagine you do." He shoved up another window sash, letting in the morning breeze. "But this pump is a bit temperamental. Best you let me show you the right way."

As if there was a wrong way to draw water. "I know you think I'm a simpleton, but I assure you, I have reached the age of twenty-one without your help and oversight. I can operate a simple water pump."

He stopped pushing up the next window, his hands dropping to his sides. "All right. How about you show me then?"

"Fine." She stalked into the cloakroom, snatched the

empty bucket from under the water crock and strode outside. Lars still tumbled with the dog in the long grass, but Rut was already busy with a broom, sweeping the steps.

Savannah kept her chin in the air as she rounded the building, aware of Elias behind her. The pump stood twenty yards to the west of the schoolhouse, surrounded by a wooden platform. Sunshine had warped the boards a bit and a few nails stuck up, pulled loose by the wood shrinking over time. She dropped the bucket beneath the spout with a clank and grabbed the iron handle.

Up, down, up, down. Though she pulled and pushed with all her might and the pump squealed and squeaked, no water came out. Elias stood to the side, arms crossed, face bland. Savannah blew a few wisps of hair off her forehead, regripped the cold iron and tugged with vigor.

Still nothing.

She let her hands drop. An uncomfortable prickling raced across her skin. She couldn't even pump water. What was wrong with the wretched thing? What was she doing here?

Slowly, she forced herself to look Elias in the eye, prepared for his gloating. He would have every right, since she'd shoved his offer of help back into his face.

"Are you done?" He had one eyebrow raised, the very picture of long-suffering patience.

Nodding, she stepped back. He turned and put his fingers to his lips, letting out a piercing whistle that brought both children and the dog at a run. A couple of quick words to Lars in Norwegian had the boy running back to the school and returning with the small pail he'd brought from home.

"This pump hasn't been used in a while, and like I said, it's temperamental. You have to prime it with a little water, even if it's only been a couple of days. Always remember to fill a bucket on Friday afternoon before you leave, so it will be ready for Monday morning." He took the pail of water from Lars and poured it carefully into the top of the pump, working the handle gently at first.

When the water from the pail had disappeared, he gave half a dozen strong pulls on the handle and was rewarded with a gush of water from the spout. He filled the larger bucket, but dumped it on the grass in a rusty, brown arc. After another bucketful, the water ran clear and clean.

Savannah forced herself to remember her manners. "Thank you for your help, Mr. Parker." Her lips were stiff, and straight vinegar tasted better than this particular slice of humble pie, but she got the words out.

He shook his head. "The kids can help you inside. I'll sluice down the privies and make sure the lean-to and corral are tight while you clean. If you need anything—not that I'm assuming you will." He held up his hands. "But if you do, holler."

He strode across the grass, leaving Savannah staring after him. His walk was powerful, his upper body swaying slightly, his arms swinging. Girard had been graceful, with a long, easy stride and loose limbs, but he lacked Elias's muscular shoulders and chest, tending more to the lean side in build. More intellectual than physical. Everything about Elias Parker spoke of hard work and capability.

But he wasn't to be trusted. No man was. Elias offered help one moment, but in the next, let her know he was certain she would fail. Girard had asked her to marry him, but at the last moment, he'd fled rather than go through with the wedding.

Even her father wasn't reliable, never home for more than a week at a time, always traveling, always putting business first.

No, a woman shouldn't put her trust in a man. She was better off on her own.

It might be lonely, but it was better than a broken heart.

Trust a woman to kill herself just to prove a man wrong. Elias hammered another nail into the corral fence, jerking the board to make sure it was tight. Savannah Cox had scrubbed and polished and sorted and cleaned all morning without a break and without a word.

She'd feel it tomorrow, he figured. No way was she used to hauling buckets of water or washing windows or scrubbing floors. Not with her manners and clothes and all.

Elias picked up his toolbox. His brother had better appreciate this.

Miss Cox headed back to the pump with another bucket. She'd shed her jacket and rolled up her sleeves, making her look a little more approachable. Water gushed from the pump and hit the bucket, tipping it over. Elias chuckled as she righted the pail and held it up with her foot. Why didn't she use the knob on top of the spout like a normal person?

Probably because she didn't know sic 'em from c'mere when it came to practical matters. She hadn't even known how to prime a pump in the first place. He'd had to force himself not to laugh out loud at her consternation. And her apology had nearly choked her.

Still, she *had* apologized, which was more than some folks would've done. He watched her tote the full water bucket, leaning away from the weight as she hefted it up the stairs and into the schoolhouse.

Captain lay in the shade beside the porch, but he sat up when Elias drew near. "Hey, Cap. You're sure working hard." The dog trotted over and put his nose under Elias's hand, inviting a pat. "Shall we go in and see the progress?"

Captain's nails clicked on the entryway floor, and the smells of vinegar and soap prickled Elias's nose.

"Don't bring him in here." Savannah knelt in one of the doorways into the schoolroom, a scrub brush in her hand and a pail of soapy water on one side, a bucket of clean water on the other. "Dogs don't belong inside, and if he marks up this floor, you're going to be the one scrubbing it next."

Still touchy.

Elias put his hand on Captain's ruff. "Sorry, boy, the boss has spoken. Outside." He pointed to the door and snapped his fingers. Captain gave him a sorrowful look but turned around, clicking his way out.

Elias went to the other doorway and surveyed her progress, inhaling the aromas of lemon polish and lye, vinegar and ammonia. Every surface gleamed. She'd accomplished more than he'd thought she would.

Stubborn or efficient? Maybe both?

Savannah dipped her scrub brush in the bucket again, scooting backward toward the door. The boar-bristle brush scraped against the floorboards in rhythmic circles. She rinsed with a cloth from the clean-water pail. The floor glistened damply, but when it dried, it would be dull until she waxed it properly.

The bow on her apron, so perky this morning, had gone limp. Her rolled up sleeves revealed pale, slender arms. The brush looked too big for her small hand,

and her neat hairdo had become a bit bedraggled, with wisps escaping the braided knot at the back of her head.

"Where did the kids get off to?"

She wiped her forearm across her brow, sitting back on her heels. "I sent them on home. They worked hard all morning, and there wasn't much left for them to do once I started on the floors."

Flo-ahs. Why was it that every Southerner made one-syllable words into two? Still, it sounded kind of cute when she did it.

"I mended the corral fence and tightened a couple of loose boards on the privies. And I took a scythe to the grass. You won't have to mow here. Tyler has a contract with Ole Oleson to cut it once school starts. There's some hay in the shed, but a couple of the farmers will deliver more soon. And Tyler will see that coal's delivered before it gets cold. The coal shed is a lean-to on the back of the schoolhouse, but you have to go outside to get to it." He pointed to the coal hod by the stove. "Usually, one of the older boys is in charge of keeping the stove supplied, but you'll have to light the fire in the mornings."

"I saw that on the list of teachers' duties." She switched arms for scrubbing, her movements slower.

"Is there anything inside that needs fixing? Might as well tend to it while I'm here." He held up his toolbox. "Any loose floorboards or wobbly desks?"

She scooted the buckets backward the last few feet, and he edged back through the doorway. With a couple swipes, she finished the floor. He reached for her elbow to help her up, an instinctive gesture. Her skin was soft and warm, and so smooth, as if it had never seen the sun, never been scoured by cold wind. As delicate as a flower petal.

When she was on her feet, she eased her arm from his grasp, rolling down her sleeves and buttoning the cuffs. "There is one thing that needs fixin'."

"Oh?" He focused on her face again.

"One of the shelves here in the cloakroom. There's a broken bracket and the shelf tips." She reached out and rocked the empty shelf. "I would hate for anything to fall on one of the children."

Elias bent to survey the damage. The bracket hung by one screw. "This will be a quick fix." Digging through his toolbox, he found a screw that would work. "If you'll hold the shelf steady, I'll fasten it back together."

Savannah took hold of the shelf, and he went to his knees to work on the underside. Soon the job was finished and he stood. "You've done a good job today. The place looks great."

"You sound surprised." Her chin went up a notch.

"Don't get all defensive. I'll admit I didn't think you'd ever been on the business end of a scrub brush, but you proved me wrong."

She rubbed her shoulder, blushing a bit. "Would you believe me if I said I had never washed windows before today? Rut had to show me how to use the vinegar and newspaper. I tried it first with soapy water and it looked terrible."

"You got the hang of it. Everything's bright as a new penny now."

A smile touched her lips, but when she looked at her skirt, dirty and water-splotched, the smile faded. "If my aunt Georgette could see me now, she'd have a fit of the vapors."

Vay-pahs.

"Everything will be shipshape as soon as you wax

the floor." He put his hands in his pockets and leaned against the now-sturdy shelf.

"Wax the floors?" Her eyes went wide.

"Sure. You scrubbed off the dirt and most of the old wax. Soon as everything dries, you have to put down a new coat of wax to protect the floors." Elias pushed himself off the shelf with his shoulder and opened a cupboard in the corner. "Tins of wax are in here along with rags."

"Does it have to be done today?" Savannah sounded forlorn and her shoulders drooped.

It really should be done before school started on Monday, but he didn't have the heart to tell her. "How are you making out at the Halvorsons?"

She shrugged. "Fine. They're all very nice. I just wish they spoke a little English or I spoke a little Norwegian." She spread her damp hands, palms up, and something caught his eye. Every fingertip had a callus along the edge.

Now where had she gotten calluses, and in such odd places?

She gathered cleaning supplies, returning them to the basket she'd brought. He picked up the water buckets. "I'll sluice these out for you."

When he returned, she had the basket and his toolbox on the porch.

"I'll give you a ride back to the Halvorsons'." He put a full pail of water just inside the door to prime the pump on Monday.

Once they were headed down the road, he remembered what his mother had asked him to do. "Say, tomorrow, after church, my ma would like to have you over to dinner at our place. Well, my folks' place, but I'll be there for Sunday dinner."

Savannah didn't answer right away, and he began to be irked. Was she too good to have dinner at his parents' home? His ire rose. If that's how she was going to be, then fine—

"I'd like that. Tell her thank you for me." Graciously said.

He calmed down.

She shielded her eyes from the sun and looked up at him. "Will your brother be there, as well?"

Elias frowned. "No, he'll still be in the Cities. Why?"

"I looked through the desks and shelves, and there are hardly any school supplies. I couldn't find chalk or ink or paper. There's a ruler and a new attendance book in the teacher's desk, but that's about it. If I'm to have nearly a dozen pupils, I'll need some slates and readers and tablets at the very least."

He pulled the buckboard to a stop. "You do understand how things work out here, right? This is a poor school district. The kids bring the supplies they have at home, and if they don't have any, you make do."

Savannah's eyebrows rose, and she looked at him as if he was a simpleton. "How can the children get a proper education if they don't have the tools they need? There's not even a dictionary or globe in the school. Not to mention the condition of the few readers and spellers I found."

"I guess that's why they need a teacher as smart as you." Elias slapped the reins, sending the mare into a trot, and smothering a smile at her gasp of outrage.

For a teacher, Miss Savannah Cox sure had a lot to learn.

Chapter Four

Elias chirruped to the mare, the Sunday morning breeze whipping up the sorrel's mane as the buckboard rolled along. Normally he would ride his saddle horse, but he was supposed to bring Miss Cox to his parents' home for dinner after church.

Early mornings were the best, when everything was clean and new, the sun fresh in the sky and birds awakening in the long grass. The day promised to be another scorcher, but for now, the temperature was tolerable.

Ahead, the church steeple pierced the sky. He loved that the church was the oldest building in Snowflake, the first permanent structure erected by its inhabitants when they'd reached their new home on the Minnesota prairie.

And he liked being a deacon in the church, responsible for the building and grounds. He liked being the first one there on a Sunday morning to unlock the door, to spend a little time in prayer as he swept the steps and made sure the hymnals were straightened in the racks.

The varnished brown doors opened without a sound, and he left them wide, letting in the fresh air. Six pews on either side of a central aisle led to the pulpit. His boots sounded loud on the red-painted floor, and he glanced up to the pale blue arched ceiling with exposed white rafters like ribs.

In an alcove behind the pulpit, the church's prized stained glass window glowed in the sunlight. Ruby, turquoise, emerald and gold pieces of glass created flowers and vines around a cross. The window had come all the way from Germany, paid for by the saving and scrimping and generosity of the small congregation.

Elias opened windows, propping them with short pieces of wood to allow the cross breeze to circulate. In winter he hauled coal and had the place toasty by the time the first parishioners showed up, but in summer his job was to get the building as cool as possible.

People began arriving, neighbors and friends, greeting one another, filing into their customary seats. The pastor came in, holding his big Bible, his thinning hair combed over his pink scalp. His little wife, her hair in tight silver curls, edged into her front-row pew.

All the while, Elias kept an eye on the doorway. The Halvorsons were late. Per Halvorson had a well-earned reputation for being early, often arriving at the same time as Elias and helping ready the church, but today there was no sign of him.

Had something happened? Was there an illness in the house? Everyone had seemed fine yesterday when he'd delivered Savannah home.

His parents entered. Pa nodded and put his hand on Ma's lower back, guiding her to a seat. Elias liked that about his folks. They weren't inappropriate, but they were affectionate toward one another in small ways, even in public. If he ever married, Elias wanted to still be that close with his wife after almost thirty years.

Ah, there was Per Halvorson, but his normally sunny

face looked like a thundercloud. He ushered Lars and Rut ahead of him, and Agneta hurried in behind.

Where was Savannah? Hadn't she come? Surely she was a churchwoman. Tyler would never hire someone to teach who had no faith…

Savannah came through the doorway, and Elias's breath hitched. She looked just as if she'd stepped off the cover of the *Godey's Ladies' Book* his mother liked to pore over. The pale green material of her dress shimmered as she walked. Tucks and frills and furbelows everywhere, even more elaborate than the dress she'd worn on the stagecoach.

And her hair, that ripe-wheat-in-the-summer-sun hair, was swept up and back on her head to a mass of ringlets and curls tucked under a pale green hat that sported ostrich-tip feathers.

Heads turned, eyes widened, elbows hit ribs and whispers scurried through the air. She paused in the doorway. Most seats were full, and the pastor was headed to the front. Mr. Petersen plucked the single string of the *psalmodikon* as the pastor took his hymnal and found the correct page.

Savannah caught Elias's eye, pink flying in her cheeks. Her eyes asked, *Where do I sit?*

He moved to the door and took her elbow. "Good morning." The congregation got to its feet, rustling and moving. "My mother would be pleased if you sat with us."

Savannah gave him a grateful nod, and he led her up the right-hand side of the church, letting her enter the pew before him to sit beside his mother. Elias edged in after her, and when he sat, her voluminous skirts brushed his leg.

It seemed to take forever for her to arrange her

furled parasol, her handbag, her fan and her Bible. Elias waited, holding the hymnal as the congregation began to sing. At last she was ready, stood, and grasped her half of the book.

She took one look and gave him a bewildered glance. Of course, the hymnal was written in Norwegian. All around him the hearty voices of farmers and housewives and children sang of the Rock of Ages in their native tongue, but Savannah was mute.

Elias sang, but his mind was on her. Overdressed, nearly late, and everyone around her spoke a different language. What kind of church experience would this be for her? Why hadn't Tyler found someone from this part of the country to be the new schoolteacher? The poor girl had to be miserable.

Then she began to hum the tune. Her eyes closed, as if the music was seeping into her soul.

Elias sang softly so as to be able to hear her. She had a nice voice. Admiration rose for her. Worshipping in spite of the unfamiliar surroundings.

The song ended and they sat. She fussed with her skirts again, arranging them just so. Why did women wear such cumbersome garments? When she turned to smile at his mother on her left, the ostrich feathers on her hat brushed Elias's head. He leaned away, swatting them out of his face, but the tickle made him sneeze.

"God bless you," she whispered, oblivious to the cause of his predicament. "What is that instrument?" She looked at where Mr. Petersen sat.

"It's a *psalmodikon*. Most Norwegian churches have one."

She nodded and watched as Mr. Petersen played it while the offering was gathered in.

The sermon was probably excellent, but Elias had

a difficult time concentrating. Her dress rustled with her every movement, and every time he inhaled, he breathed in her perfume. Roses? Violets? Some sort of flowery, girlie smell. In profile, her pert little nose tilted up a bit at the end, and her lashes skimmed her cheeks when she blinked.

He caught a movement down the way—his father leaning forward with a one-eyebrow-raised look and a nod Elias's way.

Which was when Elias remembered telling Pa that the new teacher was pretty. That was Pa. Subtle as a sledgehammer through a windowpane.

Evidently Pa wasn't the only one who thought Miss Cox pretty. After church, everyone flocked around, waiting for an introduction.

"This is Peder Bergdahl. Peder, Miss Cox, the new teacher." Elias spoke in Norwegian, translating for Savannah.

She nodded to the burly young man. "A pleasure."

"This is Samuel Eggleston. Miss Cox."

Knut Dotseth.

Jespar Rosedahl.

Magnus Haugen.

Every bachelor in the county. Elias shifted his weight and looked at his watch as, one after another, they elbowed each other out of the way to meet her.

Then came the families with children. He translated greetings and pointed out her students. The women hung back a little, whispering, eyes troubled. Elias caught snatches of their comments, and he found his jaw tightening.

Savannah excused herself and sought out Mr. Petersen. Thankfully, he spoke a bit of English and was only too happy to show her his beloved *psalmodikon*. He

pointed out the flat stick marked with the finger place-
ments for various notes and the pegs for tightening the
single string. Savannah nodded, asked a question, and
Mr. Petersen beamed. Stepping aside, he motioned for
her to go ahead.

Elias was amazed. Sven Petersen never let anyone
touch the musical instrument. He'd made it himself as
a young man in Norway and brought it to America. He
cherished and guarded it and played it with loving care.

Voices stilled as Savannah played, picking out the
tune to "A Mighty Fortress is Our God." She never
missed a note, and when she finished, everyone was
smiling. Her own smile was especially bright, and Elias
sucked in a breath. How had she conquered the instrument so quickly? She hadn't known what one was before, and yet she played it well.

Finally, only a few families remained, including the
Halvorsons. Per Halvorson took Elias aside. "You need
to tell her we leave for church at nine-thirty and not a
minute after. Never have I seen a woman take so long
to prepare for church. The dress, the hat, the shoes.
And then the hair. Did you know that women heat up
an iron stick and wrap their hair on it to make curls?"
He snorted. "If God did not give you curls, then why do
you want them? Straight hair is good enough for church
if it is what God gave you. You tell her." He crossed his
arms, and Elias got an image of what Per had endured
that morning.

"I'll let her know."

"Yes. Already I think I am going to have to add a
room to the house for her belongings. Never have I
seen a woman with so many things. There is no room
in the loft, no room anywhere for the boxes and cases.

She brought enough for five years. Do you think she will stay even one?"

Elias shrugged. "I hope so, for the children's sake. They need schooling. But it will be hard."

Per nodded. "It is good for the children to be in school. I hope she is a good teacher. She will teach them fine manners and good English if she can stay. They will become real Americans, not rough Norske farmers."

Savannah stooped to say hello to little Ingrid Langerud. Ingrid would be Savannah's youngest student this term. The child, big-eyed, twirled the end of her blond braid as she gazed at her teacher. Savannah took Ingrid's hand and drew it to her skirt, letting the little girl feel the heavy, shiny fabric. Ingrid's shy smile had Elias smiling, too. Women and their fripperies. It sure started young.

"You were right."

"Huh?" Elias turned to where his father had taken Per's place.

"She's pretty."

He slanted Pa a sideways glance. "And she's small and from the South and green as spring grass."

Pa chuckled. "She might surprise you."

"What makes you say that?"

He shrugged. "It's just that most women are full of surprises. You think you know them. You think you can predict how they'll act or what they'll say, and then, wham! Out of nowhere, they surprise you. Your mother's done it to me a thousand times."

"This one seems pretty cut-and-dried. Just cleaning the school yesterday about did her in. She didn't even have the stamina to finish the job properly. The floors got washed, but they didn't get waxed." Elias shook his head. "The first time she has to shovel a path through the snow to the coal shed, she's going to collapse and call it quits."

Pa glanced out the window. "No sign of snow yet, though. And the floors will be fine for another week, I'm sure. You should go fetch her, so we can head home for lunch. Your ma cooked special most of yesterday."

When he approached, Savannah looked at Elias as if he was a lifesaver and she was drowning. "Are you ready to go?"

"If you are."

He followed her outside into the sunshine. She popped open her pale green parasol. How many of those things did she have?

As they drove toward his parents' place, Elias asked, "How did you like church?"

She shook her head. "I couldn't understand the words, but the feeling in the room was familiar. God speaks all our languages. I worshipped, the rest of the congregation worshipped. It was good. I especially enjoyed the music."

Elias didn't know how he would've fared under the circumstances, if he'd been dropped into a church service where they spoke only Russian or Italian or some other language he didn't know. He'd have been too distracted to worship—and, if he was honest, disgruntled at not being able to understand what was going on.

"I did have a question, though." She slanted the parasol back on her shoulder. "What's the reasoning behind the color scheme inside the church? I've never seen one painted like that before."

He shrugged. "The colors are symbolic, I guess. The sky-blue ceiling represents heaven."

"And the red floor?"

He grinned. "Like I said, symbolic."

They traveled in silence for a while as Elias tried to decide how to broach the subject Per Halvorson had asked him to tackle. This really should be Tyler's job, running interference between his teacher and her landlord.

"Savannah, about this morning. Per wanted me to talk to you."

"He seemed out of sorts. Did something happen to upset him?" She adjusted her skirt to keep it from flapping. "He's been nothing but kind until this morning."

Elias eased his tight collar. "Well, the thing you have to know about Per is that he hates being late, especially to church."

"We weren't late. We arrived precisely on time."

"Well, to Per, on time means fifteen minutes early. He's known for coming well ahead of time to any function. He thought all your primping made him late today. I'm just giving you a little warning to either cut some of the getting-ready steps, or start sooner, that's all." Elias shrugged. "Is that what you wear to church where you're from?"

Her look got a little frosty and her chin went up. "What's wrong with what I'm wearing now? Surely it's acceptable to wear nice clothes to church? You're wearing a suit and tie."

"Well, there's nice clothes and there's nice clothes. But what I'm trying to say is, you need to be ready to go to church earlier so Per can get there at a time when he's comfortable."

"Fine, why don't you tell me when that is? I asked several times when we needed to be ready, but nobody in the house understood me."

"Per said he wanted to leave his house by nine thirty.

If you could make it earlier, that would be even better. To Per, on time is late."

"I didn't know I was making him late. In the future, I'll be sure to be ready sooner." Frustration colored her voice. "But there isn't anything I can do about my wardrobe, and I wish you'd stop twitting me about it. It isn't a crime to wear the latest fashions or have nice clothes."

"It is if you're the only one for a hundred miles dressed like that and it makes the mothers of your students feel like you're lording it over them that you're better off than they are."

Her mouth fell open. "Is that what you think I'm doing? Is that what the ladies think?"

"They were whispering about it, about how they never saw clothes like yours, and how you were a foreigner who must be rich, and what were you doing way out here nearly to the Dakotas." The hurt in her eyes had him backtracking. "I'm not saying you're lording it over them, I'm just saying that might be how they feel."

"That's wonderful." She sank back into the seat. "Without speaking a word, I've managed to alienate at least half the county."

Elias propped his elbows on his knees, wishing Tyler was here to take this whole situation off his hands.

The women thought she was a snob. Savannah didn't know whether she wanted to scream or cry. How was she supposed to disabuse their minds when she couldn't even talk to them?

What if they got Elias's brother, Tyler, to fire her? Where would she go? She couldn't face Raleigh yet, and she'd hate to admit failure in her first job before she even got started.

"Here's the farm. Pa homesteaded it right after the

war. He held on through the grasshopper years, and now it's doing pretty well. When the option came to buy the two sections to the west, Tyler and I purchased them, and we run the farm together." Elias turned the horse in through an open gate. "We run sheep and cattle and raise wheat and corn. I raise and train a few horses every year and help Pa on the farm when I can."

"And do you live here?"

"Sort of. Since I'm the town sheriff, I have a room on the back of the jail, but half the time I stay out here. It's only a couple miles from town, and I have a part-time deputy, Bjorn. He lives in town, so he keeps an eye on things." Elias shrugged. "Upholding the law isn't too difficult in Snowflake. There's usually time for a bit of farm work."

A pretty frame house with flowers in pots on the porch sat at the end of the drive. A few trees had been planted, giving the place a settled, homey look. A large barn with lots of fences took up a big part of the farm-yard, and beyond the barn, crops stretched far away.

If only she could board here, she would have a bedroom she could stand upright in.

Savannah struck down that ungrateful thought. The Halvorsons were generous to board her, and she should be thankful, cramped loft or not.

Mr. and Mrs. Parker met them at the door. "Come on in, Miss Cox. We're sure glad you're here," Mr. Parker said in greeting. He was tall and broad like Elias, with silver dusting his dark hair and crow's feet showing at the corners of his eyes.

Mrs. Parker nodded and smiled. "*Ja*, ve are glad. Tyler vas very happy to haff a teacher for this fall for the *barn*."

Savannah blinked, both at the word and the accent. "I'm sorry. The barn?"

"Oh, my pardon. Elias?" Her brows scrunched together as she looked to her son.

"*Barn* is the Norwegian word for children."

"I'll tuck that away to use on Monday." Savannah smiled at Mrs. Parker. "Perhaps I can come to you for some lessons in speaking Norwegian. I think I will need them in order to best teach the *barn*. Now I understand how it is that Elias speaks fluent Norwegian and English."

"Yep." Mr. Parker beamed, putting his arm around his wife. "I am a blessed man to have found my sweet bride fresh off a boat from Norway. I grabbed her up before anyone else could." His pride in his wife shone in his eyes.

The meal was delicious, though Savannah had never seen food prepared the way Mrs. Parker had done it. Creamed rutabaga, dilled cucumber and a roasted meat, either beef or lamb, she wasn't sure.

"Elias…" Mr. Parker sat back after patting his wife's hand. "Why don't you take Miss Cox outside and show her around. I'm sure she'd enjoy a bit of a walk after a meal like that."

Savannah laid her napkin aside. "Let me help clear the table first."

"Nonsense. I can help my wife clean up. You go get some fresh air."

Elias pulled out her chair for her and held the door.

"Son, while you're out there, walk round the sheep, will you? Captain's keeping watch. They're in the close pasture."

"Yes, sir."

Savannah and Elias strolled past the sapling trees toward the barn. A breeze brushed her cheeks, and though it was warm, she was grateful for it. Without any wind, the day would be stifling. How a place this warm got the name Snowflake, she'd never know.

"Captain watches the sheep all by himself? I mean, with no shepherd?" She tilted her parasol to shade her face.

"Yep. Pa can't afford to hire a shepherd just for the couple hundred sheep he runs, so he relies on Captain to look after the flock. He has another dog, too, but she's expecting puppies any day now, so Pa's keeping her close to the house. I'm not sure if he was as excited about his own sons' births as he is about this litter." Elias bent and plucked a long grass stem from along a fence line, bending it and snapping off little pieces as they walked.

"You said you have horses here?"

"Sure, almost a dozen head right now. They're in the pasture behind the barn."

"Could we see them?" Savannah lifted her hem to step across the dusty ruts left by farm wagons.

"You like horses?"

"Oh, yes. I'm a very good equestrienne. Many Southern women are. I had riding lessons from the time I was a child." A pang hit her heart. Girard had taken her riding many times. It was one of the things they shared, a love of horses.

"Too bad you're not dressed for it. I'd saddle up a couple of horses. We could ride round the sheep that way." He threw away the last piece of grass stem.

"It wouldn't matter how I was dressed if you had a sidesaddle. I'd risk my Sunday silk for a chance to ride." It had been much too long since she'd been on horseback.

"Are you serious?" He tilted his head, studying her.

"Of course I am."

"I forgot, you're always serious." He shrugged. "As it happens, we do have a sidesaddle. If you're sure, I'll bring in the horses."

Elias ducked into the barn and emerged with a pail half-full of grain in his hand and two halters slung over his shoulder. "Come around this way."

At the pasture gate, he whistled and clanked the handle against the bucket, shaking the oats. Heads came up from grazing, and several horses started toward him. Bays, chestnuts, a gray with a black mane and tail.

Elias scattered some of the grain on the ground, shouldering his way among the horses. "Which one would you choose?"

Savannah eyed them, knowing he was testing her. "The buckskin with the blaze. He looks like he could move."

"Hmm, you've a good eye. That's my horse, Buck. And you're right, he's fast. But he's not a lady's mount."

"How about the gray mare?"

He paused. "She's new, and I haven't ridden her much. I bought her over in Pipestone for a broodmare. She's got good lines, and I think I'd get some nice foals out of her. But she's a quick mover and she likes to run." He frowned. "Maybe I should put you up on my ma's horse, Gresskar." Pointing at a round little chestnut with a shaggy mane and knobby knees, he reached for the halter on his shoulder. "*Gresskar* means pumpkin."

"I told you I could ride. I'd like the gray. She won't unseat me." Savannah gripped her parasol. The man didn't think she could do anything. "What's her name? The gray?"

"Elsker."

Was that a blush reddening his cheeks?

"Elsker? What does that mean?"

He shrugged, not meeting her eyes. "*Elsker* means 'love' in Norwegian. She came with the name. I didn't give it to her." Elias busied himself getting halters on Buck and the gray mare. He dumped the rest of the grain on the grass for the horses left behind, and led the two mounts through the gate. "You're sure you want to do this? You're not dressed to ride, and if you get thrown, your dress will never be the same."

"I'm sure." She put conviction into her tone.

In short order, Savannah closed her parasol, leaning it against the barn wall, and went to Elsker's side, patting the mare Elias had saddled and speaking softly to her. While Elias was busy tacking up his horse, she checked the girths, making sure they were tight. The plain saddle bore only a scant resemblance to her ornate velvet-and-leather one at home, but it was serviceable and well cared for.

"I'll give you a leg up since we don't have a mounting block." Elias bent and laced his fingers for her to place her knee into. He lifted her easily, and soon she was gathering her skirts, tucking them in, fitting her foot into the stirrup and picking up the reins. Elsker sidled a bit, tossing her head.

Soon they were walking down a farm track, side by side. Savannah thrilled to the movement of a horse beneath her again, letting her body sway with Elsker's long-legged stride. The mare toyed with the bit, swishing her tail, sending Savannah all kinds of messages that she felt good and would like to move out of a walk.

"The sheep are in here." Elias stopped at a gate, leaning down to unlatch it and pull it open for her to ride through, all without getting off his horse. Buck piv-

oted like a seasoned professional as Elias closed the
gate behind them.

The sheep grazed in a bunch near the center of the
pasture, and Captain rose from the tall grass, loping
over, his tongue lolling and his tail curving up, like a
great bottlebrush. Elias pulled to a stop, and Captain
rose on his hind legs, planting his forepaws on Elias's
knee. The collie licked his hand and gave a bark before
bounding away toward the flock.

Elias stood in the stirrups, counting heads. "It's a
well-fenced pasture, and the dogs keep predators away,
but it's always a good idea to count noses."

They rode completely around the flock, and Elias,
finding nothing amiss with the sheep, opened the gate
again. "There's a creek about a mile east of here. Let's
head for that. Are you comfortable trotting?"

She tried not to be offended. He didn't know her
very well, after all, but his condescension grated. "I'd
be more comfortable at a canter." Savannah lifted the
reins and put her heel to the mare's side. This was all
the cue Elsker needed. She picked up her feet, leaping
into a gallop.

Elias shouted, but Savannah leaned forward, urging
the mare on. The wind whipped against Savannah's
cheeks, pulling at her hair. Her hat gave up the fight,
flying off, and her skirts flapped against the horse's
side.

For the first time since she was left standing at the
altar, Savannah felt as if she could leave the hurt behind
and be free, if for only a little while. Free of the stigma
of being a jilted bride, free of her fears and insecurities. Embracing the wind, skimming over the ground,
exulting in the rushing speed… A laugh escaped her
throat, surprising her.

Hoofbeats pounded the ground, and she glanced back. Elias urged his buckskin on, yelling, but the wind tore his words away. As he drew nearer, Elsker stuck her neck out, eating up the ground in long bounds, determined not to be passed. Buck fell back.

Savannah noticed a gully ahead. It wasn't wide, but it was deep. That must be what Elias was shouting about. With a reckless abandon that telegraphed itself to her mount, she leaned forward, her hands high on the mare's neck. With a huge leap, Elsker soared over the ditch, landing gracefully on the far side and galloping onward. At the horizon, trees appeared where the creek must be. Savannah eased back in the saddle, gently pulling the mare up, asking rather than demanding.

Elsker resisted for a moment and then dropped to a lope, then a trot, then a walk, tossing her head and prancing, her sides pumping. Savannah patted the mare's warm neck, pleased and exhilarated.

Elias pounded up on Buck, his face like a thundercloud. "What were you thinking? You could've broken your neck!"

Savannah tried to make some sense of her hair, which had come loose from its pins and lay about her shoulders in a tumbled, curly mess. "I was in no danger. I saw the ditch in plenty of time and knew we could jump it easily." She patted Elsker again. "This is a very fine mare."

"You knocked about ten years off my life. I saw myself trying to explain to Tyler how I killed his teacher on the eve of the first day of school." Elias didn't seem to be quite over his temper yet. "That was a foolish thing to do."

Savannah blinked. He really was upset. "I told you I was a good rider. There was nothing to fear."

"You raced an untried mare over unknown ground with no thought to prairie dog holes or gullies or anything else. You knew I was hollering at you to stop, but you just kept going faster. You have no idea of the dangers you could encounter here. This isn't a bridle path in some city park, you know." He whipped off his hat and slapped his thigh. "What if you'd come up against a barbed wire fence? The mare wouldn't have seen it in time, running full out like she was, and you'd have come a cropper for sure. As it is, you had no idea how that mare would react to having a woman in flapping skirts on her back. What if she'd started bucking, shied or flat out run away with you? Plenty of danger to you, but what about the danger to the mare? You could've killed her along with yourself."

Savannah held up her palm to stop the flow of words, remorse flooding her as she realized the truth in his tirade. "I'm sorry. I didn't think. It just felt so good to be riding again, and the mare wanted to go." She dropped her hand and gripped the reins.

"Walk her and cool her out a bit before we get to the creek." He pressed his hat back on his head and nudged Buck into a walk.

Savannah wanted to say that she knew enough to cool out a horse before allowing it to drink, but she clamped her mouth shut, aware that she'd transgressed. She followed Elias across the open ground and down the creek bank, keeping Elsker to a leisurely walk, feeling the mare's breathing slow.

They arrived at the water's edge. Elias slid from the saddle, then reached up for Savannah. His hands spanned her waist, and when she kicked free of the stirrup, he lifted her to the ground. How many times had Girard done the same for her after a ride? But Elias had bigger muscles, broader shoulders. Where Girard had worked inside at a desk, in a job with few physical demands, Elias worked outside, helping on his father's farm, keeping law and order in Snowflake. Handy with tools, good with animals, a man of the land. Girard had been suave in any social situation, quick to smile and flatter. Elias said exactly what he thought, pulling no punches.

She drew herself up short. Comparisons got her nowhere. And anyway, why should she care? She was over love and romance forever and beyond noticing how handsome and virile a man was.

The horses drank, Buck pawing at the water and blowing ripples in the surface. It was much cooler there under the trees, and Savannah took the time to quickly divide her tumbled hair into three hanks and braid it to lie on her shoulder.

Elias watched her, something intense in his eyes that made her self-conscious. He must still be angry. Savannah unpinned the ribbon at her throat and used it to secure the end of her braid. "I suppose I'll have to look for my hat on the way back. I only used one hatpin today, since I didn't know I would be riding. If my aunt Carolina saw me now, she'd be mortified and call me a hoyden."

"You've mentioned your aunts before. Are they such dragons?" Elias squatted at the edge of the creek, picking up sticks and breaking them, tossing them into the water.

A prickle of homesickness jabbed Savannah's chest. "Aunt Carolina is a dragon and a sweetheart. She practically raised us girls, she and Aunt Georgette. Aunt Georgette is flighty and gentle and given to dramatics, but so much fun when she forgets to worry about everything. My mother passed away giving birth to my youngest sister. There are three of us girls, me, then Charlotte, then Virginia."

"And your father?"

"Father is a banker. He travels frequently, up and down the East Coast. His job involves investing, quite often in shipping companies, and he prefers to visit business sites before putting money into them." She placed her hand on Elsker's neck, fiddling with her mane. "He makes a lot of money, but he's rarely home."

"If your family is so well off, why did you come all this way to teach school for thirty dollars a month? It sounds as if you had everything you ever needed at home." Elias stood, tucking his hands into his pockets.

She sighed. "Money can't buy everything. Maybe I just needed something more." Aware of the wistfulness in her voice, she firmed her tone. "We should be getting back, don't you think?"

They rode back to his parents' at a slower pace, heading into the afternoon sun. Elias found her hat and retrieved it for her. The feathers were broken, and the spot where the hatpin had been was torn clean through. Savannah shrugged. The ride had been worth it.

When they were in the buggy on their way to the Halvorsons', Elias asked, "Are you nervous about tomorrow?"

Savannah searched the horizon as thoughts of the school came flooding back. Should she be honest or bluff her way through?

"Yes, very." The truth slipped out, the confidence she'd gained racing across the prairie on Elsker drifting away like mist. "I'm more worried now than I was before church. What if the parents don't think I can do a good job? If I've managed to put off all the mothers because I dress and speak differently, then will the children be put off, as well? What if, right now, they're sitting around their tables wondering if Tyler made a big mistake? You seem to think he has, so why should they be different?" All his questions and comments about her lack of competence came charging back, all the more powerful when paired with her own misgivings.

Elias pulled up before the house, his face grim. No doubt he still thought she'd make a hash of teaching here. She climbed down before he could help her, and disappeared inside without a backward glance.

Chapter Five

Savannah unlocked the schoolhouse door, her fingers chilly. Stepping inside, she inhaled. Though she'd expected the scents of soap and vinegar, another smell overlaid them. What was that? She entered the schoolroom and stopped.

The floor gleamed in the early morning light. Not from the scrubbing she'd given it, but from a mirror-like layer of wax. From the depth of the shine, several coats of wax.

Only one person could've done it, and she'd spent the past night disgruntled with him. Chagrin tugged at her lips. It must've taken him hours…all evening. The whole time she'd been fuming at Elias, he'd been here polishing the floor, doing her job for her.

Small didn't begin to describe how she felt.

Glancing at the clock, she took a deep breath, pushing thoughts of Elias from her mind. She had too much to do before the students arrived to allow herself to be distracted.

A half hour later, Savannah forced herself to relax… again. Should she greet the students at the door? Should she be seated behind her desk when they came in?

Checking the clock for the third time that minute, she willed herself to remain calm.

The cloakroom, that's where she should be. To ring the bell. She hurried down the aisle, though it was only quarter to eight. Her skirt trailed the floor in a navy fall of tucks and drapes, and she smoothed the pin-tucked white blouse. She fingered the gold locket she'd put on this morning, her only jewelry for the day. Surely this outfit was sober and prim enough to satisfy any critic.

Taking a moment, she flicked open the hasp on the locket to study the portrait inside of her beautiful mother. Savannah barely remembered her, being only five when she'd died, but she'd committed every feature to memory. Would her mother be proud of her for striking out on her own? If her mother were alive, would Savannah have left home at all?

Closing the locket, holding it in her fist, she sent up a quick prayer. *Lord, help me get through this day. Give me wisdom and strength to teach these children.*

Young voices reached her ears, and her eyes popped open, her heart kicking up a notch. Footsteps clattered up the stairs. Savannah put on a smile.

Lars and Rut Halvorson.

Relief had Savannah shaking her head.

"Good…mor-ning, Miss Cox." Rut beamed, remembering the English greeting Savannah had taught her at breakfast.

Lars nodded, his blond forelock hanging nearly to his eyes. He glanced at the water pail—which Savannah had filled first thing this morning, remembering to prime the pump and fill not only the drinking crock but the pail—and grinned.

Within moments, several more children arrived, chattering away to one another. The smallest, Ingrid, whom Savannah had met at church, hung back behind her older sister's skirts, keeping her finger tucked into the corner of her mouth.

As the hands on the clock hit eight, Savannah tapped Lars on the shoulder and pointed to the bell rope. He grinned and gave it a hearty tug. The mellow peel of the bell filled the air, vibrating in the cloakroom. The children filed into the schoolroom and found seats.

They seemed to know just where to go, organizing themselves at the desks with the youngest in front and the eldest in the back rows. Savannah went to her desk, picked up her ruler and rapped it on the desktop.

"Good morning, students." She smiled. "Let's open our day and our school year with prayer."

They stared back. She laced her fingers under her chin and bowed her head. Understanding dawned, and they followed suit.

"Dear Father, we ask Your blessing on our work here. May we be diligent, kind and industrious. Amen."

Tyler had left a list of students, and she called each name, making a check beside each one, trying to match the name with the face. Several times the children corrected her pronunciation, smiling as she tried to wrap her tongue around the unfamiliar syllables.

Her oldest student, Hakon, was sixteen, nearly grown, with broad shoulders and a sunburned fair face. He barely fit in the last desk. The youngest, Ingrid, sat alone on the front bench, her feet dangling inches above the board floor.

After reading aloud Psalm 1, Savannah took her seat behind the desk. "First primer class, please come forward." With so many children of different ages, she would need to assess where each was in their education and how to arrange them into classes.

Ingrid remained in her seat.

"First primer class."

Johann raised his hand in the back of the room. "Miss Cox, Ingrid is not speaking the English." His broken speech sounded like music to Savannah. A student who could understand her, at least a little bit... She had to restrain herself from running down the aisle and hugging the boy. Elias had led her to believe her students wouldn't know a word in any other tongue but Norwegian.

"How many of you speak at least a little English?"

Two hands went up, slowly. Johann and Hakon. The oldest students in the school. The ones who had attended under the previous teachers, perhaps?

All right, not as many as she'd hoped, but two was better than none. "Johann, will you ask Ingrid to come forward, please, and bring her books?"

Ingrid slid off her seat, gathered her two books and stood in front of Savannah's desk. Savannah's heart went out to the child, and she motioned for Ingrid to come to her side.

The schoolbooks proved to be a speller and a primer, both written in Norwegian. Savannah pointed to the first word in the speller, but Ingrid shrugged and shook her head.

Savannah sent her back to her seat, smiling to let the girl know she wasn't displeased.

But she was daunted.

One after another they came forward so she could examine their supplies and books and get a feel for where they were in their schooling.

Johann and Hakon helped, translating where they could, though their own English was limited. Johann had a history book written in English, and Hakon had a *McGuffey's Fifth Reader.*

By the end of the school day, Savannah had a headache and a heartache. The children were obviously frustrated by not being able to communicate with her or understand what she wanted. They had almost no books or tools, and she didn't know how to reach them, to educate them when they couldn't communicate.

She dismissed the students, remaining behind as they streamed out the door as if being released from prison. What would they go home and tell their parents?

Probably the same thing she was thinking herself: that she was the worst teacher in the whole world.

Elias rubbed his aching shoulder and tried to concentrate on the new batch of wanted posters he'd received in the mail. Hardly likely that any of these desperados would pass through Snowflake, but he liked to keep up-to-date on the latest news.

His hands still smelled like floor wax. What had compelled him to finish the floor at the schoolhouse last night? And by lamplight, no less?

It certainly wasn't to win favor with Savannah Cox. Or to apologize for speaking his mind on the subject of her unsuitability for the job of Snowflake, Minnesota, schoolteacher.

He shuffled the papers into a tight stack and shoved them into his desk. The hands on the clock crawled toward three. Things were quiet here. Maybe he'd take a little ride.

After all, he'd promised Tyler he'd look after the school.

Buck waited at the hitching rail out front, and Elias swung himself into the saddle. They quickly left the town behind, traveling between the wheat and corn-fields. The sun shone down hot, and from the nearly harvest-ready wheat fields arose the aroma of baking bread—one of Elias's favorite scents in the world. Next week, every farmer would be scrambling to get reapers into the fields, and in a couple more weeks, threshers would arrive. Everything in the community would come to a halt until the wheat was threshed and sacked and stored.

And after that, the corn would be ready. And if enough rain fell and the cold weather held off, perhaps another cutting of hay. Elias would rely more heavily on his deputy, Bjorn, to keep the jail while he helped his father on the farm.

When the schoolhouse came into view, he slowed Buck to a walk. He was just in time to see the door fly open and a stream of children emerge, tumbling down the steps like lambs let out of the barn. He pulled Buck up at the crossroads and let the kids go by, greeting them as they passed.

He walked his horse up to the school, but though he waited several minutes, Savannah didn't emerge. How much after-school work could she have on the first day? Or maybe she had to keep someone behind? He hadn't counted noses, so perhaps one of the kids was still inside with her.

The door stood partially open, and he pushed it back with the flat of his hand. Nobody in the cloakroom. Then a faint sound caught his ear. Not conversation.

It sounded like…crying.

Soft, but for sure, weeping.

His gut knotted.

What should he do? He knew nothing about dealing with a crying woman.

And yet leaving felt like deserting the field of battle.

He eased around the partition. She sat at the desk, her head on her arms, her shoulders shaking. Sunshine fell across the desks and gleamed off the polished red oak floor. The room smelled of children and lunches and wax and chalk dust.

Elias didn't want to startle her or to intrude, so he eased back into the cloakroom, went to the door and closed it with a loud click.

He heard stirring noises inside the schoolroom, sniffing and—he grinned—someone delicately blowing her nose.

"Who's there?" Her voice sounded watery and ended with another sniff.

"Just me." He rounded the divider again, sauntering in. "Thought I'd see how the first day went."

She blinked a few times and squared things up on her already tidy desk. "Fine."

Not a good liar.

"Kids behave?" He stepped up onto the platform and perched his hip on the corner of the desk.

"They were fine." Her lashes stood out in damp points, and her eyes glistened.

He waited—a trick he'd learned from his pa. Truth often came out of being quiet and giving the other person some empty space to fill.

She stared at her hands, her desktop and out the window. He counted to ten, slowly.

"It was awful." Her blue eyes locked with his. "It was nothing like I imagined. How on earth am I supposed to teach them when we don't speak the same language, we don't have proper books and materials, and there are so many different ages?" She gripped her fingers together on the blotter, so tight her pale skin whitened even more. "My practice teaching didn't look anything like this."

"You mean you didn't train in a one-room schoolhouse where the students didn't understand you?" He put a teasing lilt in his voice.

"No." She regarded him gravely. "I received my education at the Raleigh Women's Normal School, and my classroom teaching experience was in a large city school. We only had one grade per room, and I taught children who could already read and write. I had a seasoned teacher in the room the entire time, which only lasted for two weeks. After that they gave us our diplomas and launched us into the world."

He resisted the urge to roll his eyes. It was worse than he thought. Two weeks of practical experience in a completely different environment.

"And I never thought I'd actually *be* a teacher." The touch of bewilderment in her voice caught his attention.

"Why study to be a teacher if you didn't intend to teach?" That was like studying to be a doctor and never treating any patients.

She grew still, her face losing all expression, sadness invading her eyes, leaving them almost lifeless. "I went to school to fill time. My father would've sent me to a finishing school in Europe if I had desired, but I chose the normal school in Raleigh so I could stay at home."

Finishing school? He nodded as if he understood, and then asked, "What's a finishing school? What do they finish?"

"It's a school for young ladies, teaching them all they will need to know to take their proper places in society. They teach deportment, dance, art, menu planning, equitation, elocution, decorating, needle arts, lots of things."

He covered his mouth with his fingertips. Finishing school sounded like a load of bog grass. Did anyone teach these ladies how to cook or clean or make clothes or milk a cow? Or anything about fending for themselves if the need arose? It sounded as if they learned just what they needed to snag a rich husband. "I think you chose a better path. At least with normal school training you could get a job and be useful, support yourself." Though that training seemed to be lacking, too. At least to teach out here.

"Most of the girls who go to finishing school have no need to support themselves. They are preparing for marriage."

"What about you? Didn't you want to get married?" Didn't all women?

This time her eyes resembled blue flames. "I'd prefer not to discuss my personal life. I'd rather talk about this school. How did the previous teachers handle the challenges? I need to know what has worked in the past and how to get through to the children."

She could go from bunny-soft to porcupine-prickly in a flash of gunpowder. Elias picked up a pencil and rolled it between his palms. "The first one was a fellow from Saint Paul, and he left before Christmas. Said he got a job offer to work in a lumber camp at more than twice what we could pay him here."

Elias forced his jaw to relax. "The second one was a woman, also from Saint Paul. She didn't last long, just took off one day with no explanation. Maybe she was bored away from the big city. Maybe she didn't want to spend a winter out here, shoveling snow and toting coal buckets." He tried to keep the bitterness from his voice. Britta had made some sharp comments about the "locals" when she first arrived, but he'd thought she would in time get used to the place and the people and the pace of life. He'd been willing to plan his whole future around that hope.

"Anyway, they both ran and left Tyler high and dry in the middle of the school year."

Savannah's spine straightened and blue sparks snapped from her eyes. "That's terrible. How could they just abandon their responsibilities? Abandon the students? No wonder the children are still so uneducated."

Tilting his head to eye her, Elias set the pencil down. "Don't be too quick to judge. This isn't an easy job, and this isn't an easy place to live come mid-winter. Wait until you've walked a mile in their snowshoes…literally. You might be singing a different tune by then."

She froze, studying his face. Her brows, slightly darker than her hair, arrowed toward one another. "What did you say?"

"I said this isn't an easy job—"

"No, you said 'singing a different tune.'" She tapped her lip with her index finger, her eyes getting a faraway look. "A different tune." Her bottom lip disappeared, and then she focused once more, snapping her fingers. "Oh, my, forgive my manners. A lady shouldn't use such a vulgar gesture. But thank you all the same. I think you may have given me a little crack in the wall I'm trying to break down."

"How did I do that? What wall?" The schoolhouse walls looked fine to him. She hopped from one topic to the next like a grasshopper in tall grass.

Her laugh surprised him. "Never you mind, Mr. Parker." She pushed back her chair. "I wouldn't want you to think I couldn't do my job."

She rose, her skirt hem swishing along the floor, her little shoes tapping on the shiny boards as she gathered her belongings. Her handbag fell off the corner of the desk, and when she picked it up, her cheeks pinked. "My manners have deserted me completely. I meant to say thank you the moment I saw you." She spread her hands, the bag dangling from her wrist. "The floors. They must've taken you hours. Thank you so very much."

Elias eased off the desk. The shine in her eyes and the color in her cheeks hit him in the chest like a burst of warm air from the stove on a freezing day. Last night while he waxed and polished, he'd called himself all kinds of a fool, told himself he was doing it for Tyler, for the children, because it was a neighborly thing to do. But in the privacy of his heart, he admitted he'd done it for her. To make amends for being so churlish? Yes, that must be it.

"Are you telling me that my little brother waxed floors?" A familiar voice came from the cloakroom and then Tyler stepped through the doorway. Dust covered his checked suit and bowler. He wore an annoying smirk.

Heat prickled across Elias's chest, and his ears got hot. *Great.* "I thought you were in Saint Paul."

Tyler grimaced. "I never made it that far." He turned to Savannah, removing his hat. "Miss Cox, so nice to see you again." He surveyed the room. "You've got the place looking well. Though I can't imagine how you got Elias to wax floors. He'd rather unload a wagon of wheat a grain at a time than use a scrub brush." Tyler accepted her hand, holding it a tick longer than necessary, in Elias's opinion.

"Your brother has been most helpful." She withdrew her fingers from his clasp, smoothing her skirts. "Are you here long, Mr. Parker?"

He grimaced. "I'm afraid not. I had barely reached

Mankato on Saturday when I received a telegram from the state board. Since I was unable to fill the vacant teaching position in Kettinger, I'm told I will be teaching there this term. Kettinger is on the southern edge of the county, about an hour's ride from here. I'll head down there tonight and start school in the morning."

She pursed her lips. "I had hoped to talk with you about the conditions here. The school is almost completely unsupplied."

Tyler nodded, turning his bowler around and around in his hands. "I am aware, believe me. There is just no money in the budget for books and the like. I can try to get you some chalk and paper, but most of the school's allowance goes for coal and your salary. There's not much left after that."

Elias tucked his hands into his pockets. "The kids have some books, don't they?"

She nodded and then shook her head, a contradiction. "None that are of much use to me. Most of them aren't even in English."

Tyler sank onto a front bench and let out a long sigh. "I've been telling the board for three years now that they're neglecting the children in this part of the state. It seems like if you don't live in the Twin Cities, you have to fight for every bit of attention and help you get."

The clock chimed four. "I'm sorry." Savannah hurried down the aisle to the cloakroom. "I must be getting back to the Halvorsons. I don't want to make dinner late. Mr. Halvorson is a stickler for punctuality."

Tyler and Elias followed, and Elias was pleased to see that she checked the water bucket before closing the door and locking it.

"Thank you again, Elias, for doing the floors, and for helping me find something to try tomorrow that I hope will give us a better day." She gifted him with a small smile, nodded to Tyler and started down the road.

Elias watched her intently until he realized Tyler was doing the same. "Humph."

"What?" his brother asked.

"So you're going to teach down in Kettinger? For the whole term?"

Tyler nodded. "That means I need you to keep watching out for Miss Cox. Now more than ever."

Something in Tyler's tone grabbed Elias's attention. "What do you mean?"

His older brother took off his hat again and ran his fingers through his hair. "That telegram I got? It was a long one. Basically, they're not pleased with the reports from Blue Stone County in regards to the education system, and they say if we lose another teacher, they'll remove me from my position. If that happens, I can kiss my future political career goodbye."

Visions of Savannah crying after her first day, of her realizing she'd made a huge mistake coming here, of himself on his knees begging her to stay, drifted through Elias's mind and stuck there.

"You're going to owe me after all this," he told his brother.

Chapter Six

Getting Mr. Halvorson to understand that she needed him to take her to school in the wagon the next morning nearly tipped Savannah's frustration over the edge. She finally resorted to drawing what she needed on a piece of paper.

Lars took one look at her stick horses and boxy wagon and burst out laughing. He fired a couple quick sentences to his father and then pointed to the large case at the foot of the stairs. Savannah almost wept in relief when realization dawned on Mr. Halvorson's face.

They rode in style to school on the second day, rattling along in the farm wagon, harness jingling. Mr. Halvorson dropped them off, and before he left, he asked Lars a question. The boy tugged his earlobe and shrugged.

"Come get?" Lars asked Savannah. "Later?"

Pleased that he had used English, Savannah smiled and squeezed his shoulder. "No. I will walk home." She pantomimed with two fingers walking. Pointing to the case, she motioned that she would leave it in the school for now.

When class started for the day, Savannah couldn't

help but smile at the curious looks cast toward the case she'd placed in the corner.

Prayers, Scripture, roll call. She matched names and faces, and evidently did better this morning at pronouncing names, because she was corrected only twice.

When they'd finished the preliminaries, Johann raised his hand. "Miss Cox, vat is that?"

"A surprise. For later. First we have some work to do."

"Do I say in Norwegian for class?"

She shook her head. "Not right now, thank you. For now, I want to use only English, to see how much everyone understands."

From his bunched forehead, she suspected *he* didn't understand. Still, they would learn faster if she taught in English. And they'd start with the basics.

She went to the blackboard and wrote the alphabet in capital letters. Using her ruler, she pointed to each letter, saying it aloud and waiting for the class to respond. Frustratingly, the letters looked the same in Norwegian, but nearly every letter had a different pronunciation in English. Perhaps it would be better to start with whole words? She just didn't know.

Then she drew a picture of a cat's face, and put together *C*, *A* and *T.*

"Cat." She pointed to the animal, then the letters one at a time.

A few snickers.

"Cat," she repeated. "Johann, what is the Norwegian word for cat?"

He grinned. *"Katt."*

Startled, she set her ruler down. "If it sounds the same, why did they seem to have such a hard time with it?"

"Dat does not look like *katt*." He shook his head. "Meow."

Giggles sounded.

"All right. Come here." She held out the chalk to him. "Draw me a cat."

He slid from his desk and sauntered up, confidence in every line of his frame. With a few quick strokes, he drew a cat so lifelike Savannah's jaw dropped.

"That's amazing."

"Vat is…a-may-zing?"

"It means good."

He beamed.

"I think I will keep you busy making me some flash-cards." She tore three sheets of her precious paper into fourths and handed them to him. "Do you have a pencil?"

Johann shook his head.

"Use one of mine." She gave him one of the two she had. This really was ridiculous, trying to teach without the proper tools. She'd give up some coal to have tablets and pencils and pens and ink.

All morning they struggled through reading and arithmetic, though the numbers looked the same in either language, which was a plus. Savannah resorted to drawing pictures again, using tally marks in place of numbers, adding and subtracting to show what she wanted the children to do.

By noon, she was worn through and not sure she had made much progress. The youngest children seemed to be trying and learning, but the older students… They were holding back, as if they didn't trust what she was teaching them.

Or didn't trust her.

At lunchtime, all the students went out into the sunshine to eat, leaving Savannah alone at her desk. The laughter of the girls opened a hollow ache in her chest. They sounded like her sisters. How often had Charlotte and Virginia's hijinks irritated her? How often had she chided them for their hoydenish behavior?

How much wouldn't she give to be with them right now?

She peeked into her lunch pail. What wouldn't she give for some real Southern food, some cornbread and greens and fried ham? Though she'd been to Europe and sampled fine cuisine in the best hotels, she was a Southern girl at heart.

They all slogged through the afternoon until almost two, when Savannah set her pencil down and called for attention. She went to her case and hefted it onto her desk. Aware that every student watched, she unsnapped the hasps and unbuckled the straps. Opening the case so that the lid rested on the desk, she reached in and touched her most precious possession.

Without her bidding the students gathered around. Nestled in its velvet-lined bed lay her Celtic harp. The wood gleamed, glowing with a patina that bespoke the harp's age. As always, her heart thrilled at the sight of her beloved instrument.

Synove sucked in a breath, and Ingrid stood on tiptoe to see over the edge of the case.

Savannah raised the harp, sat in her chair and put the instrument on her lap, reveling in the familiar weight. With the back of her thumb, she strummed from the bass strings to the treble.

Wincing, she reached for her pitch pipe. After so much travel, bouncing and jouncing, and the change in climate, the harp was sadly out of tune. One by one she adjusted the strings until a harmonious sound vibrated through the schoolroom when she played. The children's eyes were round, and she held their attention with ease.

Margrethe reached out to touch the carved rosewood frame and then drew back. Gently, Savannah clasped her hand and drew it to the ridges and valleys of the Celtic knots and ivy decorating the harp.

After that, each student wanted to touch the instrument. She allowed them to pluck and strum the strings, stroke the woodwork and finger the pins. When they'd each had a turn, she adjusted the harp, leaning it gently on her shoulder, and played the first line to "Rock of Ages."

Faces lit up, recognition dawned and a couple students hummed along. She nodded to encourage them, and they began to sing, just as they had in church.

When the children reached the end of the first verse, she placed her hands flat on the strings to still their vibrations. "Now my turn." She plucked the strings and sang.

"Rock of Ages, cleft for me,
Let me hide myself in Thee;
Let the water and the blood,
From Thy wounded side which flowed,
Be of sin the double cure,
Save from wrath and make me pure."

Savannah knew she had a more than pleasant voice, especially after all her elocution and singing lessons, but the way her students listened to every word gratified her heart.

"Now you sing with me." She began again, slowly this time. "Rock of Ages…"

Synove caught on first and sang the line with Savannah. Soon everyone was singing. Savannah would sing the line, and then they would all chime in to repeat it. Over and over they sang, until everyone knew every word.

Setting the harp aside, she asked Johann to write the first verse in Norwegian while she did the same in English, side by side on the blackboard. This was where they would begin. Music was a universal language.

A bit later, dismissing school for the day, Savannah felt optimistic for the first time. When the last student had scampered out the door, she picked up her harp and strummed quietly. Before she knew it, the strains of Pachelbel's Canon in D Major filled the schoolroom. Something about the melody, the rhythm, the rich tapestry of the piece soothed her, and at the same time made her long for home and her sisters.

Charlotte played the violin and Virginia the pianoforte, and the three of them had spent many long hours sharing their love of music and playing together. Thinking of them, she dropped Pachelbel and strummed "Oh, Susanna."

A knock on the door startled her, and she yelped, plucking a wrong string.

Elias entered, eyebrows tilted at a skeptical angle. "That doesn't sound like the refined music I would expect from a cultured Southern belle." His lips twitched.

Rattled at being caught playing at all, much less a folk song, Savannah pressed her cheek against the shoulder of the harp and her hands against the strings. "I'm sorry. My aunt Georgette deplores what she calls our 'pedestrian tastes' when my sisters and I play Foster."

He shook his head. "I was only funning you. You're so serious." His long strides brought him up the aisle. "So this was what you were hiding in that big box."

"I wasn't hiding anything. I just didn't open all my baggage for your inspection."

"It also explains your hands." He removed his hat and set it on the desk, brim up.

"My hands?"

"I noticed the calluses on your fingertips, and I couldn't think how you got them."

Savannah decided not to be offended. "Hours of playing." She held up her hands. "They were hard won, though my deportment teacher despaired of me ever having ladylike hands. She used to make me do them up in goose grease and gloves at night, hoping to soften them."

He grimaced. "The things girls worry about and the lengths they'll go to."

Savannah lifted the harp and stood, only to have Elias remove the musical instrument from her hands and lay it carefully in the case.

"That's pretty heavy for a little thing like you. How'd you get it here to the schoolhouse?"

"Mr. Halvorson drove us this morning."

"How did today go?" He looked at the blackboard. "Hymn singing?"

Savannah closed the lid on the harp and snicked the clasps. "Yes. Today went fine. You don't have to check on me every day, you know."

"I know. I'm playing postman." He reached into his back pocket and withdrew a letter. "I thought you might like this now instead of waiting until Saturday to come to town and get it."

Savannah snatched the letter from his hands, scanning the return address. "It's from my sisters." She pressed the envelope to her chest, blinking hard. "I'm surprised, since neither of them likes to write much. But a letter from home is just what I need."

"Then you'll be mighty happy, because there was another one." He pulled it out. "This one is from a Miss Carolina Cox. Aunt Carolina, I presume? She of the sweet heart and dragon nature?"

This time he laid the envelope in Savannah's outstretched hands. The heavy cream stationary bore her aunt's embossed name and address. She'd written Savannah's name in black ink, her personality leaping off the paper in those few bold strokes.

Savannah stood there, staring at the letter, homesickness washing over her like a rain shower. The letter was fat. It must be several pages long. She couldn't contain her smile.

Elias rubbed his jaw. "I think that's the first time I've seen you smile since you got here—a real smile, I mean. You should do it more often. It looks good on you."

Flustered, she reached for a hairpin and slit Aunt Carolina's envelope first. "I hope you don't think me rude, but I can't wait. She must've mailed it the same day I left Raleigh for it to arrive so soon. She's thoughtful that way."

Savannah pulled out the pages, surprised when another envelope dropped out onto her desk.

She froze. Recognition was instantaneous. Her heart and throat squeezed tight.

Elias picked up the envelope. "Girard Brandeis? A relative of yours?"

With icy fingers, she plucked the missive from his hand. "No."

Why would he be writing her now? What was there possibly to say? She stuffed everything back into Aunt Carolina's envelope. "I believe I'll read these later."

Savannah cleared her throat, angry at the smallness of her voice. "Thank you for delivering them. I am most appreciative."

"Hmm." He scrubbed his hand through his hair. "Guess I'll be going, then. You want a ride to the Halvorsons'? I have the buckboard today."

"No, thank you."

"Are you sure you're all right? You look a little pale."

"I'm fine, really."

He picked up his hat, but lingered, his gray eyes clouded. Why didn't he just go so she could fall apart in private?

"I'll see you, then. Probably not until Saturday, when the Halvorsons come into town, unless you need me before then."

She shook her head. "I'm sure I won't need to bother you."

When he finally closed the door, she sagged onto the front bench.

Aunt Carolina had been right. Savannah might've left the whispers and stares behind, but the hurt had come north with her.

Savannah should've taken Elias up on his offer of a ride, but she'd wanted to be alone to make sense of her feelings after seeing Girard's handwriting. With each step on the journey back to the Halvorsons' she regretted her decision. She'd elected to wear an impractical pair of shoes, ones that matched her pale yellow gown perfectly, but pinched. Because Mr. Halvorson had given her a ride this morning, and because she spent a great deal of her day seated behind her desk, she hadn't realized how unsuitable these kidskin boots were for walking on dirt roads.

Less than halfway to her lodgings, her heels screamed over new blisters, and her toes ground against one another at each step.

As she crossed over the wooden bridge that spanned a small creek, she gave in to the urge to stop and soak her feet. Easing down the bank, she found a reasonably clean patch of grass and unlaced her shoes. With quick jerks, she hiked her skirts to her knees, stripped off her stockings and lowered her burning toes into the water.

Savannah let out an unladylike sigh and rotated her ankles. The tall grass swayed, and the water drifted lazily. This was the perfect spot to read her letters unseen. Half dreading, half anticipating, she opened her sisters' letter first.

Savannah, darling,
Charlotte here. I know you've only been gone a few hours, but I thought it might be nice to get a letter from home pretty soon after you arrived there. How have the first couple of days gone? Do you like teaching? I can't imagine keeping control of a classroom and lessons and all that tedium. I don't like school enough for myself that I'd want to inflict it on other people.

Aunt Georgette's begonia, the one she wanted to enter in the Garden Fair, is showing signs of rebellion. Something about wilting leaves or black spots or some such. Anyway, she's in a perfect dither about it.

That's all I can think about to tell you, since you haven't been gone long enough for anything to really happen. Hope all is well with you, and write soon. I'd love to hear about your adventures up there in the Great North.

Charlotte Louise Cox

Savannah smoothed the pages on her knee and read her youngest sister's note.

Savannah,
I wish you'd write to Aunt Carolina and convince her that it isn't at all scandalous for young girls to visit the ice cream parlor as long as they are in a group. She has some notion that mobs of young men hang about such places just waiting to prey upon unsuspecting girls. I mean, really. If a group of us girls happen to be at the ice cream parlor at the same time as some young men stop in, we can't really be blamed for that, can we? And it isn't wrong to visit and be polite, is it?

Anyway, ask her, will you?

I see above that Lottie mentioned Aunt Georgette's problem. I've dubbed it The Begonia Disaster of '87. It's quite comical, except that I do feel sorry for her. She sets such store by those flowers and her garden club and all.

Miss you lots. Write and tell us what life's like up there. I can't imagine.

Is it snowing yet?
Ginny

A blanket of homesickness settled around Savannah. Funny, she hadn't thought how much she would miss Charlotte and Virginia. They'd been close, but then Savannah had met Girard, and he had taken all her time and focus. She'd neglected her sisters, and they'd grown apart from her over the past year.

Thoughts of Girard drew her to Aunt Carolina's letter. Susannah found herself sitting straighter, smoothing her skirts…even as her feet splashed in the creek. A laugh forced its way past the tightness in her throat. If Aunt Carolina could see her now, she'd be scandalized. A lady simply didn't drop down by a stream, disrobe her feet and plop them into the water.

Susannah pulled the pages from the envelope, keeping Girard's on the bottom and opening her aunt's letter first.

Savannah,

I had thought to wait a week before sending you a letter, but then this envelope arrived in the post. I was of two minds whether to even send it on, but in the end, I decided that you deserved to hear whatever explanation Mr. Brandeis cared to submit. He owed you that much.

I have many things I would like to say on the subject of your ex-fiancé, but I will merely caution you to be careful. He was always one for fine words, and I would hate for you to be swayed by them into forgiving him and accepting him back into your life. In this respect, I'm grateful that you took a job so far away. It would appear that Girard is not aware of your relocation, therefore, unless you choose to tell him (which I strongly hope you will not) he will be unable to contact you directly.

Your father will be making a brief visit home in a fortnight. He has been informed of your absence here, but a letter from you wouldn't go amiss.

We're all most curious as to your situation there, your accommodations, the reception you've received and how the first few days have gone.

Write soon,

Sincerely,
Aunt Carolina

Savannah could hear her aunt's voice in every word,
see her concentrating as she wrote at her desk. Tears
pricked her eyes. Aunt Carolina had never been de-
monstrative and wasn't one to endure overt emotion,
but Savannah had never doubted her love.

Her heart picked up an erratic rhythm as she fingered
Girard's envelope. The temptation to flick it into the
river and let it wash away flashed into her head. And
yet she wanted to hear what he had to say for himself,
how he could possibly justify what he'd done.

Finally, she slit the envelope and drew out the single sheet.

Savannah,
It was never my intention to hurt you, though I
know I did. I apologize for that. At the last moment I realized that I couldn't go through with our
wedding. I am not in love with you, and I know
now that I never was.

The truth is, just before I met you, the woman
I had been courting for over a year broke off our
relationship. I was angry and hurt, and I had to get
out of New Orleans for a while. When I agreed to
go to that party at your house with my cousin and
I saw you, I thought you would be just the thing
to take my mind off Jeanette. You were sweet and
young and beautiful. Before I knew it, things had
gotten out of hand, we were engaged and the wedding plans escalated.

My heart will always be Jeanette's. When I left
you at the altar, it was to return to New Orleans to

plead my case with her one last time. To my joy,
we are reunited once more and will marry by the
end of the month.

I know this is crass, but would you please return the engagement ring I gave you? It's a family heirloom.
Girard.

The blood drained from Savannah's head and diz-
ziness swirled before her eyes. *He never loved me. He
used me.*

He wants the ring back to give to her.

Crumpling the paper, Savannah tossed it into the
water. It bobbed and swirled, then disappeared under the
bridge. Nothing made sense anymore. He had courted
her only as a distraction for his broken heart? What
kind of man did that? What kind of woman grieved
over such a man?

"Well, not this one." She dusted her hands together
and drew her feet out of the water. "I'm shutting the
door on that chapter of my life forever." Using the edge
of her petticoat, she dried her feet and restored them
to her stockings and the too tight shoes. She rose and
began the walk back to the Halvorsons'. "From now on,
Savannah Cox, you rely on yourself and no one else.
There's not a man on this globe that is trustworthy." She
wouldn't be foolish enough to rely on a mere male again.

Chapter Seven

Elias looked up from cleaning one of his rifles as a shadow darkened the doorway of the sheriff's office.

He hadn't seen her for almost two weeks, and he was struck afresh at how pretty she was. In spite of her parasols, the sun had kissed her cheeks, giving her some color. She wore a blouse almost as blue as her eyes.

"Morning." He set aside the gun and rose. Cap's tail thumped the floor and he waggled to his feet, his nails clicking as he trotted over to greet her.

"Good morning. I hope I'm not interrupting." She stepped over the threshold. Her fancy bonnet framed her face, all ribbons and flowers and ruffled lining. He hated that it covered her bright hair. She hesitated and then patted Cap's broad head.

"Not at all. You come into town with the Halvorsons?" The community bustled beyond the door, busy with farmers and their families in town to do their Saturday trading. He'd seen his pa down by the harness shop. Today was the date set for scheduling the harvest, so all the men for miles around were gathered at the far end of the street to get on the list for the threshers.

"Yes, I had some things to mail. I hoped to see you

last Sunday." She toyed with one of her cuff buttons. "Your father said you had to travel for your work?"

He ignored the thump of his heart at the notion that she might've missed him while he'd been away. "The US Marshal's office asks from time to time when they're stretched thin if local law enforcement can transport prisoners. I had to take a fellow they apprehended over in Pipestone to stand trial in Mankato." Elias wiped his hands on a rag. The smell of gun oil lingered in the air. "It only happens maybe once or twice a year."

She studied the room, his desk, the small cells in the back, the potbellied stove, the gun rack in the corner, and she kept fidgeting with her sleeve button, as if she couldn't quite make up her mind what to say.

"Was there something you needed, or is this a social call?" He'd be surprised with either circumstance, since she'd been pretty clear that she didn't need his help or interference. But why else would she be at the jail?

"It's most awkward. I would take care of the problem if I had any notion how, and I'd ask Mr. Halvorson, but there's still quite a communication gap..." Two small lines appeared between her brows, distracting Elias for a moment. "I need some assistance with a small matter."

She paused.

"Just ask." He leaned against the desk and crossed his arms.

"Well, there's a terrible odor lingering around the school. At first I thought one of the boys was playing a prank, but now I understand that a skunk has taken up residence under the front steps of the schoolhouse. I'm at a loss to know how to remove the animal. I've never seen one, and I've certainly never smelled one." Her pert little nose wrinkled. "Johann drew one and pointed to the front stoop so I would understand what had occurred."

Elias grinned. "Never smelled a polecat before? You *were* sheltered. I guess I could come out and take care of it for you."

"Thank you." Her face relaxed and she actually smiled. "I didn't know what else to do."

"I warn you, it's going to smell for a while. Aside from the nuisance of having one under the stairs, skunks are often hydrophobic." Elias bent to open a drawer and withdraw his sidearm. Better to use the pistol rather than a shotgun under the steps. He didn't want to splinter the treads and risers using a scattergun. "We can't risk you or one of the kids getting bitten, so I'll have to shoot the varmint. When I do, he's going to stink up the place. But the odor will diminish over time. In a week or so, you won't smell it much at all, hopefully."

"Thank you. I've been carrying a handkerchief soaked in rosewater, but even that hasn't been enough." She tugged a hankie from her sleeve, all lace and embroidery, and the floral scent drifted toward him.

What a feminine bit of frippery. He buckled on his gun, glancing at the clock. "I'll go now. That way you'll have the rest of today and all of Sunday for the place to air out."

"Could I go with you? I still have some cleaning to do. I could just let the Halvorsons know."

"Sure. I've got the buckboard."

While she tracked down Per and Agneta, Elias ducked into the feed store to let someone know where he'd be for a while.

"Don't hurry back." Gar Joren grinned, his teeth gapped like a broken comb. "Wouldn't mind driving around the countryside with a pretty teacher myself if I was twenty years younger."

Mikkel Torgerson elbowed him. "If you were *forty* years younger, you mean."

They all shared a laugh, and Elias made his escape. His step was light, but he refused to examine why he felt so good. Cap trotted at his side and leaped into the buckboard.

"You go in the back today, old son." Elias pointed to the short bed behind the seat. Cap gave him a morose look, but hopped over and plopped onto the dusty boards.

Elias helped Savannah into the buckboard, noting the soft blue-and-pink plaid of her skirts. The colors reminded him of the rosemaling his mother did on winter evenings. Coming from the mountain valley of Valdres in the Old Country, she had learned the skill of folk painting from her own mother, creating works of art out of the most mundane objects.

He glanced at Savannah. Ever since he'd delivered those letters from her home, he'd been wondering how they would affect her. Would they make her so homesick that she would leave? And who was Girard Brandeis? And why was his letter tucked inside one from her aunt?

But Savannah was as self-contained and remote as ever. He'd seen her truly relaxed and free only twice, once when she was racing Elsker across the prairie, and then when she'd been playing that harp. In those moments, she'd let down her guard. At all other times, she held herself tight and controlled. Was that her natural state, or had something happened to make her wary?

They clipped along at a good pace. Huge, puffy clouds drifted lazily across the sky, and the heavy heads of grain waved in the sunshine. "Harvest will start soon. Tyler explained that there's no school during harvest, right?"

"Actually, it was your father who told me, just today." She frowned. "I asked why there were so many men in town, and he told me about the threshing crews and how everyone pitched in, including the children."

"And you don't like the idea?"

"What makes you say that?"

"Because you're a teacher. All teachers hate to lose school days. Every schoolteacher we've ever had grumbled about time out for harvest." Elias flicked the lines, anchoring his elbows on his knees.

"I can't say I like the idea of missing school, but I see the need, especially once your father was so kind as to explain it to me. He said the women help with the cooking and feeding of the workers, and that at the end, there's a community dance to celebrate."

"Highlight of the year around here. Folks come from as far as fifty miles." Elias imagined her at the dance, fancy clothes, light steps and a score of young bucks just waiting to lead her out onto the floor. His fingers tightened on the reins.

"If that many people come, you must need a large place. Do they hold the party at the church?"

He sat up straight. "Of course not."

"Did I say something wrong?" She turned troubled blue eyes his way.

"Norwegians like to go to church and Norwegians like to dance, but they don't mix the two. The party is held outside unless it's too cold or rainy, then they move everything into Larson's barn. Larson's got the biggest barn in the county, so there's plenty of room."

She smoothed her hands along her skirts. "It's so frustrating. I'm trying to fit in, and to understand, but

there are so many little things that are different. I feel
as if I'm in constant danger of making a faux pas. Not
only are things different because I'm from the South
and this is the North, but throw in an entirely different
culture on top, and I don't know where I am. I dress
wrong. I speak wrong. I don't know the food or the customs. Just yesterday I made the mistake of opening Mr.
Halvorson's cupboard. I didn't know. I thought it was a
spice cupboard, like the one in the other corner. I think
everyone gasped, and Mrs. Halvorson hurried over and
closed the door, leading me away like a naughty child.
It's like walking the edge of a precipice."

"I never even thought to tell you about the man of the
house's cupboard." Elias shrugged. It was such a part
of his life, he hadn't thought it needed explaining. A
Norwegian man's cupboard held his pipe and tobacco,
or his special knives, or his important documents. Nobody in the house touched it. The woman of the house
had her own wall cupboard for her things. He hadn't
considered all the small ways that would seem foreign
to Savannah.

She smoothed a stray hair off her cheek. "I should
write a book, a list of things for the next schoolteacher
to know and be aware of so she doesn't make a complete fool of herself."

*The next schoolteacher. Here only a couple of weeks
and already talking about her replacement. Don't forget
what happened last time. Keep your head, boy.*

A hundred feet from the schoolhouse, the unmistakable scent of polecat wafted on the breeze. "That's
a skunk, all right." Elias pulled the buckboard up near
the corral fence. "Don't want to get the horses sprayed. I
wish I had thought to leave Cap in town. Nothing worse
than a dog who gets skunked."

Savannah took his hand to climb down. "I could keep him with me. I have to do some outside chores. I scrubbed the pails and the water crock yesterday and left them out to dry, with all the cleaning rags."

"That'll be fine. It shouldn't take me too long to sort this out. From the smell, I'd say the skunk must've gotten disturbed close by the school, so he might be skittish if he's still under there. Just keep Cap with you and we should be fine."

She disappeared around the building, and he sent the dog after her.

Elias surveyed the steps. Sure enough, one of the vertical boards along the side had loosened and stood askew, the perfect doorway for a varmint. The animal hadn't even had to dig to get under the porch. Elias studied the opening. The trick was going to be taking care of the skunk without getting sprayed himself. Perhaps he could lure it out, get it away from the school before he shot it?

This was going to be tricky.

He leaped up the stairs and fetched a lantern from the shelf in the cloakroom. Easing down beside the broken board, he shone the light into the darkness under the porch. Two bright spots glittered back at him from the far corner.

Hmm. He was under there, all right. Elias stood and blew out the lantern. Maybe he was glad he had brought Captain, after all. If they made a racket on the other side of the porch, perhaps the skunk would dart out and take off. Then Elias could follow at a safe distance and take care of things away from the school. He put his fingers to his lips and let out a piercing whistle. His collie bounded around the school.

"Don't worry about him, Savannah. Just stay back there," Elias shouted.

Cap plopped onto his rump beside him, ears up, eyes bright.

"All right, boy. Come around here." Elias led Cap to the far side of the porch, opposite the broken board, and near where the skunk crouched under the front step. "Speak."

The dog gave a small woof, his tail stirring the grass. That wasn't going to be enough to make the skunk come out.

"Speak, Cap. Speak!" Elias clapped his hands and raised his voice. He kicked the step where the skunk had crouched, hoping to drive it out.

Cap obliged, giving a loud bark.

"Good boy! Speak!"

Lifting his muzzle, Cap let loose a long string of barks, bounding to his feet. Elias put up his hand. "Good boy."

Leaning to his left, he grinned. "Success. Sit! Stay!"

Sure enough, the skunk had vacated the steps and was waddling along the foundation, head low, tail low, scurrying through the tall grass. Perfect.

Elias drew his gun. The animal disappeared around the corner, and Elias moved to follow, slowly, careful to keep his distance. Just a few more steps and it'd be back in sight. Once the skunk left the shadow of the school, he'd—

A scream filled the air, along with the unmistakable tang of eau de polecat.

A sharp whistle startled Savannah, and she jerked, knocking the edge of the water crock against the pump handle. A chip flaked off the crock and hit her in the cheek.

Cap shot up from the grass and tore around the edge of the school before she could stop him.

Wincing at the damage to the pottery, she eased the heavy water jar to the ground and started after the dog. Elias shouted something, but she couldn't hear him clearly, so she picked up her hem and hurried, anxious to get Cap back before he got in the way.

The dog began barking, and Savannah broke into an unladylike jog. As she rounded the back of the school, something moved in the grass at her feet. Stunned, she froze, but it was too late.

The skunk turned, lifted its tail and let fly.

The stench hit her like a wall. She screamed, instantly regretting opening her mouth. Her eyes filled with stinging tears and her nose began to run. Throwing up her hands, she whirled and ran back toward the pump.

Gagging and choking, she dropped to her knees. Plunging her hands into a bucket of water, she doused her face. She sniffled and coughed, repeating the water treatment, but it didn't seem to penetrate the stench. Horrible, horrible smell!

It was everywhere. Her clothes, her hair, her skin. The air she breathed was coated in skunk aroma.

A gunshot split the air and she yelped. Face dripping, eyes streaming, she looked over her shoulder. The furry black-and-white animal lay still on the grass.

Elias ran toward her, but stopped twenty feet away. His face screwed up and he backed off. "What happened?" He paused. "Never mind, I can tell what happened. What were you doing, charging a skunk? Why didn't you stay back?"

Her ire rose from the shards of her shattered dignity. "This isn't my fault. Cap ran when you whistled, and then you shouted, and I thought you wanted me to come get the dog. I ran, and then the skunk was there and…" She hiccupped. "You were going to shoot the skunk, not chase it right at me."

"I hollered for you to stay put, not to come belting at us. I wanted the dog so I could scare the skunk out from under the porch." Elias edged backward with every sentence, covering his lower face with his hands. "Anyway, I shot the skunk."

"Wonderful." She stood, arms out, water dripping from her face, creating huge damp blotches on her dress. The water seemed to make the smell worse, if that was possible. The brim of her bonnet trapped the horrendous odor near her face, and she shoved the hat back, facing into the breeze, which didn't help much. "What am I going to do?"

"Um…wait here. I'm going to get a shovel and bury the culprit." He crossed the yard toward the lean-to stable.

"Wait here. Where else am I supposed to wait?" Savannah grabbed the dipper hanging from the pump and took a drink, swishing the water in her mouth and turning away to spit it on the ground. It didn't help. She could still taste skunk.

Elias returned, scooped up the carcass and walked off, holding the shovel at arm's length. He buried the skunk out behind the privies and sauntered back, again stopping a good distance away.

"Now what?" She dug for her rosewater handkerchief, but the sodden mess stank of skunk.

He pushed his hat back and scratched his head. "I guess I'd better take you to Ma. She'll know what to do."

Captain took one whiff of her and whined, backing away, sneezing and rubbing his nose on the ground. Wonderful. She smelled bad even to a dog. When she reached the buckboard, the horses stamped and shook their heads, sidling and snorting. This really was too much. Tears burned her eyes, both skunk-induced and shame-caused.

"I think you'd better ride in the back." Elias sounded apologetic, but she pounced on the hint of smothered laughter in his voice.

"You think this is funny?" Humiliation burned her skin and shriveled her heart.

"No, of course not." His denial fell flat because it was drowned in a strangled snicker. He swallowed and composed his face, still keeping his distance, making a wide arc around her to get to the other side of the buckboard. "Can you get aboard by yourself?"

Without answering, she scrambled into the back, hiking her skirts and edging onto the bed. Her feet dangled off the small tailgate, and she gripped the low iron rails on either side.

Cap refused to jump up, tail low, skulking ten yards away with a wary look in his eyes.

Elias slapped the team and urged them into a fast trot. The horses settled down, and Savannah shrank into herself, fighting her tears and not succeeding. Her beautiful dress, her hair...the tremendous smell. And Elias thought it was funny. She was mortified.

They whipped down the road, and she realized he was driving fast, not to get her to help quickly, but to create a breeze that kept the worst of the smell behind him.

Captain must've known staying upwind was the smart course, because he loped ahead of the team as if being chased. Savannah hung on as they bounced and rattled, kicking up dust.

The drive seemed to take forever, even at their rapid pace, but finally the Parker farm appeared. Elias pulled up in front of the house and shouted for his mother.

Mrs. Parker came out, drying her hands on a dishtowel. "*Ja*, Elias, I did not think you were coming today. Ah, Miss Savannah…" She stopped. The dishtowel came up to cover her nose. "Vat has happened?"

"She got skunked." Elias stood away and put his hands into his pockets. "I thought you'd know what to do for her."

"Oh, you poor *barn*." Mrs. Parker jumped into action. "Elias…" She rattled off several commands in Norwegian that Savannah didn't try to decipher. She was too miserable to care. Now that the buckboard had stopped, the smell swirled around her, as heavily as ever.

Elias nodded. "I'll put the horses away and get right on it." He motioned to Savannah. "She wants you to go around back to where the clotheslines are strung. She'll meet you there."

Savannah gingerly crept off the buckboard, keeping her head down. She was an affront to herself, much less to others, and to be dragged to Elias's mother's doorstep smelling like this… She blinked hard, but a pair of tears gave up the fight and raced down her cheeks. Even the lovely flowers planted along the front porch seemed to shrink away from her as she passed.

The clothesline poles stood behind the house in the glaring sunshine. Nearby, a huge brass cauldron hung from a tripod over spent ashes.

"*Stakkar.*" Mrs. Parker hurried down the steps carrying an armful of blankets. "*Stakkar.*" She shook her head, wincing as the smell hit her afresh.

"I don't know what that means." Savannah shook her head, wiping her tears.

The older woman began pegging the sheets to the clothesline to form a square. "Poor dear? *Ja*, poor dear. I am so sorry this happened to you. It is unpleasant, *ja*? But it is not forever. I vill help you."

Elias emerged from the barn, went straight to the house and returned carrying a tin bathtub. The outside of the tub had been painted with flowers and scrolls and lacework after the manner of so many Norwegian furnishings. He set the tub in the middle of the blanket enclosure. "I'll get a fire started and fetch the water, and then I'll make myself scarce."

"And I vill bring the vinegar and soda and the soap. I vill need much vater, Elias. Go now."

Savannah could do nothing but stand off to the side and watch until Mrs. Parker motioned her over to the little cubicle. "My husband is still in town, and Elias vill stay inside until I call him. Do not vorry. Ve can help."

The kindness in the woman's voice was Savannah's undoing. She burst into tears, giving way to her misery. Mrs. Parker tutted and steered her behind the quilts, then helped her disrobe and step into the tub. She tossed Savannah's clothes out.

"There's hardly any water in the tub." Savannah sniffed and wept, swallowing hard and hiccupping.

"Ve need de vinegar first. And de soda. It vill make a mess, but it vill help vid the smell." Mrs. Parker poured the cold vinegar over Savannah's hair and then dumped a handful of baking soda on her. The concoction foamed and bubbled up. The sharp tang of the vinegar cut through the skunk smell, and for the first time, Savannah had a glimmer of hope that perhaps she wouldn't always smell like a polecat.

With strong fingers, Mrs. Parker scrubbed and kneaded Savannah's hair and scalp. A washcloth plopped into the water. "You scrub vid vinegar, too." Something in her tone reminded Savannah of Aunt Carolina, the way she took charge of every situation and knew just what to do in every crisis. Homesickness swamped Savannah, and she cried into the bathwater as she rubbed and scrubbed.

It took three full vinegar baths before Mrs. Parker was satisfied, and even then Savannah caught whiffs of skunk when she moved. After the vinegar came the homemade lye soap. Her skin tingled and glowed redly from the fierce scrubbing. After a final rinse, Mrs. Parker wrapped Savannah in a sheet.

"You vait here. I vill bring clothes." She lifted one of the blankets. The day was warm, but Savannah felt chilled as she stood on the grass in her bare feet. And she smelled like pickling brine, which, while better than skunk, still wasn't great.

Mrs. Parker returned with a towel, as well, and wrapped Savannah's hair in it, then stepped outside again so she could dress in private.

It felt strange wearing another woman's clothes, but Savannah was grateful. She'd never worn such…rustic fabric. A homespun skirt, an ivory blouse that had probably started life white, hand-knit stockings. And a pair of square-toed shoes that had seen better days.

And yet they were loaned generously. Savannah cautiously raised the edge of the blanket and emerged. Mrs. Parker was raking the coals from beneath the kettle and gently pouring water to douse the fire. She must've given Elias the all-clear, because he stood on the back porch.

"Now you need *kaffe*," his mother declared.

Coffee. Savannah smiled, ruefully. So much like Aunt Carolina's belief that tea could fix anything.

Savannah sat at the table, feeling vulnerable with her hair wrapped in a towel. Her family would be scandalized to know she'd been seen by a young man in this condition. Of course, they'd be scandalized to know she'd been sprayed by a skunk, too. And that she shared a room with one of her students, and that her host family spoke almost no English, and that her school was so poor they had almost no supplies… The list grew every day.

Elias straddled the bench on the far side of the table and cradled a cup of coffee in his hands. "I am sorry, Savannah. I shouldn't have strayed from the plan without telling you first, and I shouldn't have laughed. What's happened to you isn't funny, and I'm sorry."

It was hard to meet his gray eyes. When word got out about today's catastrophe, she'd never live it down. Elias wouldn't be the only one laughing. But she forced herself to be brave and do the right thing. She raised her chin. "I'm sorry I snapped at you. The whole thing was an accident. Thank you for bringing me to your mother. I don't know what I would've done without her help."

He grinned at his mother, who handed Savannah a cup of coffee and pushed a plate of small cookies toward her. "You know," Elias said. "I've felt that way more than a time or two myself over the years. I can always count on Ma. She's a wonder, isn't she?"

"Always you haff been an *uregjerlig barn*, Elias, but ve love you." Mrs. Parker sat beside her son. She gave him a tolerant smile and sipped her coffee.

"She says I'm an unruly child." Elias took a cookie. "And I suppose I am."

"What happened to my clothes?" Savannah smoothed the homespun skirt and blew on her coffee.

He grinned. "I'll have you know the dress and shoes and bonnet and all were buried with the utmost ceremony and solemnity a fair distance from the house." He sobered. "I'm sorry about that, too, since they were so fine, but you realize there was no saving them?"

Another lost outfit. She'd ruined one cleaning the school, another when she'd gone riding and now this one. At this rate, she'd need a new wardrobe by Thanksgiving.

Mrs. Parker gave her an encouraging smile and came to unwind Savannah's hair from the towel. Resembling rats' tails, it hung around her shoulders in clumps, smelling of vinegar and faintly, still, of skunk. How long would it take for the odor to wear off? Would she have to cut her hair short? Savannah bit her lip.

"It is not bad. Always the smell is vorst ven it is wet. Ven it dries, it vill not be so bad. You have such *vakkert hår*. I vish I had such pretty color." The woman brought a comb and began unsnarling the tangles.

It had been years since anyone had performed so personal a task for Savannah, and having Elias sitting across the table watching made her cheeks flame. But she savored the tender care, even while she wanted to squirm, the sensations warring inside her.

Which was a tiny picture of how she felt about being in Minnesota. On the one hand, she'd made some new friends and had begun to make some progress at the school, but on the other hand, she still felt alien and strange.

Had she made a mistake coming to Snowflake, or would it turn out to be the best decision of her life? Perhaps it was too soon to tell. For now, she would have to bear up and keep on and pray that the skunk odor faded quickly.

Chapter Eight

Mr. Halvorson called up the stairs, and Savannah groaned, pressing her face into her pillow. It wasn't even daylight yet. This was supposed to be her week off from teaching, and she was being roused earlier than ever.

Lars shuffled into his clothes and clomped down the stairs, and Rut slid from beneath the covers, answering her father's call with a *"Morgen, Far."*

For the first time since arriving in Minnesota, Savannah felt a decided chill in the air when she got out of bed. Not enough that her breath showed, but enough to raise goose bumps and make her hurry to get dressed. Savannah pulled her hair over her shoulder and sniffed it. Her shoulders relaxed. No skunk odor. For the past week, she'd scrubbed it with vinegar and soda every night, and gradually the smell had faded.

She hadn't been able to hide the incident from the Halvorsons. They'd noticed her change of clothing the moment she'd come into the cabin. Striving for a light-hearted approach, Savannah had shared a good laugh with them when Elias explained it all in Norwegian, though she hadn't felt much like laughing. Of course, the children had told the news at school, and Savannah had been forced to shrug and smile sheepishly. But it was a nine days' wonder, or in this case, a five days' wonder, because by the end of the school week, the children had ceased to mention it.

Breakfast was a hurried affair in candlelight, then they carried baskets and crocks to the wagon, and were on their way to the Linnevold farm as the sun peeked over the horizon.

Only a couple wagons stood in the yard, and Savannah guessed that Per Halvorson was his customary fifteen minutes early. She noticed Elias's horse, Buck, tied to the corral fence, and she shivered, wrapping her shawl tighter around her shoulders. She hadn't seen him—except at church—since the skunk incident, and hadn't had a chance to speak with him.

"Good morning, Miss Cox." Elias's father, Mr. Parker, came out of the house and helped her from the wagon. "Glad you decided to pitch in." He grinned. "Ready for your first threshing?"

"I hope so. I've never seen a threshing before, and I'm not even sure what happens." She tightened her bonnet strings and reached into the wagon for the paper-wrapped bundle of Mrs. Parker's clothing. Agneta had laundered them for Savannah the previous week.

"By the time harvest is over, you'll be an old hand." Mr. Parker hefted a basket from the wagon. "Elias is helping Vilhelm set up the tables out back for you ladies. He'll be glad to see you."

Her heart skipped at the mention of his name, but she forced herself to take a slow breath. Elias had been much too often in her thoughts and even her dreams this week, and it was beyond time she reminded herself that he considered her a lightweight fly-by-night, too fragile for his beloved Minnesota prairie.

Mrs. Parker greeted her with a smile, coming to take her arm. "How are tings?" She sniffed. "You are smelling like flowers today." She beamed and squeezed Savannah's elbow. "I told you it vas not forever. Come, you can vork vid me. Ve are making food for de men. I vill show you how to make *blotkake*. It is Elias's favorite."

"Thank you so much for your help that day. I was a mess." She held up the package. "I brought your dress and things back."

"You can put them in our vagon. Come, meet the ladies."

The women and girls welcomed Savannah in, and before she knew it, she was stirring and mixing and chopping alongside them. Mrs. Halvorson enveloped her in a huge apron, wrapping it twice around Savannah's waist and tying it in the front. "Keep dress nice?"

At her halting English, Savannah hugged her. They'd been practicing every day. Savannah nodded and said, *"Takk."* Thank you.

Agneta's smile lit the room. Mrs. Parker patted Savannah's hand. "You are a nice girl. I tink you vill do vell here."

Of Elias, she saw nothing until the morning break. The women spent the time cooking and talking, and near ten o'clock, packed baskets with treats and carried them out into the field. Savannah brought a coffeepot, held gingerly with towels to protect her hands, and stepped across the rows of stubble, watching her footing.

The sun had come out and chased away the chill of the morning, and she stopped to admire the crisp colors, the blue of the sky, the golden grain and the bright dresses of the women. She could see clear to the horizon all around, as if she stood in the center of a huge dome. There was definitely room for the imagination here on the prairie, an expanse for the mind that she hadn't found in the city.

The smells of grain and dust and wood smoke surrounded her, and a cloud of dust and soot hung over the field. A steam engine puffed away, powering the threshing machine, which clattered and banged. Savannah spotted Elias right off. He stood atop the stack of cut grain, pitching bundles into the machine's maw. The thresher clanked and rocked, stalks disappearing inside, bright straw coming out the back and grain pouring into bags from a chute along the side.

Mr. Parker picked up a tin cup from one of the baskets and held it out to her. "I see you survived the morning so far."

She poured his coffee, careful not to spill. "I did. It's been most entertaining. But tell me, how does this all work, Mr. Parker?"

"Call me Ian." He stepped to her side so she could pour coffee for others and still listen. "There are a couple of harvester teams cutting the grain in the field. Then there's four wagons behind those. Men pitch the stalks into them, then pile it up here." He pointed with his coffee cup toward the bright mound. "Elias is the stack man at the moment, so he pitches the stalks into the thresher."

At that moment, Elias jabbed his pitchfork into the stack and slid down the side. He dusted himself off and resettled his hat before sauntering over. A man at the steam engine flipped a lever, and the belt linking the engine to the thresher stopped flapping, the gears quit grinding. At once, Savannah could hear better.

Mr. Parker continued. "As you can see, the steam engine provides the power to the thresher, which separates the grain from the chaff. The grain comes out the side there, and a couple of men fill the sacks, a couple more sew them and a couple more stack them on the wagons for a trip to the barn." He accepted a slice of coffee cake from one of the ladies. "The straw and chaff blow out the far end, and there are some stackers there. Bedding, insulation, new straw ticks—there's plenty of use for good, clean wheat straw."

"So many men. I had no idea." Savannah tried not to track Elias's progress through the crowd toward her. She poured cup after cup for others as he stopped to chat and joke before finally picking a cup from the basket and making his way to her side.

"Ah, just what I need." He held his cup under his nose and breathed deeply. "You have a good time with the ladies?"

"Yes. Everyone's been so nice. I wondered at the amount of food they were preparing, but seeing the size of the workforce, I'm thinking we didn't make enough." She poured another cup for a young man with white-blond hair and ruddy skin.

"There are a couple dozen men here. Two came with the thresher, and the rest are neighbors. If a farmer had to pay for a crew this size, he'd lose money growing grain, but when all the neighbors pitch in and share the cost of the thresher and cover the labor, it works out well. But you can see we need everybody. The schoolboys are driving the wagons, keeping the grain sack pile supplied and packing down the straw stacks." He pointed to Rut and Synove, who were carrying a basket of yeast rolls between them, offering them to the men and dispensing smiles and food in equal measure. "Even the girls are pitching in. I think it's good, makes everyone feel a part of the community. We all need each other out here."

"I realize everyone needs to lend a hand, but I miss the school time. So many of the children are so far behind. I'm praying for a quick harvest so they can get back to classes before we lose all the progress we've made." Savannah poured more coffee. The line of men stretched to six deep, and each one smiled and bobbed his head.

"Takk, frøken."

She smiled and nodded, and then turned to Elias. "I know *takk* is thank you, but what is *frøken*?"

"It means 'miss.' Thanks, miss." His brows came down as he eyed the line of young men. "Seems like you're drawing a bit of attention from the bachelors."

The next man stepped up, smoothing his mustache with one hand and holding out his coffee cup with the other. Savannah was sure she'd already served him twice. Her coffeepot was almost empty. He took the last half cup and asked Elias, *"Spør henne om hun vil være på dans, og hvis vi kan reservere danser akkurat nå?"*

Elias's lips flattened. "They want to know if you're coming to the harvest dance, and if so, can they reserve their dances with you now."

Heat started up her neck and into her cheeks, and she rued her fair complexion. She hadn't sought the attention, and yet it was flattering, a balm to her wounded heart after Girard's defection and the callous reason behind it. The ring had been left on her dressing table in Raleigh, and she'd sent instructions to Aunt Carolina to return it to him. It felt as if Savannah was finally closing a chapter of her life and perhaps opening another.

The men waited expectantly.

"I don't know what to say." She implored Elias with her eyes, putting her hand on his arm. "I don't even know how the dance will be conducted. Are we supposed to arrive with a partner, or does everyone just show up? I've never attended a harvest dance before."

"Courting couples will be partners, but everyone else just shows up. There aren't any fancy dance cards or anything like that. The men just ask the ladies to dance every time the music starts." He shrugged. "I'll let the men know that you aren't taking reservations."

Elias drew them aside, and Savannah went to put her empty coffeepot into one of the baskets. Agneta and Mrs. Parker were busy packing up the containers and crocks. The food had all disappeared, and the men were drifting back toward their workplaces.

"You are…how do you say it…popular." Mrs. Parker held up her coffeepot and gave it a slosh. "I did not run out of *kaffe* like you."

Agneta nodded. "Pretty girl like…honey for bees."

Savannah blushed again and shook her head at their teasing. But she felt good. If they could tease, they must like her.

Elias scaled the heap of harvested grain, and as he stood there, silhouetted against the sky, broad-shouldered, lithe-limbed, so sure of himself, her breath quickened. She knew he hadn't changed his mind about her being unsuited for her position, but how did he feel about her as a person? Did he like her at all?

And why did she care? She wasn't interested in him or any man. Not romantically, for certain.

But as a friend? She hefted a basket onto her hip and began the walk back to the farmhouse. She wouldn't mind having Elias as a friend.

The night of the celebration, Elias kept off to the side, holding his glass of raspberry cordial and watching the dancers as they whirled by…or rather watching one dancer when he could catch a glimpse of her in the crowd.

Savannah stood out like a rose in a cabbage patch, drawing plenty of attention. The moment she'd stepped out of the Halvorsons' wagon, his brain had turned to mashed millet, and it hadn't recovered.

The night was half-over, and he had yet to approach her for a dance. Not that it mattered. She hadn't lacked for partners. Seemed as if everyone had given her a turn on the dance floor. He looked up at the rafters of Larson's barn, breathing in the smells of hay and grain... and rain. Almost the moment the last bushel of wheat had been sacked and stowed, a steady rain had begun to fall, so the dance and dinner had been moved inside for the evening.

She went by in the arms of Knut Dotseth, and before they'd made it halfway down the floor, Jespar Rosedahl cut in. Her skirts, the color of new spring grass, belled out, and she smiled up at Jespar.

Elias's guts knotted, and he took a slug of cordial.

Lamplight gleamed on her fair hair, and her cheeks glowed, whether from the exertion of dancing or her enjoyment of the company, he didn't know. What he was sure of was that he'd never seen anyone so beautiful. Not even Britta could hold a candle to her.

"You gonna quit lollygagging around and ask her to dance, or are you going to let all the other young bucks enjoy her company?" Pa elbowed him. "She sure is setting up a stir, isn't she?"

"I noticed you danced with her." Elias made his tone desert-dry.

"And she said I danced real well, too." Pa preened. "Said I was light on my feet and easy to follow."

"What did Ma think of you dancing with the school-marm?"

"She's the one who told me to do it. She also said you hadn't danced all evening, not even with her. I suggest you remedy that before the night is out. Won't do for you to hurt your mother's feelings." He took Elias's glass. "Stop glowering like a dog in a manger. You don't want to dance with the schoolmarm, fine, but don't begrudge the other fellows who have more gumption than you. Your face looks like you drained the vinegar barrel. This is supposed to be a party."

Elias scowled. He wasn't a dog in the manger, he didn't care who she danced with, and he wasn't glowering. "Fine. If it will make you happy."

A bell rang as the song ended, and Pa nudged him again. "You waited too long. It's time to eat."

The floor cleared, and folks lined up for the buffet. Through some fancy maneuvering Elias managed to wedge his way into the line just behind Savannah, much to the obvious chagrin of several of the single men surrounding her. But Tyler had put Elias in charge of looking after the new schoolteacher. He couldn't shirk his duties, could he?

She picked up a plate and some napkin-wrapped cutlery. As Elias bent to get his own plate, the scent of her perfume captured him. Lying in a field of wildflowers must smell that way.

He'd never seen her eyes so bright. "You look as if you're enjoying yourself."

That had come out more accusing than he'd intended. He winced and shrugged.

"More than I thought I would. The music is fine, and everyone is friendly and nice. I find it difficult to believe you all have enough energy to dance, what with all the work you did this week. I didn't work half as hard, and I'm getting tired." She studied the great array of items on the table. "What should I eat? I don't recognize most of these foods."

"I'll help you out." He told her what each dish was, putting some on her plate when she nodded. They got to the end of the table, where two final dishes waited. "Now, these you have to try. True Norwegian delicacies."

"What are they?" She eyed him and then the platters.

"The first is *lefse*, a potato flatbread. It's delicious." He put one of the rolled pieces on the edge of her plate. "You put butter and sugar on them, or some of this." He pointed to the *lutefisk*, a pale, almost gelatinous mass of fish fillets. They must be from Mrs. Soderberg. She was well-known in Snowflake for her love of the lye-soaked whitefish.

Savannah's little nose wrinkled as he held up a piece of the fish. "Oh, no. I don't think so." She moved her plate out of his reach.

"Now, you don't want to disappoint the cooks, do you? They're all watching to see what you'll do, whether you have the right stuff to be an honorary Norwegian." He teased her, jiggling the fish.

She gulped, glancing at the row of matrons behind the table who were keeping the dishes filled. They whispered behind their hands, and Elias noted the mischievous gleams.

Savannah must've noticed them, too. Her chin came up in a familiar gesture. "Just a tiny piece then."

Elias relented. "You don't have to. I was just teasing. *Lutefisk* isn't to everyone's taste. Nobody would blame you if you didn't eat any."

Holding her plate toward him, she said, "I'll try it.

My aunt Carolina would never let us say we didn't like something, especially something we'd never tried. She made us say 'I have not yet acquired a taste for this.'"

"I'm liking your aunt Carolina more and more." Elias cut a small wedge of the fish and put it on the rim of her plate, careful not to let it touch anything else. "Let's find some seats."

His pa waved his long arm, motioning them over. Several pairs of jealous bachelor eyes followed Elias and Savannah across the room to where his parents had saved them seats at one of the trestle tables. The men might've been frustrated, but they weren't daunted. Elbowing and crowding, they managed to find seats close by, near enough to watch and listen.

"Having a good time, Savannah?" Pa scooted out the bench a bit so she could sit.

"'Savannah'?" Elias asked. Since when did Pa use her first name?

"Yep, she gave me leave to call her that instead of Miss Cox. And I told her she could call me Ian if she wanted." Pa grinned.

"And I am Tova." Ma bobbed her head. She wore her traditional Norwegian skirt, blouse and vest. An embroidered woolen cap covered her graying hair. Many of the ladies had opted for their traditional outfits, heavily embroidered, with silver brooches and clasps and buckles.

Elias reached over and squeezed her hand. "You look beautiful tonight, Ma."

She blushed, and Pa laughed, putting his arm around her. "The most beautiful woman here. No offense, Savannah. You look lovely, too."

"No offense taken. I've been admiring the pretty dresses. The colors are so cheerful." Savannah placed her napkin in her lap. "And the embroidery is very fine. Perhaps you can show me some of the stitches sometime."

Buttering a piece of *lefse*, Elias said, "The traditional dress is called *bunad*. Ma is wearing one from her home region of Valdres. There are lots of different styles of *bunad*, depending on where you're from in Norway."

The young men around them called out the regions they were from, showing off their vests and hats and jackets with much laughter and shouting.

Elias glanced at his own attire, a plain white shirt and dark trousers, and shrugged.

"I feel as if I have so much to learn, living here, but every little bit helps me understand my students better." Savannah poked her *lutefisk* with her fork, eyeing it. "How do you eat this?"

"Here." Elias leaned over, tore a piece of *lefse* off her portion and forked the bite of *lutefisk* onto it. He folded up the edges and gave it to her.

She took it, apprehension wrinkling her brow.

"Elias, did you goad her into trying that? Don't let him tease you, Savannah." Pa stabbed a meatball with his fork and used it to point at Elias. "Son, that's playing mean. She probably doesn't even know what *lutefisk* is."

"Now, Pa, don't scare her. She said she'd try it." Elias wrapped his own larger portion in a piece of *lefse*. "We'll do it together." He gently bumped his knuckle against her hand in a mock toast.

Benches scraped back, and Savannah's admirers crowded around, laughing and waiting to see what she would do. Jespar leaned against Elias's shoulder, and Knute crowded him on the bench.

She gulped, then closed her eyes, popped the bite into her mouth and chewed.

Immediately, her eyes opened wide and she froze. Blinking hard, she chewed another time, her lips trembling. Elias sank his teeth into his *lutefisk*, laughing. "Yum. Good, isn't it?"

Savannah reached for her water glass, gulping and coughing. Her eyes teared up and she breathed hard. Everyone erupted into laughter.

Pa refilled her glass from the pitcher on the table, chuckling. "You're a brave one, lass, I'll give you that. Most non-Norwegians take one smell of that awful stuff and run."

She reached for a bit of *lefse* and ate it quickly, as if trying to cleanse her mouth of the residual taste. "Oh, my. That was…unique." She patted her lips with her napkin, shooting Elias a glare.

"Your aunt Carolina would be proud." He finished his *lutefisk* quickly. He despised the stuff, but couldn't show cowardice in front of Savannah. He caught his pa's eye and winked. Pa laughed back, clearly in high spirits now that the grain harvest was over.

Laughter and talk swirled around them. Most of the discussions were in Norwegian, and in true Norwegian fashion, most of it, among the men anyway, centered on politics. But Jespar and Knute and the rest húng around, trying out their broken English, strutting like tom turkeys trying to get attention. Savannah was gracious and kind, maybe too kind. Did she like their antics?

Britta had relished being the center of attention, playing the young men one off the other, especially Elias. She could flirt and tease and get a man's dander up better than anyone he had ever met, and he couldn't resist her.

Until she'd up and left town without a word, abandoning her pupils and disillusioning Elias.

His appetite waned, and he pushed his plate away.

When the music started again, Pa leaned forward. "I'll take care of your plates and such. Elias, why don't you take this gal out onto the dance floor before some of these eager young fellas cut in?"

Nicely done, Pa. Now I have to ask her.

Elias rose and held out his hand, his heart banging like a barn door in a high wind. "Savannah?"

Savannah placed her hand into his, and a tingle shot up her arm and fizzled in her chest. He held her steady while she stepped over the bench. All evening she'd waited for him to cut in, to claim her for a dance, any dance, but he'd stayed on the sidelines. Even now, she had a feeling he would've liked to back out, but good manners forbade him.

Perhaps he didn't dance? Was that the reason he hadn't joined in? If so, should she let him off, claim to be tired and sit this one out?

Before she could make up her mind, Elias put his hand on the small of her back, raised her other hand in his and swung her into a waltz. Her mouth dropped open. He was so light on his feet, the pressure of his hand guiding her perfect and his sense of rhythm and timing excellent. Her dancing instructors back home couldn't have done better.

He raised one eyebrow, pivoting her. "You didn't think we were all clumsy, clodhopping farmers, did you?"

She closed her gaping mouth. "Of course not. Several of my partners have been quite good, but you're… exceptional." She relaxed in his arms, trusting his ability not to step on her toes or bump into other couples, both of which had happened several times already tonight. Instead, Savannah allowed herself to think only of the music and the company. "Where did you learn?"

"Pa's a good dancer. He taught me and Tyler. Though he grew up dancing Irish jigs and Scottish reels more than waltzing."

Savannah asked no more questions, giving herself over to the dancing and enjoyment of being with Elias. Long before she was ready, the music ended and another young man stood beside her, asking for the next dance.

"Thank you, Elias. I enjoyed that."

He shot a hard glance at the man waiting and then shrugged. "Your admirers await."

The next tune started, and she was carried away from him.

A string of partners came and went, tall, short, fair, dark, some in traditional Norwegian dress with double-breasted vests and silver buttons, some in American garb. She smiled and danced and smiled and danced, all the while watching for Elias, waiting for him to cut in.

But he didn't. He danced once with his mother and then retired to the sidelines.

During a small intermission, her partner—Rollef?—leaned in and whispered, "It is warm, *ja*? The rain has stopped. You vould like to go outside?"

It was warm in the barn, and crowded. A little space to think would be welcome. Elias's inexplicable behavior tonight had her on edge, taking away from what should've been a joyful occasion.

She allowed Rollef to guide her to a small door set into the large, rolling ones at the far end of the barn. As he opened it just wide enough for her to slip through, fresh, cool, damp air hit her cheeks. She breathed in, turning into the slight breeze, letting it cool her face. Careful to keep her hem off the wet ground, she glanced up at the clearing skies, picking out the stars in the indigo night.

"It's beautiful." Darkness blanketed the countryside, and when Rollef shut the door behind him, only faint starlight allowed her to see.

"You are beautiful." He stood close, his breath stirring the hair at her temple.

"Thank you." Savannah moved away. Alarm bells began to ring faintly in the background. Rollef had been a perfect gentleman all three times she'd danced with him. She was probably misreading him. Perhaps it was a cultural thing that she didn't understand.

"You are most beautiful woman I have seen." He closed the distance again and reached for her hand. "I say that right?"

Her heart banged in her chest, and her breath hitched. Cultural or not, this was making her uncomfortable. "Rollef, you said that nicely, but I think you've misunderstood. I only came out for a bit of air, nothing else." She untangled her fingers and moved around him toward the door.

Rollef grabbed her elbow. "Vait."

"No. Let me go."

He pulled her closer instead, grasping her by both elbows. "You dance vid me tree times, you smile, you come outside and now you…how you say it, tease?"

His eyes glittered in the darkness, and he loomed over her. Her mouth went dry, and she tugged against his grip, but to no avail.

"I vant von kiss."

"No." She twisted her head as his face lowered to hers.

A bar of light fell across them, and a man stood silhouetted in the doorway. "Fjelstad, let her go."

Elias. Relief washed through Savannah.

Rollef hung on for a moment longer, said something in Norwegian and flung her away, stalking into the barn.

Savannah's knees shook, and she pressed her hand to her throat. "Thank you. I'm so glad you came just then."

Her rescuer closed the distance between them, grabbing her elbows much as Rollef had done. "What do you think you're doing, stepping outside with a man? Don't you care at all for your reputation? It might be done at a Southern dance, but here, a girl can be ruined for such carelessness. Not to mention the parents of her students might question her judgment and fitness for teaching children."

Savannah's mouth gaped open as heat and shock blazed through her.

"Never mind. I don't care. Get back in there before someone misses you."

Stepping into the light of the barn, she blinked, feeling bludgeoned by both Rollef's advances and the anger in Elias's voice. She dared a glance up at him, and his rigid jaw and narrow eyes brought a lump to her throat.

"Elias, I—"

"Don't talk, just dance."

He took her in his arms again, swinging her out onto the floor, but his hold was stiff. He stared over her head. Woodenly, she followed his steps, her heart like a brick in her chest. Heat flamed in her cheeks, and tears burned her eyes.

How had things gone wrong so quickly?

Chapter Nine

Savannah entered the busy mercantile, list in hand, resolve and dignity wrapped around her like a cloak. She hadn't seen Elias all week and wasn't sure what she would say to him if she did. The last time they'd spoken, after their dance, he'd handed her over to the Halvorsons like an unwanted puppy, then turned on his heel and strode away.

Thankfully, the Halvorsons had been ready to leave the party, and hadn't questioned her. It seemed no one knew of her faux pas beyond Rollef and Elias.

And Aunt Carolina. Or she would soon.

Savannah had written out an account of the entire evening, everything from the charming costumes, to the noxious *lutefisk*, and Elias's inexplicable behavior.

I honestly didn't think I was doing anything wrong, but apparently I've committed quite the transgression. Did I lead Rollef on or somehow give him the impression I was inviting his advances? I didn't think so. But Elias was so angry... disgusted, really. I was as shamed as I was bewildered. I thought he was beginning to like and accept me here, but now, I think he'd just as soon pack me off to Raleigh with the next post.

Savannah felt for the letter in her reticule as she stepped to the post office counter, edging around a barrel of dried beans and one of rye flour.

"Good morning, Miss Cox. You are here for letters?" The proprietor, Karl Svenby, came down the aisle behind the counter. "Tree of dem came in for you."

His accent was so thick she had to concentrate to decipher his words. Gladly she took the envelopes, scanning the addresses. Aunt Carolina, Aunt Georgette and… Stillness came over her. A letter from her father.

He'd *never* written her before. The occasional telegram addressed to the household, but never a letter just for her.

A crowded store was no place to delve into such an anomaly, so she stuffed the mail into her handbag and withdrew her missive to Aunt Carolina. "Could you please frank this for me? I also have a list of things I would like to order."

"Ah, letters to home again? Always you write." He stamped the envelope and dropped it into the mail bag. "De stage vill pick it up on *Mandag morgen*."

The door opened, letting in a gust of brisk air. And Elias.

A quiver went through Savannah.

"Hi, Karl. Getting chilly out there." Elias blew on his hands. "Weather sure changed all of a sudden, didn't it?"

"*Ja*, I am selling much long-handles." The store owner grinned. "I tink it vill be a cold vinter, *ja*?" As he spoke, he deftly wrapped a customer's parcels in thick brown paper, tying them with string and handing them over with a smile.

"Hello, Miss Cox." Elias lowered his voice and removed his hat. "I was hoping I'd see you today."

"Really?" She couldn't keep the archness out of her voice. If he'd wanted to see her, he knew well enough where he could find her. She studied a glass case of sewing notions.

"We need to talk."

"I have nothing to say to you." Not after the way he'd treated her.

He tunneled his fingers through his dark hair. "Then you can listen."

"Miss Cox." Something thumped her leg, and she looked down into a little face.

"Hello, Ingrid. How are you?" She spoke slowly, squatting down to put her arm around her youngest pupil.

"I. Am. Vell." Ingrid paused between each word, and grinned, showing her two missing front teeth.

"Perfectly said." Savannah squeezed the little girl. "Your English is coming along better than my Norwegian."

The door opened again and several more people came in, crowding the store, separating her from Elias. Before long, she found herself surrounded by students and their parents. Hands clasped hers, words poured out in Norwegian. Bewildered and frustrated by not being able to communicate, Savannah nodded and shrugged, spreading her hands. Johann's father reached through the crowd and snagged Elias's sleeve, tugging him in.

"He wants me to interpret for them." Elias listened to them and turned to Savannah.

"They say they are very happy you have come to

teach the children. They hear good reports of you each day, especially about the music. They would like to have you visit them."

"Really? That's so nice. Tell them I'd love to come to their homes." She smiled at each of her students as he translated.

"They would also like me to accompany you." He paused. "To help with the Norwegian."

She studied him. It bothered her to be upset with him and yet need him. "Very well. It would be useful to have you along, I suppose." Dispassion laced her words. "Perhaps we could begin next Saturday?"

"Fine." He slanted her a grim glance. "I'll work out a schedule with them and let you know."

Savannah edged out of the crowd and weaved her way to the counter with her list, but Mr. Svenby and his two assistants were busy. She perused the goods for a bit, then wandered back to the rear of the store, past the stove with its pretty isinglass doors showing the bright flames inside, past the kitchen goods and shoes and ready-made clothing, stopping when she reached the high table where the catalog perched proudly.

The pages rustled under her fingers as she leafed back to the women's clothing section. She'd never ordered clothes from a catalog. All her garments were made by a modiste especially to her measurements. Savannah turned the pages, examining the offerings— every type of garment from the skin out in multiple price ranges, with or without embellishments. Fascinating.

"You shopping for Christmas presents, or for more clothes?" Elias spoke over her shoulder.

Savannah slapped the catalog closed. "I was just

looking." She could've bitten her tongue for rising to his bait. Why did he get under her skin so much?

"Listen, I wanted to talk to you about the dance." He looked around to make sure no one was listening, but there were people everywhere. "Can't we get out of here, go somewhere quieter and talk?"

"That's what Rollef said, and look what trouble that got me into. I have shopping to do." She edged away from Elias, all too disturbed by his nearness, disappointed in herself for remembering how it felt to be held by him and spun around the dance floor. Remembering the mischievous light in his eyes as he'd tempted her to try Norwegian delicacies.

"I'll help you."

"I really don't need your help."

"I'll help you, anyway. After all, Tyler did tell me to look after you." Elias took her elbow and guided her toward an open space at the counter. "Karl, when you have a minute." His voice rose above the chatter, and the store owner flung up his hand in acknowledgment.

Soon, she handed over her list. Mr. Svenby stroked his bushy mustache, his brows waggling as he read.

"Vat is dis?" He pointed.

"I need one dozen slates and two dozen slate pencils."

Elias took the list. "What do you think you're doing?"

She drew a patient breath. "I'm ordering school supplies."

"And just who do you think is going to pay for these? I told you, there's no money. These people have all come in to pay off their store bills with the cash they got from selling their grain. They have to stock up for the winter on food and clothing and supplies. There won't be anything left over for books and pencils and the like."

He rubbed his forehead as if her reasonable plan was giving him a headache.

"The children can't learn as they're supposed to without them. If the parents or the school board can't afford them, then I'll take care of it myself."

"You just don't get it, do you? The fastest way to alienate a Norwegian is to wound his pride. They don't want your charity." Elias tossed the paper onto the counter.

"They want their children to succeed, to be educated and take their place as citizens of their new country. I can't do that properly without books and slates and supplies."

"And they don't want to be in debt, not to you or anyone else. It's hard enough that they have to charge things here at the store for months at a time until the harvest. Why can't you understand that? They live one harvest to the next, and if that harvest fails, they go without. This isn't your high-class, grand life in the city. These people don't have a rich daddy to give them handouts…and they don't want one. They're making it, slowly. On their own."

Savannah pinched the bridge of her nose. How could they be so stubborn? They'd given her a task and no way to complete it.

Or was Elias trying to ensure she didn't succeed? That she went home sooner rather than later? He'd never been in favor of her, not from the moment she arrived. Savannah picked up the list, smoothing it out. "I'll make the purchases for myself then, and I'll explain as much to the families when I visit them."

"If you think anyone will buy the notion that you need twelve slates, two dozen slate pencils and a dozen sets of *McGuffey Readers* just for yourself, you're delusional. And if you think I'm going to help you insult my friends and neighbors, you've got another think coming."

His dictatorial tone set her teeth on edge.

"Mr. Parker, I have no desire to insult anyone, but I will do my job to the best of my ability, and that includes getting these children the tools they need. You seem to think I am a half-witted child who needs your help and guidance at every step. I assure you, I intend to discuss my actions with the parents, and I am confident we can reach an agreement that will satisfy everyone involved, even you."

"And I'm just as confident that you don't have any notion of what you're doing. But—" he crossed his arms "—I can see there's no dissuading you. Why is it that women are always so headstrong and sure they're right?"

She gasped. "Do you hear yourself? That's the pot calling the kettle obsidian if ever I heard it done."

Karl's laughter cut between them. "You sound like old married couple. Nobody fight like people who care, *ja*?" He picked up the list. "I haff to send away for dees tings, but I get dem here quick, *ja*?"

Savannah hardly registered his question. Like an old married couple? Fighting because she cared?

That was ridiculous.

Leaving the mercantile, she braced herself against the cold wind. Low clouds scudded across the sky, obscuring the sun. "You are a Southern thin-blood, Savannah Cox, but don't you dare show it," she muttered under her breath, drawing her shawl around her and fisting her hands in the fringe.

Two doors down, she ducked into the drugstore which also served as a small café. Her encounter with Elias had left her shaken and doubting herself. Was she going to insult her students' parents if she procured teaching materials? Was she being headstrong and stubborn?

She ordered tea, and when it arrived, she opened her letters, starting with Aunt Georgette's.

Savannah found herself smiling over her aunt's theatrics. All the news about people Savannah didn't know. Fluff and frills and fashion—quintessential Georgette.

Until the last paragraph.

Savannah, darling, we miss you so much here. The girls miss your steadying influence, and Carolina misses having someone to share responsibility with, and I miss your sweet face. Most of the furor over your broken engagement died down when you left. Until that dreadful Girard showed up married to another woman! Now sympathies are flowing very much in your favor, dear child. Everyone thinks it God's blessing that you escaped marriage to that horrible man, that's what. And I do, too. I just wish you weren't perishing up there on those stark prairies. Can't you come home now?

Perishing on the stark prairies. Savannah shook her head, restoring Georgette's letter to its envelope. If only they could see her. She wasn't perishing, she was flourishing.

Aunt Carolina's letter started with a bang.

Savannah,

I returned the ring to Girard, and I left him in no doubt as to my feelings on the matter. I am stunned that he courted you under false pretenses, giving no thought to the devastation he would leave in his wake. Then to have the gall to request the return of the ring. Still, you don't want such rubbish cluttering up your life, ring or man.

I've sent along the recipes you asked for, though the one for fried green tomatoes will be difficult to make at this time of year, I imagine.

Do write soon. We love your letters, and I worry about you up there all alone.

Several recipe cards accompanied the letter. When Savannah had written requesting them, she hadn't known she would be at such odds with Elias. Still, she would go through with her plans.

Worried about her up here all alone. Funny, after the first couple of weeks, she didn't feel alone. In fact, she was rarely alone. Living with the Halvorsons, being surrounded by her students each day, trips to town on Saturday, church on Sunday... Life here had kept her so busy she hardly had time to be homesick.

She took a bracing sip of tea before opening her father's letter. With no idea what to expect, she unfolded the single sheet. It was written on bank letterhead, dated ten days before.

Savannah,

I am concerned about your current location, and I have taken steps to approach the school superintendents of several East Coast schools, where your presence would be welcome should you choose to continue in educating children.

I am concerned regarding your income at that

school district. Do you have enough funds for
your needs? If necessary, wire any of my banks.
Funds will be made available to you.

Finally, I am concerned as to your well-being.
Carolina has informed me that I have been re-
miss in my paternal duties, but we both know that
I am not familial and have been bewildered by
my daughters since they were born. I wish your
mother was here to guide you. Thankfully, you
have your aunts.

If you should decide you would rather take a
trip to Europe instead of hiding out there on the
prairie, send me a wire.

He'd signed it with his name, not Father, not Dad,
not Pa, as Elias called his parent. Just "Jonathan Cox,
President, Southern and Textile Bank."

Savannah read the letter twice more, unsure how she
was supposed to feel about it.

He was concerned, and she supposed this was the
only way he knew to show it. Offer money, offer a trip,
offer a different job where someone could keep an eye
on her. Offer her an escape from this choice she'd made.

But she didn't want an escape. She would show her
father and Elias that she was made of sterner stuff. That
she could stay the course.

He'd tried to think of an honorable way to get out of
taking Savannah around to all her students' homes, but
his conscience wouldn't let him back out. And perhaps
he could mediate and, hopefully, avoid hurt feelings.

Savannah stepped out of the Halvorson cabin and
closed the door behind her.

"You'll need a coat. It's brisk today."

"This is a coat." She frowned, tugging on a thin pair of gloves.

"I mean a proper winter coat. You do have one, don't you?"

"I wish you'd stop fixating on my clothing. I'm perfectly warm, thank you, and I can take care of myself." She climbed aboard and settled on the bench, smoothing and arranging her skirts.

Stubborn as ever.

"Suit yourself." He flicked the reins. The mare obliged by breaking into a quick trot. Chilly air flowed over them, and Savannah gasped.

"There's a blanket in the back if you want it." Elias thought she might be too proud to use it, too set on proving she didn't need help, but after a minute she reached for the quilt and wrapped it around her shoulders.

"We're going to the Rosedahls first?" she asked.

"Yes, and then the Rambeks, and if there's time, the Magnussens. Those are the men that make up the school board. I figured if we started with them and you got their approval on the school supplies, the rest would follow their lead." Or if they shut her down right away, she'd give up on the notion.

"Good idea."

The silence between them hung heavy, and Elias chided himself. *Just say it, get it over with. You won't be happy until you do.*

"Listen, before we get there, I wanted to talk to you about what happened at the dance."

"Did I mention that I'd rather not talk about that? A gentleman wouldn't bring it up again." She held the edges of the blanket up to her cheeks to cut the wind.

"Then I guess I'm no gentleman." He flicked the

reins again, feeling grim. "I wanted to apologize. I over-reacted."

When she didn't speak, he risked a glance at her.

"So you don't think I lured Rollef out there?" Her blue eyes pierced him.

"No. I know you didn't. I was feeling sore about something else, and I took it out on you." Memories of Britta at last year's harvest celebration made his fingers fist on the reins. He'd never told anyone about his feelings for her, but he found himself wanting to tell Savannah.

"Pa homesteaded our farm just after the war. One of the reasons we settled here was because there were so many Norwegians. Pa thought it would be easier on my ma if she had some of her own people as neighbors." Elias shifted. "I think Tyler thought if he hired a teacher with a Norwegian background, they would fit in and stay. But that didn't work out. Not with Erik, and especially not with Britta." He braced himself for the sting. He hadn't said her name in months. Odd, this time it didn't hurt as much.

"Britta?"

"Britta Thoreson. She was from Saint Paul, Norwegian, about your age, maybe a little older." He cast back, but strangely, he couldn't remember her features as sharply as he once did. "She was pretty, tall and slim, and she cut quite a path through the young men in this county."

"Was she a good teacher?"

"Tyler seemed pleased enough. I knew her more outside of the school." Sucking in a breath, Elias decided to tell the truth. "I had plans to court her as soon as school was out, and I told her as much. I thought we had an understanding, but at the harvest dance, she flirted and carried on with every man there. The dance was outside that night, and I lost track of her in the crowd. When I found her, she'd slipped away with another man. I found them in the barn, kissing. And unlike you and Rollef, Britta wasn't protesting or trying to get away."

Savannah put her hand on his arm, dropping the blanket. "Elias, I'm sorry."

"Thanks. Anyway, that's why I got so sore at the dance. Britta laughed it off, said I had no claim on her and she'd do what she wanted with whoever she wanted. I didn't know what to do. Should I tell Tyler and let him deal with it? Before I could, she up and took off. Left without a word. Tyler tried to track her down, but she didn't go to her home." Elias shrugged. "Guess it was for the best. Anyway, I'm sorry about the other night."

He turned up a drive, ready to change the subject. "This is Rosedahl's place. He's the chairman of the board. Convince him of your plan and you'll be home and dried."

The Rosedahls welcomed them in, and warmth from the hearth hit Elias's cheeks. He breathed in the smells of bread and coffee.

"Elias, welcome," Mr. Rosedahl said in Norwegian. "Thank you for bringing the teacher to visit." He cupped the backs of two little heads. "Say hello, Peder, Synove. Jespar had to go to town." The kids greeted Savannah with shy smiles, and Mr. Rosedahl introduced his wife.

The adults sat at the table, and Mrs. Rosedahl served thick slices of rye bread with butter and hot cups of coffee.

"Mr. and Mrs. Rosedahl, first let me say what a joy it is to have Peder and Synove as students." Savannah smiled as Elias translated. "Synove is very strong in math skills, and Peder has a real talent for getting everyone to work together. He's a natural-born leader."

The parents beamed, and Mr. Rosedahl leaned back, tucking his fingers under his suspenders.

"I wanted to ask you both what your goals are for the children this year. I know what I want them to accomplish, but I'd like to hear your views." Savannah drew a small tablet and pencil from her bag.

This both pleased and flustered the parents. Elias watched as one of the most reticent men in the community opened up.

"We want them to read and speak English well, and to know about the history of their new country. They will learn of Norway and Norwegian things during the parochial term, so we want you to focus on American things."

"I'm sorry, the parochial term?"

Elias stopped translating. "Didn't Tyler tell you about the parochial term at school?"

"No, what it is?"

"It's a two-week period each semester where the children are instructed in their Norwegian heritage and faith. Since the school is public and run by the state of Minnesota, but the parents want religious education incorporated into the curriculum, parochial terms are a compromise. The teacher, Mr. Birk, travels from school to school throughout this part of the state, staying for two weeks and teaching, then moving on. I can't believe Tyler didn't mention it."

Elias reminded himself to have a word with his brother the next time he saw him. This issue had been a bone of contention with the first teacher, and Britta hadn't stayed long enough for it to be a problem. How would Savannah react to having her school interrupted again?

"I see." She tapped the pencil on her pad. "What a wonderful idea. I can certainly understand the parents wanting their children not to lose their heritage. I wish all school districts were as sensible."

Elias blinked, and then translated for the Rosedahls.

"She is a good teacher for the children." Mrs. Rosedahl refilled her husband's coffee cup. "I think she has settled in very well. Agneta Halvorson says she is much easier to board than the other teachers, even if she does have many cases and bags. You don't need to tell her that part." The woman blushed. "Tell her we are happy with her teaching and ask if there is anything we can do to help."

Which was evidently the lead-in Savannah had been waiting for.

"There is something I wished to talk to you about, not just as parents, but because Mr. Rosedahl chairs the school board." She laced her fingers together. "One thing that is sorely lacking at the school is proper materials and equipment for the children. I understand that times are tough and the parents don't have the funds at the moment to spend on books and papers and such. However, the need is great, and I've taken it upon myself to order supplies."

As Elias let them know what she'd said, Mr. Rosedahl's eyelids descended to half-mast, and his arms crossed his chest.

"I understand from Elias that this could be seen as a breach of manners, and I assure you that is not my intent. My goal is to help you accomplish your dreams for your children. We are a team in this. You provide the schoolhouse and my wages, the coal to heat the school, the hay to feed the horses the children ride, and the support here at home to ensure that they do their lessons. My part is to teach them, and in this case, to supply some of the materials."

Mr. Rosedahl rubbed his chin, his eyes narrowing. "What things did you order, why do you need them and how will you pay for them?"

Elias expected nothing less than a succinct summing up by the man.

"Excellent questions." Savannah leaned forward, her eyes glowing. "I ordered slates and readers for each student. And for the classroom, I ordered a globe and a dictionary. If the children are to read and write in English, as you wish, they need to practice. Slates are much less expensive for practicing than ink and paper. In order for the children to understand both where in the world they come from and where they live now in relation to other nations, the globe is so helpful. I like flat maps, but a globe helps the children understand the distances and relationships better, both for current world borders and for history."

Her enthusiasm reached out and grabbed each of them, and Elias found himself nodding. To his surprise, he found Mr. Rosedahl nodding, too.

"As to how the items are paid for…" She shrugged. "I would pay for them now, but I thought I would work out an exchange."

Eyebrows rose. "What sort of exchange?"

"I am in need of winter clothing, a heavy coat, mittens, woolen garments. Where I come from, it rarely gets below freezing and never stays cold for long. I don't have the appropriate garments for a winter in Snowflake." She glanced at Elias. "So I thought perhaps the mothers of my students might be willing to either trade some of the winter clothes they no longer want, or even make clothes that would work for me. I am especially enamored of the lovely embroidery I saw on several of the costumes at the harvest dance and would love to have a few pieces of my own."

Elias sat back, leaning against the log wall, and stared at her. She tilted her head a fraction and gave him a what-do-you-think-of-that? look, all saucy and proud of herself.

And she had reason to be. Charity would not be accepted, but a trade? Norwegians loved to trade.

He laid it out for the Rosedahls, and Mrs. Rosedahl jumped up and ducked into the bedroom. She came out with a pair of woolen puttees, beautifully embroidered with red-and-gold flowers.

"She wants to know if these are what you might be looking for."

Savannah took the puttees, stroking the silk embroidery. She touched the wool to her cheek. "Oh, my, these are so beautiful, it will be a pleasure to wear them. And so warm. That walk from the Halvorsons' to the school won't be as daunting now."

When they left, Elias helped her into the buckboard. She held the leg wraps in her lap, waving to the Rosedahls in the doorway as he pulled out of the farmyard.

"How did you do that?" he asked when they reached the main road.

"Do what?"

"Didrik Rosedahl is the most skeptical, proud man I know. You not only turned him to your way of thinking, you had him agreeing with everything you said. You got him to not only agree to your proposal, but now he's championing your cause. I'm flummoxed."

Her laughter rang out in the chilly air. "I didn't think

of it until midweek. At first, I was so mad at you for telling me I would offend everyone by ordering supplies that I couldn't think what to do. On Wednesday, I was so cold walking to school, and Lars and Rut were saying this was a mild fall and it would get much colder. How was I going to get warm clothing, and how was I going to convince parents to let me buy schoolbooks? Then it all snapped into place."

Elias soaked in her laughter. She sounded happy and carefree, easy in his presence and buoyed by her success with the chairman of the school board. As well she should be.

She clapped her hands "And just think, not only will the students have the things they need to learn, making my job easier, but I'll have a winter wardrobe and some truly lovely pieces to show my sisters when I go back home to Raleigh."

His happiness cracked like ice on a lake. *When she went home.*

A good warning. He could easily fall for someone like Savannah, and he needed the reminder that she had no intention of staying in Snowflake.

Chapter Ten

"You want to cook for us?" Elias asked.

Savannah tamped together a stack of papers, butting them against her desk. "Yes, well, mostly for your mother. As a thank-you for her help over the skunk incident."

The windows rattled, and she shivered as the November wind struck the side of the schoolhouse. "It's been doing that all day. We had a hard fight to keep it warm in here. If I kept the damper open too much, the wind sucked the heat right out, but if I closed it, the fire went out."

"It's a fine line sometimes, depending on which way the wind is blowing."

She studied him, trying not to be obvious, trying not to admit that she'd missed seeing him. After a month of being together every Saturday, visiting all her students' homes, she hadn't talked to Elias in weeks. Today he had a scarf around his throat and the stubble of a couple days' growth of whiskers on his cheeks.

"How's your coal holding up? It's one of the things I came by to check on." He used his teeth to pull his gloves off, and held his hands out to the stove.

"We've made a dent in the coal store, but there's still quite a bit left. Mr. Rosedahl stopped in earlier this week to check on it. He thought it would last through Christmas at least." Savannah tucked the papers into her grade book and put the book into her satchel. She'd read and review them tonight after supper.

"How's the teaching going?" Elias turned from the stove and unbuttoned his coat. He reached inside and pulled out a crinkled yellow paper.

"Good, better than I imagined it would when I started." She chuckled. "Though the children's English is coming along much faster than my Norwegian. The singing helps. Somehow I can remember the words better when they're put to music."

He surveyed the room. "Where's your harp?"

"I had to take it back to the Halvorsons'. There's no heat here at night, and the fluctuations in temperature aren't good for it. If you just look at a harp wrong it falls out of tune." She tipped her head. "What's bothering you? Is it that paper?"

He shrugged and nodded. "It's from Tyler. Bad news. Mr. Birk, the teacher for the parochial term, can't make it to Snowflake this term. His horse bolted on him up near Big Stone Lake and flipped him out of his buggy. He's got a broken leg and some broken ribs."

"Oh, the poor man."

"Yeah, poor him and poor me. Tyler says I need to teach the parochial term." Rubbing his hand down his jaw, Elias handed her the telegram. "He says to work out the time with you, but the last two weeks before Christmas break might be best."

He sounded so grim a chill that had nothing to do with the weather raced across Savannah's skin. "That's as good a time as any. Are you worried about teaching?"

"No. I can handle that." He picked up one of the new readers off a desk and thumbed through it, set it down and moved to the globe, giving it a spin. "Guess you'd like that, huh? That would give you a month to go home for the holidays."

Savannah quit reading Tyler's telegram. Her head snapped up. "Is that what has you on edge? My going home for Christmas?" Her hands went to her hips. "You think I'm going to decamp, don't you? That if I leave, I won't come back and finish the term?"

With each sentence, she stepped closer, until they were toe to toe. "Well, thank you for thinking so highly of me. I'll have you know I wasn't even planning on going home for the holidays. I intend to spend Christmas in Snowflake and be right here in this classroom come the New Year." She punctuated the last sentence by poking him in the chest at every word.

He grabbed her hand, his face relaxing into a grin. "All right, all right, put your weapons away, ma'am. I'm guilty."

Savannah stilled. The same fizzy feeling she'd experienced when they'd danced together crackled through her hand and up her arm. From this close, she couldn't help but notice his strong jaw, the sturdy column of his neck and his well-shaped lips. What would it be like to stand on tiptoe and press her lips to his, to feel the rasp of his whiskers against her skin, to feel his arms wrap around her and draw her towa— She halted that thought and stepped back. He let her hand go when she tugged.

She strove to clear her head. "When will you stop lumping me in with those other teachers? I'm nothing like them."

"So I'm beginning to realize." His voice had a low, husky quality she hadn't heard before, a sound that made her heart knock against her ribs like a trapped bird. "So the last two weeks before Christmas break, I'll teach."

"And perhaps I will attend as a student." She gave him a saucy grin, striving for lightness. "You can teach Norwegian history and culture and catechism, and the students and I will learn. And in exchange, I will come to your parents' house and cook real Southern food for them."

"You will, will you?"

"I will. And all of it will taste better than that dreadful *lutefisk*. That isn't fit for man or beast." She wrinkled her nose.

"Where will you get Southern ingredients way up here?"

"I'm resourceful, remember? My aunt Carolina has shipped me a box of staples and sent along the recipes I need. If you would ask your mother if I could come over Saturday afternoon, I'll prepare dinner for you all." Savannah edged around him to bank the fire for the night, and then picked up her satchel and headed for the door.

Elias went with her and helped her into her coat. When she turned around, he nudged her hands aside and fastened the top button, lifting the fur collar to surround her face. "Where did this one come from?"

"Margrethe's mother. I told her it was too much, but she insisted." Savannah did up the rest of the buttons. "Isn't it fine?"

"Beautiful."

Again that husky tone. Did he think the coat was beautiful or did he mean *she* was beautiful?

He tugged on his gloves, suddenly brisk and businesslike. "Next time, take your coat into the schoolroom and warm it at the stove while you finish up your paperwork. I'll tell Ma about Saturday."

They stepped outside, and Savannah sucked in a quick breath as a cold blast of air hit her face. She didn't relish the walk home, though she was grateful that, since the harvest, she could tramp across the fields instead of going the long way around by road. Elias's buckskin stood tied to the porch railing.

"Do you want a ride home? Buck can easily carry two." Elias climbed aboard and turned the horse to stand alongside the steps. "You can ride behind." And without waiting for her say-so, he reached down and swung her up. Her feet dangled down Buck's left flank and her hip pressed against the cantle. "Put your arms around my waist and hold on." Elias raised his elbows to allow her room.

She obeyed, clasping his waist. He pressed his forearms against hers to anchor her, and legged his gelding into a walk and then an easy canter. Savannah ducked her head and rested her cheek against Elias's coat to cut the wind. She had to concentrate to keep her feet from banging against Buck's side, but she felt quite secure. Elias's back formed a sturdy wall and he moved rhythmically with the horse. It felt altogether too much like a dance, and it was over before Savannah was ready.

"I'll be by to pick you up on Saturday," he said, as he lowered her to the ground in the Halvorsons' yard. "Stay warm."

Oddly, Savannah was warm right through after that ride, and it had nothing to do with the temperature.

* * *

"It's grits." Savannah ladled up a bowl and set it before Elias.

"It looks like *rommegrot*." He quirked his eyebrows and poked the steaming bowl.

"Trust me, it doesn't taste like *rommegrot*." She turned back and rescued the fried green tomatoes. Breathing a sigh, she transferred them to a platter and put them on the table, gloating silently about their golden-brown texture.

"Lass, I've never seen the like, though that cornbread looks mighty good." Ian Parker tucked his napkin into his collar. "Howsabout we say grace so we can dive in?"

Savannah whipped off her apron and took her place at the Parkers' dining table. She took Tova's offered hand, and Ian's, bowed her head, sending up her own prayer that everything was cooked properly and that her hosts would like it.

When she raised her head and breathed in the smells of ribs and cornbread and collard greens, she had to blink fast. All the flavors of home. The same feelings had hit her all week as she practiced in Agneta's kitchen.

Elias dipped his spoon into his grits, lifting them to his nose and giving them a sniff.

"I like mine with butter and salt." Savannah took a bit of butter off the beautiful mold in the center of the table. "And I mixed the cornbread with a cake recipe so it's light and fluffy and sweet."

"This is what you eat every day at home?" Tova asked.

Laughing, Savannah shook her head. "Not all of it. I just wanted to share as many foods as possible with you. Normally, we'd have only a third of these dishes at one meal. Or less if it was hot outside. Some days, I only eat chilled watermelon, drink iced lemonade and pray for a rainstorm."

Elias cut a wedge of fried green tomato and held it up. "I never even heard of eating green tomatoes, much less frying them up."

"And I never heard of eating fish rotted in lye before, either," Savannah retorted. "I still can't believe you goaded me into trying *lutefisk*. It was horrible."

Ian laughed, making his napkin quiver. "They say of the great Norwegian migration to America that half of them came to escape *lutefisk* and the other half came to spread it to the world. Ask Elias how much he enjoys *lutefisk* and how often we have it here at the house."

"Now, Pa, you don't have to tell all our secrets." Elias tasted the tomato. "Hey, this isn't bad."

"If he won't tell you, I will. Elias detests *lutefisk*. We all do. Never have it about the place."

Savannah glared at Elias. "You made me eat that horrible stuff and you don't even like it? Just for that, I should make you eat…actually, there's nothing that awful tasting in all of Southern cuisine."

"Best spareribs I ever ate, and that's a fact." Ian reached for another. "You're going to make someone a wonderful little wife someday, Savannah. Pretty as a peach, fine manners, musical, smart and you can cook. What more could a fellow want?"

"That's most kind, but I'm not looking to get married. I'm enjoying teaching."

"All girls say that until the right fella comes along, don't they, Tova?" Ian clasped his wife's hand and squeezed. "I meant to ask you, Savannah, how'd you wind up here in Minnesota? You can't tell me there weren't teaching positions available closer to home."

Dabbing her lips with her napkin, Savannah scrambled for an answer. She'd told no one here about "the humiliation" and wasn't sure she wanted to now. Was a partial truth lying?

"My father is a banker, and when he's home, he often has business acquaintances at the house. One of them was from Minnesota, and he had a copy of the *Pioneer Press* that he left behind. When I read the advertisement for a teacher, I applied." Embarrassment prickled her skin. "I had a…disappointment…in a relationship, and I needed to strike out on my own and get away from the unhappiness."

She looked at Elias from under her lashes. The past three months had done a lot to restore her self-confidence, but she still had some tender spots.

Ian beamed. "We're sure glad you answered that ad. You've been a blessing to the community. Tyler was at the end of his rope. Nobody wanted to come out here to a mainly Norwegian community for the little bit we could afford to pay."

"How did there come to be such a concentration of Norwegians here?" It was something Savannah had wondered for a while.

Elias took a piece of cornbread and slathered it with butter. "How familiar are you with Minnesota history?"

"Not as much as I should be, I suppose." She passed him the platter of fried chicken.

"Have you heard of the Dakota Uprising of '62?"

She shook her head. "I'm afraid most of my knowledge of 1862 is centered on the South. A fair bit of history was being made in my part of the country."

"That's natural, I guess. Well, in this part of the state that year the Dakota Indians, who had been confined to a reservation along the Minnesota River valley south and east of here, went on the warpath. There was plenty of fault to go around and everyone has an opinion on it, but the upshot is that several hundred settlers were killed and plenty of folks taken captive. Eventually the captives were released, thirty-eight Indians executed and the Dakota run out of Minnesota."

"That's terrible."

"Some of the frontier settlements in Minnesota were abandoned by their occupants. Those that weren't abandoned got hit hard in the next decade by the Rocky Mountain locust. Year after year crops failed and people had to leave their farms."

Ian nodded, chewing and swallowing. "Those were some tough times, all right. I was a private at Fort Ridgely during the Dakota War. After I mustered out, I went up north to see the logging camps, and right away I meet Tova in Duluth, fresh off a boat from Norway."

"I came vid my family and many others from my town. Ve had met a...what vas he called?" She turned to Ian.

"A land speculator."

"A land spec-u-lator in Norway dat told us of the great farmland of Minnesota dat any man could haff for free."

Elias leaned forward. "This fellow went to Norway with a bunch of brochures and promises and convinced a hundred people from Valdres to emigrate to America. He had a ship, and he had homestead maps."

Tova nodded. "Most people in my country are tenant farmers. Dey vork for others. The chance to own land and be free is..." She spread her hands.

Ian set down his knife and fork. "Lots of folks jumped at the chance, left everything and came to America. When I met Tova and her people, I decided to return south and take up a homestead here near Snowflake with them. We had some rough years. Those 'hoppers nearly did us in. I had to go away to find work and leave Tova and the boys here." He shook his head, his eyes staring into the past as he stroked his beard. "We were all mighty close to giving up."

Tova stood and put her hand on his shoulder. "Ve do the tings ve must. You are a good provider. Ve ver glad ven you came home."

"We did fine, Pa. I'm glad we stuck it out," Elias said. He turned to Savannah. "So that's how there got to be so many Norwegians here in one place. They all used the same land speculator and all homesteaded here together. Some have moved on or gone back to Norway, and some new folks have come into the area, but newcomers are often Norwegian, too, because it's easier to settle in a new place if the culture is familiar."

Savannah pushed her collard greens around on her plate. "And yet the parents seem eager for me to teach the children to be Americans, while still having them retain their Norwegian heritage."

"Norwegians are realists," Elias said. "They understand that while Snowflake is 99 percent Norwegian right now, it won't always be, and neither will all their children stay here forever. They'll need the skills you can teach them. But they are concerned about losing their culture. That's why they pushed so hard for the parochial school. More than anything, the parents are concerned that the children will lose their religious roots."

Tova resumed her seat. "You see, in Norway, dere is a state religion. Religion is taught in the schools, and churches are provided. Pastors are state-trained and supplied and paid. Dat vas one of the hardest tings about living here dat I did not expect. Ve had to write home for a minister for our new little church because America government did not train pastors and send them out."

Savannah had never considered that. In America, everyone was free to worship—or not—as they pleased, without oversight or interference from the government. A state religion was a new notion to her.

"Speaking of church," Ian said. "Elias tells me you're pretty good on the harp. The pastor was wondering if you'd be willing to play for us on Sunday."

"What about Mr. Pederson? Won't he be playing the *psalmodikon*?"

"He's the one who put in the request to begin with. He heard about you playing at the school from his grandchildren, and he'd like to hear you play in church."

Savannah's heart lifted. "If you're sure I won't be intruding. I would love to play." Here was a chance to really contribute to the worship, perhaps not be such an outsider.

Elias's smile sent warm tingles through her, and she had to take a firm grip on herself. Thoughts of him had filled far too much of her time lately. She found herself reliving their encounters, the way his smile flashed, the strength of his hold on her as they rode double across the prairie, the easy way he had with people and animals.

Stop it, Savannah. He hasn't changed his mind about you, and he isn't likely to anytime soon. He still thinks you'll run when things get tough. Concentrate on your job and stop reacting like an infatuated child.

Elias met the Halvorsons, early as usual, at the door of the church and reached up to swing Savannah down from the wagon. "Hurry inside. I got the stove going early. I'll bring your harp."

She did as he bade with a quick smile. Shaking his

head, he hefted the case out of the back and toted it up the steps. Never would he have imagined, when he first laid eyes on her back in August, that by Thanksgiving she'd be playing her harp in church, learning Norwegian, charming the school board into accepting her gifts or wearing Norwegian winter clothing.

It would be so easy to let his guard down, to fall in love with her. She was everything he wanted in a mate—smart, sweet, kind…everything except Norwegian. But she was brave. Did she have what it might take to leave the world she'd known forever to marry a small-town sheriff and farmer?

Yesterday she'd mentioned some personal unhappiness that had sent her running from her home. What sort of disappointment could that be? He'd spent a rather wakeful night at the jail, tossing on one of the bunks in the back cell, wrestling with the notion. It surely couldn't be anything too serious. Certainly nothing that compromised her character or reputation. It could be anything, really. A family scandal? A failed romance?

She'd clearly been uncomfortable talking about it, and it wasn't any of his business. He had no claim on her, and she had no obligation to unburden herself further. He couldn't pry, and yet he longed to know.

He lugged the harp up the steps, disquiet swirling in his chest. Perhaps someday she'd tell him. Perhaps someday he'd have the right to know.

She opened the harp case, cheeks pink from the cold ride to church, eyes bright. He brought a chair for her and placed it to the left of the pulpit. Lifting the harp to her lap, she took a small pitch pipe and blew on it. She plucked a single string in the middle of the harp, turning a small peg along the top with a special key.

Her fingers moved so quickly, so dexterously, like little bird wings. She was so at home with the instrument. Each string received attention, and when she strummed them all, from lowest to highest, the sound filled the nearly empty church.

Per Halvorson's mouth opened and he breathed deeply. "More beautiful than a symphony."

Elias translated for Savannah, and she blushed. "Ask him if there is something he would like me to play."

He chose "Amazing Grace," and Elias sat on the front pew, watching as first she plucked out the familiar melody, then, on the second verse, added runs and chords. Now he understood why she kept her nails so short, and saw again how she'd earned those calluses. Her body moved slightly with the music, as if she felt it as well as played it.

When the song ended, she placed her hands flat on the strings to stop their vibration.

"Vakker," Per breathed.

Elias had to agree. She was beautiful.

The church filled up and the service began. When it came time for the first hymn, Savannah left Elias's side and took up her harp. The congregation stood, and he craned his neck, but couldn't see her.

Harp music welled out, and he noted several people smiling and nodded. He almost wished the congregation wasn't singing, partially drowning out her playing.

She stayed up front during the next prayer and played during the offertory, which he liked better, since he could see her and hear her music. He didn't recognize the song she'd chosen, but it didn't matter.

When the preaching began and Savannah took her seat beside Elias, it was all he could do not to grasp her hand in his. She'd chosen to wear a dark blue woolen dress that made her eyes glow and her hair shine more than ever. The dress itself was plain, sewn by one of her students' mothers, but true to Savannah, she'd embellished it with a nosegay of silk flowers at her shoulder and a froth of lace at her throat.

When she opened her Bible, a bookmark fell out. He bent quickly to retrieve it for her, but when he glanced at it his fingers froze on the pasteboard.

A little bundle of pressed violets decorated the top, and underneath, "Girard loves Savannah" was written in fancy script. She reached for the bookmark, and had to tug a couple of times to free it from Elias's grip.

He blinked, brought back to the church service, a thousand questions jamming into his mind. Girard, the same name as on the envelope he'd seen.

She pressed her lips together, glanced at the names and shoved the bookmark into the back of her Bible before returning her attention to the sermon.

She looked so sweet and innocent, but what secrets was she hiding?

Chapter Eleven

"**C**'mon, Cap. It's cold and I want to get home." Elias whistled for the dog and struck out for the livery. The bad mood he'd been toting around for the last week or so—ever since he'd seen "Girard loves Savannah"—lingered over him like a storm cloud.

Hunching his shoulders and shoving his hands into his pockets, he trudged through the snow. The storm had started last night and fat, wet flakes were still falling, piling up. It wasn't bitterly cold, probably midtwenties, with lots of moisture in this storm. But cold enough for early December.

"Elias, you want your horse?" the livery owner asked as Elias ducked in out of the snow.

"Yep, but I'll get him."

"You think this snow will last?" He pitched a forkful of hay over a stall door.

"Hard to say. It's plenty wet." Elias took his bridle from the peg beside Buck's door. Captain stood in the center aisle and shook, scattering snow and water in a wide arc that included Elias. "Knock it off, boy." He scrubbed his dog's wide head and rubbed behind his

ears. Cap's mouth split in a grin, and his tongue lolled
as he plopped down to enjoy the attention.

"Children will be happy. A white Christmas, maybe?"

"Maybe. I won't be back tonight. Going to stay out
at the farm." Elias led Buck out of his stall and tied
him before running a brush over his back and saddling
him up.

"Tell your folks I said hello."

Elias opened the big doors and took Buck outside,
swinging into the saddle and tipping his hat to the livery owner. He pulled his collar higher around his ears
and pointed Buck in the direction of the farm.

Snow fell all around him, muffling noise, blanket-
ing the landscape and obscuring its features. Elias loved
the snow, the crisp cleanness, the freshness. He loved
postholing his way through deep drifts in the bright
sunshine after a big snowfall. He loved the artful way
the wind sculpted the piles into ridges and swales. He
loved sitting by the fire and hearing the wind howl and
the snow scour the roof and walls, trying to get in but
unable.

But he also respected the snow and the cold. He
dressed for it, he watched the horizon and the barom-
eter, and he planned and prepared for it, as did anyone
who lived in this climate. To do less was to court disaster.

Elias could barely make out the white schoolhouse
in the snowy gusts and low light as he passed by. Saturday, the place would be deserted, anyway. Inevitably,
thoughts of Savannah invaded his mind. He'd wrestled
all week with his doubts and fears about her, and in the
end, after much prayer, he'd determined to wait. If she
lasted through the winter here, come spring he'd get the
whole story. If she decided winters here were too tough,

home too far away, and decided to leave, then there was no point letting himself get in any deeper. He'd bide his time, watch and wait. He'd learned to be cautious.

Buck shook his head, jingling the bit, snorting out clouds of hot breath. The wind had swung around to the northwest, and the snowflakes weren't as fat and soft now. Elias anchored his hat and ducked his head into the gusts. His hands and feet began to feel the cold as the temperature dropped.

Cap had been nosing around, plowing through the snow, bounding from one side of the road to the other, squandering energy like a playful puppy, but now he stopped, stuck his nose in the air and barked. Shooting off the road and through the ditch, he headed back in the direction of the schoolhouse.

Now was no time to be chasing rabbits. Elias called to him, but to no avail. Finally, he ripped off his glove, put his fingers to his lips and let out a piercing whistle that had Buck sidling in the half-foot-deep snow and swishing his tail.

Through the wind, Cap's bark came, faint and insistent. What had he found? Elias swung his horse around and headed back toward the school. Perhaps there was another animal taking refuge under the porch. *Please, Lord, don't let it be another skunk.*

The woofs grew louder, and Elias urged Buck on. Uneasiness rippled through his chest as the barking grew sharper. No sign of the dog in front of the school. He rode around to the back.

A dark shape huddled beside the pump. Cap whined and ran to Elias, then back to the form. Elias was off his horse and plowing through the snow, his heart thudding.

"Savannah?"

"Elias, oh thank…you…Lord!" She lifted her face to his, white from cold, her teeth chattering.

"What are you doing out here?"

"Stuck." The words came out on a stumbling sob. "Wet hands."

Her lips were blue and obviously too stiff to talk. Elias touched her bare hands, firmly frozen to the pump handle. "Hang on. I'll get you free." He turned and plowed through the snow toward the schoolhouse, praying there was some water in the drinking crock and that she'd lit the stove.

A warm blast of air hit him when he opened the front door. She must've been washing the floors. Her scrub brush lay in the doorway. The priming pail sat beside the door, full to the brim. He snatched it up and hurried outside, splashing water in his haste.

She crouched by the pump, sobbing softly, and Cap crowded close, whining and wriggling. Snow covered her shoulders and hair, and her coat hung open.

"I'm here. Can you stand?"

She shook her head. "Legs numb."

"I'll try to do this without getting you too wet. I'm going to pour water on your hands. It should melt the ice and you'll be free." Elias lifted the bucket and poured a small stream onto her topmost hand. She gave a small cry as the water hit her skin. He increased the flow, and one by one, her fingers released from the frozen metal.

Elias threw the bucket aside and reached for her, lifting her into his arms and striding toward the schoolhouse. He slipped on the steps and nearly fell, but righted himself. Using his foot, he shut the door behind them and stood with her in his arms, eyes closed, resting for a moment. His heart still pounded away in his chest, and he took a deep breath.

Her head lay on his shoulder, snow-covered and pale. Blue tinged her lips, and her cheeks looked ashen. The danger wasn't over yet.

Carrying her into the schoolroom, he set her in the corner farthest from the stove. "I'll be back." He caressed her hair, brushing off the snow. Then he hurried outside. He led Buck into the lean-to and gave him a forkful of hay. Then he ran through the deepening snow to the pump to fetch the priming pail, which he filled with fresh snow.

Captain wriggled and whined, following him from task to task. Elias took a moment to pat the dog's head. "You can come inside. I don't think she'll mind this time."

Together they entered the schoolhouse, and Elias kicked the scrub brush out of his way. Captain trotted into the schoolroom, and Elias grabbed the only garments he could find in the cloakroom, a couple hooded capes the children had left behind.

"Savannah?"

No answer. Captain had gone right to her, laying down beside her and scooting close, instinctively sharing his warmth.

Elias called across the room, "Savannah, talk to me. Don't you go to sleep, you hear me? We have to thaw you out and get you warm." He spread the cloaks on the desks nearest the fire to warm, poked the coals and added more fuel, then brought the bucket of snow to where he'd left her.

"Savannah, you have to wake up. You can't sleep now."

She opened her eyes slowly, her lashes fluttering. "Elias?" she whispered.

"That's right." He crouched beside her. "Let's get

you out of this wet coat." Her lethargy concerned him. How long had she been out there? "Savannah, sit up. Help me with your coat."

She behaved as if in a dream, as if she had to think hard before every movement. Slipping first one arm, then the other from her navy blue woolen coat, she sighed and shivered. A good sign. When the body stopped shivering, it was time to really worry.

"This is going to hurt, but we have to thaw your hands slowly." He reached into the bucket of snow and took up a handful. "I'm going to rub your hands. Tell me when you start to feel something." Her fingers were white and stiff, and she gave no resistance when he chafed them with the snow.

After a few minutes, she whimpered. Captain sat up, leaning into her, sniffing her face and hair and giving her cheek a swipe with his raspy tongue.

"Can you feel that?" Elias squeezed her fingers.

Savannah nodded. "Hurts."

Relief charged through him. "Good. It means the blood is flowing again." He didn't have the heart to tell her it was going to hurt worse soon.

"Can't feel my feet."

Elias shoved aside her hems and petticoats to get to her shoes. "How do you even get these things off?" The buttons were impossibly small. In the end he managed them and peeled off her stockings. "I'm sorry, but we have to get your feet warmed, too."

Her feet were tiny...and pale. He rubbed first one, then the other between his palms. Almost immediately she shifted her weight and frowned. "They're tingling."

"That means they're not frozen. Hang on." He brought one of the warmed cloaks and wrapped it around her lower limbs and feet. "It's your hands I'm worried about." He unbuttoned her cuffs and shoved them up, and then began rubbing her forearms and wrists, pulling downward toward her hands, trying to get the blood moving.

"What were you doing out there with your coat open and no gloves?" He continued to work on her hands.

"Needed one last bucket of water. Just ran outside for a minute." Twin tears leaked from her eyes and tracked down her cheeks, cheeks that had begun to show a little color. Her hands, too, had gone from grayish-white to dull pink to angry red.

"So you decided to go outside in the teeth of a snowstorm for one last bucket of water, with wet hands and an unbuttoned coat? And you grabbed a frozen pump handle? Haven't you got more sense? Even little Ingrid knows not to touch bare metal when it's this cold, even without wet hands." It made Elias feel better to scold Savannah…until she sobbed in earnest.

"I'm sorry. I didn't know." Her shoulders shook, and her hair fell over her face as her chin tucked toward her chest. "I thought I would die out there. I tried to pull free but I couldn't. At first it hurt too much, and then I couldn't feel anything at all."

"It was a blessing Cap found you." Elias stopped rubbing, opened up his coat and sat back against the wall, spreading his legs before him. Reaching for her, he gathered her up and settled her on his lap, wrapping the open sides of his coat around her, tucking her head under his chin.

She smelled of snow and soap and female. He freed a couple buttons on his shirt and nestled her frigid hands against his chest. The cold bit through his long johns, and he winced.

"I'm lucky *you* found me." Her breath whispered against his throat. "No, not lucky. Blessed. I prayed, and God sent you."

Things grew worse before they got better in the days right after her trial. The ride to the Halvorsons' was torture for Savannah. Elias had bundled her up in her coat and the extra cloaks, and had taken her up before him on his horse, but still the cold got through.

The pain was intense, especially the first few nights. Her hands swelled and burned and ached. Everyone kept telling her how the pain was a good sign, but it was difficult to see it as such. She stayed home from church the next morning, the first time she'd missed a service since coming to Snowflake.

Monday morning, however, she was determined to go to school. She could've stayed away, since it was the day Elias was supposed to start teaching the parochial term, but she wanted to be there.

Mrs. Halvorson popped two hot baked potatoes into her pockets for the walk to the schoolhouse. Lars took the lunch pail and headed out first, breaking a fresh trail through the snow for Rut and Savannah.

Everything sparkled in the sunshine. Millions of rainbows glittered on the snow, and the sky was a clear, deep blue. The wind had died down in the night, and Savannah stopped and turned in a slow circle. The vastness of the open prairie made her feel small. She drew a deep, clean breath, the icy air flowing into her lungs like water.

Though her hands hurt, and she'd had to wear a pair of Mr. Halvorson's gloves because her fingers had swollen so much, she couldn't help but be grateful. Grateful to be alive. Grateful to be here in this place at this time.

Snow clung to her skirts and long coat, but the exercise of plowing through it had her cheeks warm and her blood pumping.

"Are you looking forward to school today, Rut? Something different?"

The girl looked back over her shoulder, her braids swinging from beneath her woolen cap, her eyes squinted against the snow glare. "*Ja*, I like church school. Singing *und* Bible stories."

And Elias. Rut doted on Elias. Savannah was eager to see him again, as well. He was her rescuer. If he hadn't come by when he did, if he hadn't known what to do, she would've died there in the snow and cold. Savannah didn't know how to thank him.

Smoke rose from the schoolhouse chimney, and Elias's horse stood, blanketed, in the corral. Cap shot off the porch and galloped through the snow until he reached Lars. The dog cavorted and barked and had the boy in giggles, tumbling into a drift. When Cap spied Savannah, he quit Lars and raced to her side, wagging his tail, tongue lolling. He raised his head for her caress, his mouth split in a doggy grin. He walked the rest of the way to the school by her side.

When they reached the schoolhouse door, Savannah broke her own rule and let the dog come inside. In the foyer, they brushed off snow and hung up their wraps. "Here, Lars." Savannah slipped the potatoes from her pockets. "Put these in the lunch pail. We can eat them later."

Elias stood at the blackboard writing the Norwegian alphabet, including three more letters than the English one, as Savannah and the children came in from shedding their wraps. He turned and Savannah's heart flip-flopped. He wore a black vest and white shirt, and the vest accentuated the breadth of his shoulders and the span of his chest. His long legs were encased in black pants, and he'd shined his boots. She appreciated that he'd dressed up to teach. Somehow it put more value on the exercise than if he'd worn jeans and a flannel shirt.

The stove was cherry-cheeked, sending out billows of warmth against the frosty day. Savannah stayed in the doorway as the children put their books on their desks and Lars set the lunch pail near the stove. This was her little kingdom, and to have another in charge left her feeling adrift, without a place. Should she sit in the back, or go to her desk, or...?

Elias dropped the chalk into the tray. *"God morgen."*

The children greeted him in Norwegian.

He dusted his hands and came to Savannah. "How are you feeling?" he asked, again in Norwegian.

"My hands are swollen and painful, but otherwise, I am well."

"No, only speak Norwegian here this week during class time."

She thought for a moment how to say I am well. *"Jeg har det bra."*

"Godt sagt," he complimented her. "Show me your hands, please?"

She translated his question in her head and held up her swollen fingers. His brows came down as he took her hands into his, gentle and slow. "They pain you?"

His touch was pleasure and pain. Her skin was so sensitive, she shivered, but she shrugged. "I am getting better." She wanted to tell him so much more, to thank him for his help, but with her limited Norwegian vocabulary, she had to keep things simple. Perhaps later, after the parochial term, they could find some time to talk.

Cap nudged her side, looking for some attention.

"So, he can come inside today?" Elias asked.

"*Ja*, he has…how do you say earned in Norwegian?"

"*Opptjente.*"

She tried again. "Cap has earned the right to come inside."

"I was going to let him inside but have him stay in the cloakroom." Elias gestured toward the foyer.

The rest of the children filed in, laughing and ruddy. Everyone sat, and Savannah took a place at the last desk, resting her hands lightly on the slanted top. The kids grinned and took a moment to settle. To her surprise, they started the day the same way as regular school, with a Psalm and a prayer.

Savannah followed instructions, practicing her Norwegian spelling list aloud with the primer class, reading history and Scripture with the older children. The pupils seemed to enjoy the notion of their teacher becoming a student, and knowing more than she did about their curriculum, correcting her pronunciation. Through it all, the shaggy collie stayed by her side, resting his head in her lap from time to time, thumping the floor with his tail when she stroked his fur.

Elias was a good teacher, entertaining and interesting, and he had a thorough knowledge of the subjects: language, history, Scripture, politics.

Savannah's hands limited her. She couldn't hold a slate pencil and turning pages proved difficult. But she listened and learned as much as she could. When Elias read Scripture, she soaked it in, thrilling to his manly voice, trying to grasp the meaning of the words from her knowledge of the same passages in English.

At lunch, the children gathered around the stove, and Elias invited Savannah to sit with him at the teacher's desk. He pulled up the only other chair—the one disobedient students had to sit on in the corner, though Savannah hadn't needed to employ that particular punishment yet—and joined her.

"I think it's safe to speak English at lunchtime." He unwrapped a packet from his lunch pail. "Thanks for giving my ma the recipe for that cornbread. We have it about three times a week now. Pa can't get enough." Elias showed Savannah a wedge of the golden bread.

"I hope you don't get tired of it." She slowly opened her own lunch, wondering what Agneta had packed this time. *"Stekte pølser."* She laughed. "Here I am having pork sausages from Norway, and you're having cornbread from North Carolina."

"Not only cornbread, but fried chicken, too." He tipped his lunch pail toward her so she could see inside.

"I might make a Southerner out of you yet," she teased.

"Or I'll make you into a *Norske*." He grinned back. But when he looked at her hands, his levity faded and concern crowded his eyes.

She wanted to hide her swollen fingers. "Jesting aside, I wanted to thank you for coming to my aid the other day. I don't know what I would've done."

"Thank Cap. He's the one who found you."

Stroking Cap's broad head with the side of her little finger, she nodded. "I'm grateful to both of you." With a guilty grin, she gave Cap the rest of her sausage. He gulped it down, looking up at her with an expectant gleam.

"Now you've done it. You'll never get rid of him now."

She wrapped her arm around the dog's neck and hugged him. "I don't want to. Rescuers rate very highly in my estimation. He's welcome to all I have, including my devotion."

When Elias's eyebrows rose, she realized what she'd said, and she scrambled to change the subject.

"You're a good teacher. I enjoyed your lessons today. You could easily be the teacher here in Snowflake year-round. I'm surprised Tyler didn't tap you for this job." She folded her napkin slowly and placed it in the lunch pail.

"I appreciate the compliment, but I wouldn't want to teach all the time. I like being the sheriff, and I like farming with my pa. Training horses is more to my liking than training children, though a week or two here or there isn't so bad."

Savannah nodded. "Teaching is much more fulfilling than I thought it would be. I'm thrilled with the progress the entire class is making. They're so quick, and their minds are so agile. Most of them could enter any regular school and do well now. There are a couple coming along in English a bit more slowly, but I suspect that has more to do with it not being spoken at home." She looked at her pupils clustered around the stove, pride warming her heart. "Did you know that most of the kids are teaching their parents English at night? They take what they've learned here, teach it at home, and reinforce their lessons. I don't think they even know how beneficial that is."

Margrethe broke away from the group and edged over. Shyly, she held out two cookies. "For you, teachers," she said in Norwegian.

"Takk," Elias replied, taking them and handing one to Savannah.

"Miss Cox?" Margrethe stroked Cap's head. "Are you going to be our teacher for always? Hakon says nobody ever stays that comes from outside, and that you will not come back for next year."

Savannah caught the gist of her question. Her heart was torn. Elias looked at her expectantly, as did the rest of the class. She swallowed.

"I don't know, Margrethe." She didn't know what to say, especially in her halting Norwegian. "I planned to return to my family."

"But you will come back, won't you? I like you best of all the teachers." Margrethe crowded close and laid her head on Savannah's shoulder.

Putting her arm around the little girl, she gave her a squeeze. "I like you, too, sweetie. I don't know what God has in store for me, but I will be praying for Him to show me."

This seemed to satisfy Margrethe. "I will pray, too, and maybe you will stay."

When she rejoined the rest of the class, Elias swept crumbs off the desk. "Your family must miss you. Is there anyone else waiting for you? Anyone special?"

He said it so casually, and yet Savannah's senses went on alert. He'd seen the letter from Girard and that ridiculous bookmark she'd forgotten about until it fell on the floor, yet he hadn't questioned her about it. Had he been thinking all this time that she had a sweetheart at home?

"No, there's no one special waiting for me. Not anymore."

Elias pursed his lips and tapped the desktop with his fingers, giving a slow nod.

"That's all right then, isn't it." He didn't make it sound like a question, but rather a conclusion he'd come to.

And just what was she supposed to make of that?

Chapter Twelve

"Welcome. Come in, come in. Come in out of this cold." Ian Parker stamped his boots and clapped his hands, his breath billowing out in icy clouds. "Guess we're not in danger of missing out on a white Christmas, are we?" Snow banked up against the sides of the Parker farmhouse and scudded along ahead of a cutting wind. Idle flakes swirled in the air, settling and blowing like thistledown.

Savannah slid out from under the buffalo robe, hopped down from the sleigh into the shin-deep drifts and carried her valise up the steps. "Thank you so much for opening your home. I wasn't much fancying staying alone over the holidays, what with the Halvorsons traveling."

Ian showed her into the house, taking her valise from her hand. "We couldn't be happier. Tova has been baking and cleaning and getting ready. She's looking forward to your visit."

Slipping off her hood, Savannah inhaled the heady aroma of spices and yeast. In the ten days since the December 13 festival, she'd become familiar with the scent of Saint Lucia bread. Not only the smell, but the taste of the sweet, golden treats, and her mouth watered.

Elias brought her harp case in. "Where is the best place for this?"

"Anywhere not too close to the hearth." Savannah let Ian help her with her coat. "The heat dries out the wood too much."

Elias placed the case on a bench beside the staircase. "I'll go take care of the team."

Tova set the coffeepot on the table. "Come, get warm. It is cold riding in the sleigh."

Boots sounded on the hall floor upstairs and echoed down the staircase, and Savannah turned. Who else was in the house?

"Hello, Miss Cox." Tyler Parker came into the main room, dressed as dapperly as ever. "Glad to see you made it through your first semester."

Of course he would be home for the holidays. She offered her hand, praying he wouldn't squeeze too hard. Her hands had healed well. The swelling had gone down and the burning subsided. Thanks to copious applications of Mrs. Halvorson's homemade ointment, her skin had healed well, too. But Savannah was still cautious.

Tyler must've heard about her injury, because he cupped her hand in his as if he was holding a wounded bird. "I've been hearing good reports about you since I got back."

An uprush of pleasure had her smiling. "Thank you." It was silly to be so happy at his approval, but she couldn't help it. She was making a success of teaching.

"We've put you in the guest room here off the kitchen. It stays warm, backed up against the fireplace like it is." Ian carried her valise there and emerged to take her woolen coat and hang it on a peg beside the door. "We're glad you're here."

Elias stomped the snow from his boots on the front porch and came inside. He removed his gloves and blew into his cupped hands. "I sure hope we get our January thaw this year. It's frostier than a Greenland glacier out there."

"We're bound to. As cold as it's been so early, the weather's bound to moderate soon." Ian nodded, glancing out the window as if to check his forecast.

Tyler slapped Elias on the shoulder. "I hear you didn't make a total hash of the parochial term."

"Thanks. Pretty sure everyone survived it."

Savannah trailed her fingers along the lovely rosemaling on the back of a chair. "He did a wonderful job. I learned so much, and I know the children did, too. Norwegian history is so fascinating. That was my favorite part of the day. And the way he tied everything together—the Scripture, the hymns, the church history, the political history... The students just ate it up."

Tyler looked from her to Elias, and Savannah's cheeks warmed. Why had she felt the need to defend Elias's teaching? Even to her ears it had sounded a bit gushy.

Elias put his hands in his pockets and rocked on his toes. "You would've gotten an A anyway, but buttering up the teacher never hurts, I guess." He winked, and her heart fluttered.

Really, Savannah, get ahold of yourself. Remember how you got here. Use some discernment.

Her heart refused to listen and kept up its hyperawareness of him.

"Come," Tova called again. "Sit and eat, or I vill be trowing it out."

The coffee and bread warmed her, as did the easy way the Parkers treated her, more like a family member than a guest.

"You'll have to educate me on Norwegian Christmas traditions. I learned a lot during the Saint Lucia festival earlier this month, but I'm sure there are more things I need to know."

"And you will be teaching us about your family traditions, *ja*?" Tova asked.

"I will. And thank you for having me here for the holidays. It's most kind of you."

She waved away Savannah's thanks with a smile and a blush. "You are no trouble. It vill be nice to have a voman in de house."

Elias leaned his cheek on his fist and yawned. Belatedly, he covered his mouth. "Excuse me. Late night."

"You should've woke me up." Ian poured himself another cup. "This boy of mine spent all night in the barn with a sick horse. Silly beast had colic, and Elias walked her up and down the aisle in the barn for hours."

"Had to. Every time I stopped, she tried to lie down and roll."

"And that's bad?" Savannah asked.

Elias nodded. "The worst. Colic is when a horse has a bellyache, and if they roll, they can twist their gut into a knot. It's called a torsion, and it can be fatal."

"Which horse was it?"

Rubbing his hand down his jaw, Elias stifled another yawn. "Elsker. She opened her stall door, the little minx, and ate half a bag of grain that was sitting in the aisle. Just as well she only got colic. She might've foundered altogether. Anyway, she's fine now, and unrepentant. I tied her door closed this time, now that I know she can open the latch."

"Why don't you go take a nap before supper?" Ian drained his cup. "I'll be out in the barn cleaning up the tack room, and Tyler says he has paperwork to accomplish."

Tova stood and began clearing up cups and plates. "I vill be baking, and Savannah can be helping me."

Throughout the afternoon, Savannah stirred and kneaded and tasted. The more time she spent with Tova, the more she loved her. The woman reminded her to some degree of Aunt Carolina, but mostly of what she imagined her own mother had been like. Savannah had few recollections of her mother, but had created a mythical image, an "if only" idea of the relationship they might have had if she hadn't died so young. Being with Tova stirred up those feelings.

"You are an excellent teacher, Tova. I see where your sons get their teaching abilities." She sampled a gingerbread man cookie. "Delicious. I fear I'll be unable to fit into my dresses if I stay here too long."

Tova slapped a mound of dough into shape and dropped it into an oiled pan to rise. "You can use some feeding, I tink. Now to make de *kransekake* and ve vill be done for today."

Ian came in through the back door, letting in a gust of cold air. "Did I hear someone say *kransekake*?" He shrugged out of his coat.

"You did. Always you come to find me when I make *kransekake*. Sometimes I wonder if it is only my cupboard you love." Tova gave her husband a saucy grin.

"Never you fear, darlin'. I'd love you if you couldn't cook a lick. But *kransekake* is my favorite." He put his cheek against hers. "You're nice and warm."

"And you are cold. Go sit by the fire."

Savannah envied them their closeness, the obvious

affection they shared. "What is *kransekake*, and how do we make it?" She dusted her hands on her apron.

"It means wreath cake." Ian took one of the gingerbread men. "Lots of cakes baked in a wreath shape, smaller and smaller, then stacked one atop the other into a tower. Tova drizzles it with sugar icing or honey sometimes, and puts candied fruit on it, too." He smacked his lips. "One of the best things about Christmas week."

As they were mixing the almond-flavored batter, Elias came downstairs, hair tousled, eyes heavy with sleep. Savannah watched him from under her lashes, very aware of him as she laid the soft dough into the ring pans of decreasing size. He looked even more handsome than usual, boyish even. Girard never would've allowed anyone to see him looking less than perfectly turned out, but Elias was different, casual and sure of himself, especially on his home turf.

"Have a nice sleep, son?" Ian shook out the pages of a newspaper, holding it at an angle toward the windowpane.

"Felt good. I can't remember the last time I took a nap." He wandered over to the table. "Ah, my favorite."

Tova swatted his hand away from the cake batter and handed him a fat sugar cookie instead. "You say everything is your favorite."

He grinned, chewing. "Everything is…except *lutefisk*."

Tyler trotted down the stairs, removing his glasses and pinching the bridge of his nose. "You never know how many ways there are to do something wrong until you grade it a dozen times. These students are going to be the death of me."

"Trouble, big brother?"

Rolling his shoulders, Tyler took a cookie for himself. "Some of my students are a handful, that's for certain. The school is almost all boys, and at the moment, most of them are struggling with grammar."

"How old are they?" Savannah gave the last pan to Tova and wiped her hands on her apron. Before she knew it, she and Tyler were deep into a discussion of teaching methods and sentence diagramming. She lost all track of the time, enjoying a long conversation on a subject about which she was confident.

"You learned all this in normal school?" Tyler examined the sample sentence she gave him. "I'm amazed. I can't wait to try this method on my students."

Savannah sat back, pleased at his approval. "I went to a very good school, and the teachers wanted us to learn more than just facts. They wanted us to know how children take in and retain information, and at what age levels you can expect changes. My math teacher said the most difficult time for a lot of students, particularly boys, is that twelve to thirteen age range. They're growing so fast you can almost hear it, and they're being asked to think abstractly for perhaps the first time in their lives. It's a lot to process."

"Time for dinner." Elias stood and adjusted his suspenders on his shoulders. "You've talked enough shop for a while, don't you think?"

"Is it really that late?" Savannah glanced at the window, which showed full dark. "Oh, Tova, I'm so sorry. I should've helped you clean up the baking and make the supper."

"No need. You were vorking. But all is ready now. Come."

Savannah found herself seated beside Elias, her sleeve brushing his. When he held out his hand, her heart started bumping against her ribs.

"Time to say grace."

Slowly she rested her hand in Elias's and bowed her head. Ian prayed the blessing, but Savannah had a difficult time concentrating on the words.

This has got to stop. You are going to return to Raleigh heart-whole, remember? Your time here is temporary, and you're not going to fall—

"Amen."

She realized she was still holding Elias's hand, and snatched hers away.

This was getting ridiculous.

Elias passed plates and filled his own, all the while trying to get ahold of himself. What was the matter with him? Savannah had been a burden around his neck for the past four months, and he'd wanted nothing more than for Tyler to come back and take her off his hands. And yet when they'd been engrossed in their parsing sentences and teaching methods, Elias had sat there like a stump.

A jealous stump.

Ma caught his eye, a question gleaming in her expression. She was too shrewd by half. Not much got by her, especially where her sons were concerned.

"So, Savannah," he said, seeking to get Ma's focus off him. "Tell us about Christmas in North Carolina."

A wistful look came over her face, a half smile and a middle-distant stare. "Christmas at home is wonderful. So many parties and balls. All month, it's a whirl. Every afternoon there is visiting, teas and gatherings. And nearly every evening a dance or a symphony or opera to attend. And lots of charity work, too." She sighed. "My aunts are on several charity boards, and we get to work alongside them." Tugging at her lower lip, Savannah laughed. "One of Aunt Georgette's charities sees to clothing for those in need, and a few Christmases ago she wanted all of us girls to knit stockings. I am a hopeless knitter." Her laughter grew. "I talked more than I knitted and ended up dropping stitches or adding too many. My attempt at a stocking turned into a real mess."

"Did you ever figure it out?"

"Knitting? No, crocheting turned out to fit my temperament better."

Tova nodded. "I like the crocheting better also."

A look of such fondness passed between his mother and Savannah, Elias had to smile. His ma was a good judge of character. Better than he'd given her credit for, since she hadn't warmed up to Britta at all.

"What else do you do for the holidays?" He stabbed a slice of ham from the platter.

"Well, on Christmas Eve, we have a party at our house. Guests arrive for dinner at eight. There are speeches and toasts and dancing. It's one of the few times the ballroom on the top floor gets used." She leaned her forearms on the table. "Then, just before midnight, we all get in our carriages and drive to the church."

"That sounds nice," Tyler said. "We have a Christmas Eve gathering at church, too, though earlier than midnight. It's my favorite service of the year."

"Oh, that will be lovely," Savannah said. "On Christmas morning, we're supposed to sleep in, but that never happens. Aunt Carolina used to insist we eat breakfast before we exchange gifts, but we finally wore her down. Now we have brunch afterward. I think she secretly likes it better this way, though she would never admit it. She can be a bit of a Tartar, but I love her."

This time, the homesickness in Savannah's voice was unmistakable, reminding Elias that she was far from those she loved and held dear. He noted her hands in her lap, fingers laced gently. He wanted to reach out and cover them with his, but he hadn't the right. He wasn't going to court her. She might last through this one school year, and he prayed she would, but by her own admission, her home was in North Carolina and she had every intention of returning there come spring.

He'd do well to keep that in mind, especially over the next week or so while she stayed here in his parents' house.

Christmas Eve afternoon, with all the baking done and the presents wrapped, Savannah sat at the table penning a letter to her family. An ache sat heavily in her heart. Had they forgotten about her? None of them had written in the past couple weeks, and Savannah had given up hope of hearing from them before Christmas. She'd mailed off her own gifts to them in plenty of time, objects she'd bought from the neighbors, beautifully rosemaled jewel chests for the girls, a stunning silver brooch for Aunt Georgette and a hand-crafted knife with a carved wooden handle for her father. Aunt Carolina had been the most difficult to buy for, but then again, she always was. Finally Savannah settled on a Hardanger-embroidered dresser scarf. The cut and open work was so precise, it reminded her of her aunt.

She imagined what her family must be doing right now.

The house would be in an uproar, preparing for tonight's party. Her sisters would be primping and dressing, calling out to one another from their rooms upstairs. Aunt Georgette would be fussing with the flower arrangements, and Aunt Carolina would be sailing from room to room, overseeing the staff, serene and in charge.

How Savannah wished she could sit and talk with Aunt Carolina, who would give her some perspective on her current disquiet of heart.

"Brace up, child. You have much for which to be thankful."

And she did. God had brought her through so much these past few months. And yet she longed for home. This would be the first Christmas Eve party Savannah had missed since she was old enough to attend.

A pang hit her chest as she imagined the lights and music and dancing. One year ago tonight she'd first laid eyes on Girard Brandeis. He'd come in with a large group of friends, but he'd stood out among them. One look at him and she'd been swept away in a rosy fog of romance. And he'd paid court to her all night, treating her as if she was the only woman in the room, in the world. And all along he'd been hopelessly in love with another.

A knock on the door jerked her back to Snowflake.

"Come in, Svenby. Merry Christmas." Ian held the door open, and a gust of cold air swirled into the room.

"Afternoon, Ian." He unwound his muffler to reveal red cheeks. "Was passing through and thought I'd deliver these letters to Miss Cox. Had a feeling they might be greetings from home."

Savannah rose from the bench. "Oh, thank you! I was just indulging in a bit of homesickness." She took the fat envelopes, holding them to her chest. "This is such a blessing."

"Then you're going to like what else I brought. Left

it on the porch." He turned and retrieved a large parcel. "Package came with the letters."

They hadn't forgotten her. She pressed her lips together and blinked hard against the happy tears. "Thank you so much for bringing them out. I was feeling rather sorry for myself."

Elias grinned from the corner where he was repairing a saddle cinch. "You realize you have to wait to open those until tomorrow, right?"

She gasped. "Tell me you're teasing. I can't possibly wait."

Tova gave him a quick slap on the shoulder. "Do not be playing, you rascal." She pulled the coffeepot to the front of the stove. "You can stay for *kaffe* and *kake*, Mr. Svenby?"

"I shouldn't. I need to get home and do the chores before it gets any colder. Merry Christmas to you folks." He wound his muffler around his face and slipped out the door.

Savannah cradled the package in her arms, uncertain. She wanted to rip into it, but perhaps it would be more polite to wait until tomorrow morning?

"Go ahead." Elias stood and slipped his folding knife from his pocket, snapping it open. "I was just kidding. I wouldn't be so mean."

Setting the box on the table, she stepped back so he could cut the cords. "There you go."

Eagerly, she opened the flaps and sank her fingers into the excelsior.

"Oh, they remembered." She shook the curls of packing material off a box.

"What is it?"

"Pralines from my favorite chocolate shop in Raleigh." She smoothed her hand over the picture on the top, of a beautiful antebellum home with white pillars and large trees. "I can almost smell the jasmine and magnolias."

"What's a praline?" Ian leaned over her shoulder.

"Only the best candy ever made." Opening the box, she drew out one of the candies in its little paper cup. "Try this."

He bit into the confection, and his eyes closed. "Mmm."

"Isn't it wonderful?" She offered the box to Elias and Tova.

"That just might be the tastiest treat I've ever had." Ian licked his fingertips. "They make those in your town?"

"Yes." Savannah gave one to Tyler, who had laid aside his book. "A few blocks from my home. Tonight, there will be trays of pralines on the buffet table at the party. My aunts must've known how much I was missing them. There's nothing like a taste of home."

Elias tried his. "That's good candy," he said, gruffly. He had a thoughtful look she couldn't decipher.

"What else did they send?" Tova asked.

Savannah set the candy box on the table and withdrew a long, slender package wrapped in tissue. A painted silk fan. Flicking it open, she fluttered it under her chin. "Isn't it pretty? I love fans. Did you know there is an entire communication system based on fans? How you carry them, how you move them."

"Might be some time before you need a fan around these parts." Elias looked out the window, where fat flakes piled up on the mullions. "What sorts of things can you say with a fan?"

"Oh, lots of things. Everything from 'I am spoken for' to 'Please ask me to dance' to 'I wish to speak to you in private.' Even 'Stop bothering me' and 'Go away'."

She set the fan on the candy box and reached through the packing material once more. This time she withdrew a bulky parcel in brown paper.

"A new riding habit." She gathered the green wool in her arms, then shook out the jacket and held it up. "Isn't it smart? I left my other riding costumes at home, but I mentioned to Aunt Carolina that I'd had the opportunity to go horseback riding. I told her it had ruined one of my dresses. She must've remembered." Savannah smoothed out the skirt, checking for the button and loop along the right side, so she could bustle it up out of the way when riding. The day she'd gone riding with Elias, racing across the prairie with the wind tugging at her hair, had been the day she'd first begun to heal from Girard's betrayal, the first day her heart had felt a ray of hope. The memory was dear to her.

The last thing in the box was a packet of sheet music for the harp: "The Skye Boat Song," "I Love to Tell the Story" and Carl Bach's "Sonata for Harp in G Major."

"Vill you play for us?" Tova asked. "Ven you played in church, it vas so beautiful."

"I'd love to." She went to the harp case and opened the clasps. Her beautiful harp lay in the velvet bed, and she drew it out. "I'm sorry about the tuning process, but I'll be quick."

Using her pitch pipe and peg wrench, she started with the middle strings and tuned the harp as fast as she could. Plucking one string at a time, she frowned. Something wasn't right. Not with the harp, but with her hands.

Her joints ached, and she felt clumsy and slow, as if she was trying to play while wearing mittens. When she finished tuning, she placed her hands on the strings and slowly picked out the tune to "Silent Night." She stilled the strings and began again, but her hands seemed trapped in treacle, almost as if she was playing underwater. She hit several wrong notes, and stopped again, shaking her head.

"What's wrong?" Elias leaned forward, his forearms on his knees.

"My hands." She looked at them, feeling as if they belonged to someone else. "I can't…"

"Are they paining you?"

"A little, but not like they did before. They don't burn. It's my joints. They feel stiff and achy." A flutter of panic rose in her breast. "Is this normal? After frostbite?"

Tova rocked in her chair, her crochet hook poking in and out of the heavy wool yarn. "I haff seen dis before. It vill take time."

"But will it get better? Will I be able to play again?" The flutter grew. Not to be able to play her harp? What would she do?

Ian scrubbed his jaw. "Most likely, you just need more time, like Tova says. And you'll have to be careful, since once you've suffered frostbite, you're more susceptible to it in the future."

"I imagine you never had to worry too much about frostbite in North Carolina, did you? I'm sorry you encountered it here." Elias came and took the harp from her, laying it in the case. "I'm sure that if you just give it some more time, your dexterity will return." He placed his hand on her shoulder for a moment, and warmth spread through her veins, making her heart trip. Tova's watchful eyes rested on them, and Elias jerked his hand away. "I'm going to go hitch up the sleigh. Don't want to be late for the Christmas Eve service."

He hustled into his coat and hat and slammed the door behind him.

Ian stood, tugged his watch from his pocket and compared it to the clock ticking softly on the wall. "Wonder what's wrong with that boy. He's edgier than a new knife."

Chapter Thirteen

Savannah chipped away at the ice coating the school-house steps. The storm on January 5 had been more sleet than snow, and had encased the stairs, making them an adventure to traverse. Now, a week later, the ice still clung stubbornly.

At least the sun was shining. The local newspaper had reported that Snowflake had received a record three feet of snow in December, and January had started out with more of the same.

She smiled grimly as a big chunk of ice broke off and skittered across the porch. Resting on the long handle of the ice breaker, she breathed deeply. The air felt different today, like a promise of spring. There was moisture in it, and the breeze blew softly from the southwest. She unbuttoned her coat. Her exertions had warmed her thoroughly.

Small dark dots appeared in the snow on the horizon, her students coming to school. How she'd come to love them, from the burly, nearly grown Hakon to tiny Ingrid with her sparkling eyes and quick smile. Savannah cheered their successes and celebrated their milestones. Even difficult days weren't that hard now.

"Hi, Miss Cox." Johann slid from his pony and lifted Margrethe down. He rode right by the Thorn place every day and picked the little girl up on his way. "Nice day, is it not?"

"Very. I hope we're in for a stretch of good weather. Mr. Parker said sometimes you get a January thaw?"

He nodded. "Almost always we get a few nice days."

Margrethe lugged her lunch pail and books up the stairs, careful to step with her little boots in the places Savannah had cleared. When she reached her side, she looked up from under the edge of her woolen bonnet. "Teacher, can ve play fox and geese today?"

Savannah looked at the trampled snow around the schoolhouse. "If we can find a clean patch to play on."

"Vill you play vid us?"

The last time they'd played, the students had cajoled Savannah into taking part. The game consisted of tramping down a giant wheel-and-spokes path in the snow, then designating someone to be the "fox" while the rest were "geese." The fox chased the geese, and the only rule was that you couldn't step off the trampled path. If you were caught, you became the fox.

"We'll see." She had enjoyed running and laughing in the snow, but she didn't want to undermine her authority as the teacher by roughhousing with her students too often.

More students arrived, and she rang the school bell to signal the start of the day. "Good morning. Lars, I believe it is your turn to read." She handed him her Bible. "Psalm 91 today."

"'He that dwelleth in the secret place of the Most High shall abide under the shadow of the Almighty.'" Lars read slowly, sounding out the words in English.

Savannah nodded each time he worked his way through a long or difficult word.

"'He shall call upon me, and I will answer him: I will be with him in trouble; I will deliver him, and honor him.

"'With long life will I satisfy him, and shew him my salvation.'" The boy looked up, closing the Bible with a grin.

"Well done, Lars. Your reading is really coming along."

Just before the midmorning break, Hakon raised his hand. "Miss Cox, can I be moving to another desk? The fire is too varm for me." As the oldest student, he sat in the back of the room nearest the stove.

Savannah gave him permission and glanced outside. Water dripped off the edge of the roof from melting snow. It was so warm in the schoolroom she contemplated cracking a window, but thought better of it lest she give the children a chill.

Rut leaned over and scratched her leg just above her boot top. She caught Savannah's eye and jerked upright, a flush staining her cheeks at her unladylike behavior. Savannah hid a smile. She knew just how the girl felt. Her own flannels were itchy and hot, and she longed to scratch the irritation away. Aunt Carolina would be mortified…though Aunt Carolina had never worn so many layers of flannel and wool and cotton on a rapidly warming day.

"You may put your books away and go outside. Although it is warm, wear your coats and gloves. You can leave your hats and mufflers off, but if you get cold, come in and get them."

They scrambled out, and Savannah leaned back in

her chair. It was good for them to get some fresh air and sunshine after so much dismal weather.

Sliding her top drawer open, she took out her aunt's Christmas letter and a clean sheet of paper.

Dear Aunt Carolina,

I'm sorry I've been so tardy in replying to your Christmas greetings. The gifts were wonderful, and I love each one. Thank you so much. I was staying at the Parker house over the holidays, and I was able to share with them some of the pralines. Cassidy's Chocolates are still the best. I have held back just enough for a special treat for my students.

I am well, though I do have something to share. A few weeks ago, I had the misfortune to get my hands frostbitten. The fault was entirely my own. Before you scold, let me assure you that I am fine. My hands are still sensitive to extreme cold, but I am getting better. I have even begun to play the harp once more, though it has been a fight to regain my nimbleness. I first tried to play again on Christmas Eve, when your package arrived, and you would've thought I was wearing bulky gloves for all the dexterity I had.

The homesickness I felt over the holidays has abated some. I find that while I miss all of you fiercely, I am putting down roots here in Snowflake. I have begun to appreciate the resourceful nature of the people here. The way they work together, the way their lives are intertwined and the way they have drawn me into their circle is so comforting. I can finally admit that Girard's defection shattered my confidence in myself. It has taken months for me to begin to feel "right" again.

Savannah set aside her pen and propped her chin in her hand. Aside from missing her family, there had been only one jarring note to the holiday season.

Elias.

She never would've thought he'd be subject to moods, but that's what it had felt like. One moment he'd be laughing and talking, and the next frowning and silent. It seemed as if every time she mentioned something about home, he'd clam up. The rest of the family had been interested in learning about North Carolina, about her aunts and sisters, about her church and her life there, but Elias would scowl, cross his arms or find a reason to head for the barn.

He hadn't seemed any happier when she and Tyler discussed school or books they'd read. Throughout the week, Elias had been restless, as if he couldn't wait for her to be back at the Halvorsons'.

It had certainly been deflating.

The children's squeals and shouts pulled her back, and she glanced at the clock. Time to call them in. A shame, considering this was the nicest weather they'd had in weeks. Maybe just a few more minutes. She turned back to her letter.

I hope you are all well. My boss, Mr. Tyler Parker, gave me an end date for the school year—May 25. Just a little over four months from now. This time away has done what I had hoped it would. I no longer grieve for Girard, and I've gained some perspective on what's truly important, both in life and

in what I would look for in a mate in the future...
not that I'm contemplating anything like that.

What she would look for in a mate... She tapped her
chin. It all boiled down to a neat little list. Faith, family and fidelity.

When Elias's face rose in her mind, she forced herself to concentrate and finish the letter. Elias might
possess all the qualities she now knew were necessary
for her to fall in love, but he would never look her way.
They were too different. She was too different.

He'd been gone for a week, transporting a prisoner
to Mankato. She told herself it was silly to miss him,
and yet she found herself listening for his footfall on the
schoolhouse steps. Last Saturday, when she'd gone to
town, she'd known he wouldn't be there, and yet she'd
looked up from her shopping every time someone had
entered the store.

Enough brooding, girl.

She finished the letter, signed her name and tucked
the pages into an envelope. She'd mail it Saturday when
she went to town. For now, she needed to get the children inside and back to work.

By late afternoon, they all, Savannah included, had a
severe case of cabin fever. She found herself distracted
and frustrated by the students' inattention. What would
they be like when spring really arrived? She'd have to
hold classes out-of-doors.

The clock hands seemed to crawl toward three. Savannah was just beginning to think of dismissing school
early when a cloud passed over the sun. At almost the
same moment, a gust of wind rattled the windows on
the west side of the building. She dropped her chalk and
hurried to look outside.

As one, the children followed her, crowding around the three tall windows. Outside, it was as if someone had blown out a lantern. Fat, dark, angry clouds boiled overhead, and icy pellets struck the glass and siding, sounding like buckshot.

Savannah's shoulders slumped. This would be miserable to walk home in. She'd have to make sure she had her mittens and glove liners to keep her hands warm.

"Children, with the weather, I think perhaps we should get going early today. Let's get our desks tidied and our wraps on. Hakon, bank the fire, please."

Everyone went to their desks and put away books and pencils. Another huge gust rocked against the building, and the sound of sleet changed to scouring, as if a giant was rubbing sandpaper against the siding. Hakon paused, poker in hand. "Miss Cox?"

She went again to the window. This time she couldn't even see the corral and shed only twenty yards away. The snow was so thick it didn't look like individual flakes, but rather a solid wall of white. She shivered. The temperature had dropped at least ten degrees in the past ten minutes.

"We'd better hurry. Get into your coats."

"Miss Cox?" Johann raised his hand. "It is snowing very hard."

"I know, that's why I want you all to bundle up well and get home."

The older boys looked at one another, and she wanted to snap at them to hurry. The walk home would be unpleasant enough, and she wanted to get it over with.

They crowded into the foyer, to find that the snow was blowing so hard it had sifted through the cracks around the door. Savannah shrugged into her coat and helped Ingrid and Margrethe with their buttons and ties.

When everyone had gathered their lunch pails and secured their mufflers, she put her hand on the door-knob. "Ready? Those of you headed to the shed for your horses, hold hands. Let's go."

She sucked in a breath and braced herself for the cold, turned the knob and took a gust of snow right in the face. Lowering her chin into her scarf, she stepped outside and collided with a solid wall she hadn't even seen.

Elias trotted Buck through the slush on the road, glorying in the warmer weather. The trip to Mankato had stretched out much longer than he'd wanted, but now he was near home, the sun was shining and he had a good horse beneath him.

Captain trotted at his right stirrup, tail like a plume, tongue lolling. Elias had brought the burly dog along to give Cap something to do. With the sheep penned for the winter, he was bored and listless. His mate, Tip, was busy with half a dozen fluffy puppies, so Elias figured the trip would do the dog good.

Cap had done Elias some good, too. The prisoner, a bank robber who had tried to escape into the Dakotas, was nasty. Cap had guarded him well. Fortunately, the prisoner was also a coward when it came to dogs, so he'd been wary from the first growl.

Elias loosened the scarf around his neck. Though he was ready to come home, being away had been good, too. Elias loved people, but he needed some time alone to think, in order to feel right.

And he had a lot to think about.

Christmas had been pure torture, and he'd acted like an idiot. He'd known he was acting like an idiot and he hadn't been able to help himself.

All because of her.

Savannah had been an itch he couldn't scratch since the moment he met her. And having her in the house for a solid week, smelling her perfume, hearing her laugh, watching her charm his family—especially his brother—had tied Elias in so many knots he could hardly sleep.

"Cap, I'm losing my mind. I should know better. You should've heard the way she talked about her family and her life in Raleigh. I knew she was rich, but a ballroom right in her house? A party for a hundred people like it was nothing? Fancy stores where they sell nothing but chocolate?" He fisted his hand on the saddle horn. "No wonder she was in such shock when she first got here. There's no way she would stay once school is done. She'll be on the first stage out of town."

The dog trotted along, accustomed to Elias talking to him.

"Then there was all that gabbing with Tyler about her schooling and the books they've both read. I felt like an ignoramus. And wasn't old Tyler lapping it up?"

Elias hesitated to name his feelings, but in his heart he knew the truth. He'd been jealous of his brother and all Tyler had in common with Savannah. If she wanted an intellectual or academic, she'd never look Elias's way.

Of course, she'd given no indication she was looking anyone's way. She didn't have to. Wealthy, pretty, smart, talented. She had her pick of Southern gentlemen. No doubt a year from now she'd be married to a rich man, and she'd talk at her tea parties about the uncouth people of the north.

"You should've seen her at the Christmas Eve service. When she came out of the guest room in that red dress, I had to hold on to the banister or else fall smack down. I tell you, I thought my heart might pound right out of my chest. She looked straight at me with those big blue eyes, and I could hardly breathe." Elias shook his head at his sorry state. "And wasn't Tyler quick on the draw, holding her coat and offering her his arm, helping her into the sleigh?"

Elias thought back to Christmas afternoon, when he'd taken Savannah out to the barn to see the litter of pups. What a sight she'd made, sinking into the straw, cuddling fluffy babies, laughing at their antics. It was the best Christmas Elias could remember.

He was so preoccupied with his thoughts that the first frigid gust of wind caught him off guard. Jerking his head up, he blinked. A low, heavy bank of clouds covered the western horizon, racing toward him. Another cold blast buffeted him, and he clapped his hand atop his hat to keep it on his head.

"That looks bad. Best pick up the pace." He legged Buck and whistled to Cap. They couldn't go too fast because of the slippery ground, but he kept the pressure on. As always, his thoughts jumped to Savannah. School would be dismissed soon. She'd be walking home into the teeth of a storm. If he hurried, maybe he could get there in time to give her a ride.

The sleet hit him about a mile farther on, hard pellets that stung. Buck wanted to turn away from them, but Elias kept him pointed west. The wind picked up, a continuous howl now. He ducked his head, letting his hat brim shield his face. The drop in temperature was amazing. One minute he was thinking about removing his coat, and the next, he was wishing he had two.

Sleet changed to snow, tiny icy flakes, the kind that were a harbinger of a big blizzard. Soon it was impossible to distinguish features of the landscape, or even see the horizon. The cold drove through his garments and into his bones.

Distance became impossible to judge. He couldn't be too far from the school now, surely. They must've crossed some invisible line in his horse's mind, because Buck stopped fighting him about facing into the storm, and put his head down, trudging for home and his stall in the barn.

"Cap," Elias shouted over the wind. "Stay close." The snow blinded him to anything beyond about six feet. He would have to trust Buck and Cap to keep them headed in the right direction. At this point, anywhere they could get inside was the goal.

If only he had started out earlier this morning. He'd spent the night in Walnut Grove, where the sheriff was a friend of his father's. Thanks to the Warners' hospitality, Elias had been late getting on the road.

Buck stumbled, and Elias lurched in the saddle. Righting himself, he patted his horse's shoulder. "Easy, boy." Snow clung to them like a second layer of clothes, clumping in Buck's mane, filling the folds and ridges of Elias's coat. He peered through the whirling flakes and thought he caught a glimpse of something large ahead.

Cap barked and bounded away. "Cap, get back here!" Elias's words were swallowed up by the storm. Buck stumbled again. Sliding from the saddle, Elias drew the reins over the horse's head and started forward. His boots sank into the snow. They must've gotten off the road. Maybe they would hit a fence line soon that would guide him.

Captain emerged from the snow, barking. The collie came to Elias's side, then turned back to the west... At least Elias thought it was west. "All right, boy. Lead the way." He was so cold, his lips were stiff.

After a few moments of steady walking, Elias thought he heard something through the wind, but couldn't be sure. He stopped and Buck ran into his shoulder, causing Elias to stagger. Cap barked and then lifted his nose in a howl. The sound came again, and from behind Elias, Buck let out a whinny.

Horses. They must've sensed Buck's approach. Elias's heart lifted. Even a barn would suffice for shelter. Cap brushed against Elias's leg and stuck close. Through a lull in the wind, Elias spied a small shelter and knew exactly what it was.

He'd reached the school, after all. The shelter was the pony shed, and half a dozen shaggy horses crowded into the three-sided structure, which was open to the east, away from the wind, fortunately. A full shed meant the children were still inside the school.

Which meant Savannah was there, too, and not wandering on the prairie lost in this storm.

After struggling through the wind, and having to dig out the gate so he could run Buck inside, Elias finally managed to unsaddle and pen his gelding. Another fight to get to the haystack and dig into it for some fodder for the horses. Water would have to wait. He shoved his way through the animals to the back of the shed with an armful of hay. By the time he'd made several trips, he was ready to drop.

"C'mon, Cap. Let's get inside." He turned to where he knew the school stood and broke a fresh path through the deepening snow. Carrying his saddle, blanket and rifle, he stumbled up the steps and collided with someone coming out of the schoolhouse.

Savannah shrieked, and he dropped his saddle to grab her before she fell.

"Elias? What are you doing here?"

A gust rocked him. "Get inside!" he shouted. The wind tore at his hat, flapping the brim and driving snow around them and through the open door.

Scooping up his saddle, he pushed her inside and slammed the door behind him. Though the foyer was nearly as cold as outside, it was such a blessing to be out of the storm, he wanted to sink to the floor. His breath came in gasps, and the relative quiet inside rang in his ears.

After a moment, he realized the room was crowded with bundled children. He tugged his snowy muffler off his face. "Where do you think you're going?"

"We have to get home before the storm gets worse." Savannah bent to tie one of the little girls' scarves tighter. "It will be dark soon."

He sagged against the wall, tugged one of his gloves off with his teeth and blew on his hand. "The storm is already worse. We'll have to ride it out here for a while."

She straightened and tugged on her mittens, the ones she'd been given by Mrs. Linnevold in exchange for Johann's school supplies. "That's impossible. These children need to be in their homes. Their parents will be expecting them." She herded the smaller ones together. "Now, you older children be sure to take care of your younger siblings. Break the trail for them through the deeper snow, and don't dawdle. Elias, if you'd just move away from the door?"

He levered himself upright, surprised at how tired and achy he was, but he didn't move out of the way. "Savannah, the children cannot leave. You can't see more than a few feet out there. They'd be lost within a few minutes. If Cap hadn't led me here, I'd be wandering out in that blizzard myself."

Savannah shook her head. "Surely, if it is so bad out there, someone will come for us. Parents in sleighs?"

"Kids, why don't you all go back into the schoolroom and warm up by the fire. Go ahead and take your wraps with you." Elias looked at Hakon, Lars and Johann, the oldest boys, and jerked his head toward the interior doorway. They nodded, and he didn't miss the relief in their eyes as they led the kids inside.

Savannah had her hands on her hips. "Elias, we cannot stay here. It might be hours before the storm abates, and by that time it will be night. They've walked home in the snow before." Her stubborn, authoritarian teacher voice irked him.

"This isn't just snow. It's a blizzard. There's a difference. We don't have a choice but to stay here. If you send those kids out in this, they'll freeze to death on the prairie. It will be touch-and-go whether we can survive here, but we stand a better chance riding out the storm inside the school." He bent to pick up his glove. "I'm not going to argue with you about this. As the sheriff and my brother's stand-in supervisor, I'm ordering you to stay here with the children until it's safe to go outside."

She pressed her lips together, her eyes a mixture of stubbornness and now fear. "It's really that bad? What if we all tried to make it to the Halvorsons'? They're the closest, and they would have food and blankets and warmth."

"It *is* that bad. No way could we make it to Halvorsons', not even on the horses right now." Yanking off his other glove, he used it to knock the snow off his coat and pants. The idea of them setting off into the storm made his muscles tense and his mind seethe. How could she have been so foolish as to contemplate such a ridiculous thing? Fear made him angry and he lashed out at her to mask it. "I can't believe you were even thinking about leaving. Nobody in their right mind would set off into the teeth of this storm. It's a good thing I showed up when I did. You'd all be lost and dying right now."

He stomped his boots, and the casing of snow fell off in slabs. "Didn't you learn anything when you froze your hands? You can't take this place lightly or it will kill you. And not just you, but those kids, too. This is what Tyler gets for hiring a Southern belle to teach here. You don't have the sense God gave a chicken."

Her face paled and her eyes glistened. He felt like a heel, but she had to know the dangers. Glancing toward the schoolroom door, he wondered if the children had heard him. He hadn't exactly been whispering. With a shuddering breath, he took her arm and led her toward the classroom.

"Let's get in there and see about making things bearable. We're going to be here for a while. Don't let the children see you're scared."

Easier said than done as another huge gust rocked the building and rattled the windows. Eleven pairs of eyes, wide and uncertain, met his, and the responsibility for their survival nearly buckled his knees.

Chapter Fourteen

A blizzard. Savannah *thought* she'd seen blizzards before. After all, it had snowed hard in November and December, drifts piling up everywhere. But the severity of this one set in every time she looked at the deepening lines on Elias's face and thought about his harsh words.

He still held to the belief that it had been a mistake to hire her. After all these months, nothing had changed. Didn't have the sense God gave a chicken?

Elias took charge right away, tossing the last few lumps of coal in the hod onto the fire and stirring it with the poker.

"Hakon, Johann, Lars, help me move these desks and benches." He spoke Norwegian to save time. "Stack them up in a semicircle around the stove to try to keep the heat near the fire."

Hakon hefted a bench easily, while Johann and Lars grabbed each end of another.

"Not too close," Elias cautioned. "We need to make room for everyone to sit or lie down." He showed the boys where to set things. "Lay the benches on their sides to form a wall. Shove the desks up against them."

Benches banged off one another and desks skidded along the floor.

"Be careful. You're dropping books and papers." Astrid and Nils followed them, picking up school supplies that fell out of the desks, and stacking them on Savannah's desk in neat piles.

"What should we do?" Rut asked, indicating the girls.

Elias put the last bench in place. "Some of you bring the water crock into the schoolroom so it doesn't freeze, and bring in any lunch pails out there, too." He winked. "Hopefully not all of you ate everything up at lunch today. And the rest of you, if there are any extra coats or cloaks in the vestibule, bring them in. We can spread some on the floor to keep us warmer."

Savannah stood like a statue, uncertain what to do. Something nudged her hand, and she looked down into Captain's soulful brown eyes. He nudged her again, and she patted his head, then knelt and hugged him. "Thank you for bringing him here. I didn't know how much we'd need him," she whispered in the dog's ear, and he licked her cheek, his tail swishing.

"Which one of you boys is on coal patrol today?" Elias asked.

Peder raised his hand. "Me. But it was so warm, I didn't bring in much this morning."

"Not blaming you, friend." Elias put his hand on Peder's shoulder. "Can you tell me how much coal is in the shed?"

"Maybe a few buckets worth?" He shrugged, eyebrows bunched.

Savannah found her voice. "A new load was supposed to be delivered last Monday, but I didn't worry about it because the weather has been so mild. I thought

I would speak to Mr. Rosedahl about it on Sunday if none had been delivered by then."

Elias ran his hand down his face, and Savannah shivered. The room was cold now and growing colder, enough that their breaths were showing in frosty puffs if they stood more than a few feet from the stove. How were they going to keep the children warm with no coal? Why hadn't she kept on top of things and demanded the coal supply be replenished sooner?

"Savannah, you and the girls see what we have in the way of food, and you—" he pointed to three of the older boys "—bring the coal hod, and anything else we have to carry coal in. I'd like to get as much of it inside in one go as I can, so we don't let in any more cold air than we have to."

"What about the horses?" Lars asked.

"They're snug in the shed. I gave them some hay, but that's all we can do right now. If the storm lets up a little, we can check on them later."

Lars nodded. "There are blankets out there. Saddle blankets."

"Good thinking, Lars. We'll make a detour out there if we can do it without getting lost. Is there any rope in the schoolhouse?"

"There's the bell rope," Hakon said.

Elias shook his head. "No, we can't use that. We will need the bell."

"Wrap up well." Savannah crossed her arms at her waist.

Elias broke the rime of ice in the pump primer bucket in the foyer and poured the contents into the top of the water crock. "I'll take this bucket. While we're out there, Savannah, you stay in the vestibule. Every five minutes, ring the school bell. If we get turned around out there, it will help guide us back. Ready, boys?"

Hakon, Johann and Peder nodded, bundled to the eyes, each holding something to carry coal in.

"All right. Link arms with each other and follow me." Elias put his hand to the doorknob, and when he opened it a cloud of snow burst inside. "Let's go!" he shouted above the raging storm. Savannah had to help them close the door.

She stood in the foyer, shivering, her hands on the bell rope. "Dear Lord, keep them safe," she prayed. "Bring them back inside. Please let this storm be not as bad as Elias fears. Get us all home safely."

She tugged the rope. The bell sounded muffled and faraway, as if it had been wrapped in a blanket. She supposed it was. A blanket of snow. Pulling harder, she sought to get more sound from the cupola, and went back to praying. With no clock in the small room, she had to guess at the five minute intervals, but surely more ringing was better than less.

"Miss Cox," Rut called from the schoolroom doorway. "Ingrid is crying."

"Is she cold?"

"She is afraid of Captain. Every time he comes near her, she cries. She got bit by a dog once, and now she is afraid."

"Bring Captain out here. He can keep me company."

The collie's nails clicked on the floor, and he whined, head low as he sidled up against Savannah's leg. "I know, boy. I'm worried, too."

The windowless foyer was dark, and she was grateful for Captain's company. Surely they should be coming back soon. How long did it take to walk around to the coal shed and back?

She rang the bell again, doubts and fears crowding into her head. The wind was so high, she didn't hear footsteps on the porch until the door burst open. Cap barked sharply as four snow-covered beings staggered inside and slammed the door shut. Whirling flakes settled on the board floor, and it was so cold they didn't melt.

Elias and the boys gasped as if they'd been holding their breath the whole time. Each lad carried a bucket of coal, and Elias carried a burlap sack filled with lumps. Under his other arm, he carried a bundle of saddle blankets.

Cap nosed each boy, checking them over, whining and wagging his tail.

"I've never seen a storm this bad," Elias said when he could speak. "I can't believe how cold it is out there now, and the wind is making it worse. Feels like thirty below."

"Boys, brush off as best you can and hurry inside by the fire. You have to get warmed up. Let me help." Savannah grabbed the broom and began swiping at their coats and pants. "We don't want this snow to melt on you."

Once fairly free of snow, the boys trudged into the schoolroom. Elias touched Savannah's arm when she went to follow. He tugged down his muffler.

"This is it. This is all the coal in the shed." He used the end of the muffler to mop his wet face. "That's what took so long. We scoured that shed, getting every last piece. Even at that, it might not be enough."

He hefted the sack of coal and headed into the schoolroom. Savannah followed with the blankets, closing the interior door behind her quickly to try to hold in some of the precious warmth.

What would they do if they ran out of coal? Could they survive, huddled together with no fire? Icy fear rippled through her limbs and settled in her middle, chilling her from within even as the storm raged outside.

Elias looked at the coal they had on hand, perhaps a bushel basket's worth, and tried to calculate how long he could make it last. The soft lignite coal burned faster than other types and would be consumed quickly, especially given the extreme cold. He glanced at Savannah and then at the wooden benches and desks, wondering how many might have to be sacrificed.

"Spread those saddle blankets here." The benches had been placed in a horseshoe around the little stove. "Then everybody find a place to sit."

Ingrid whimpered when Captain dropped down beside her. She drew away, all but climbing over Savannah.

"What's wrong with her?" Elias took a spot farthest from the stove.

"She's afraid of the dog." Savannah put her arms around the little girl, gathering her close and whispering against her hair. "Shh, he won't hurt you."

Elias drew his knees up and wrapped his arms around his legs. "Captain's a big softy who likes pats from pretty girls."

Ingrid sat up a little, her eyes doubtful.

"It's true. That's why he follows Miss Cox all over the place."

Rut giggled, and Elias realized he'd just admitted that he thought Savannah was pretty. He shrugged and grinned. Well, she was.

Savannah kept her head bent over Ingrid, and in the dim light, he couldn't tell what she might be thinking.

After a moment, Ingrid's little mitten stuck out and she touched Cap on the ear. The dog leaned into Savannah and put his head on her leg near Ingrid, looking up at her with his chocolate eyes in a gaze Elias knew all too well. Some collies were one-man dogs, but Cap's heart belonged to anyone who would show him affection.

"He's not only friendly, he's also a big ol' furnace. Somebody tonight is going to get to sleep with his fur coat beside 'em." Elias figured it should be Ingrid and Margrethe, the two smallest children.

Wind howled outside, trying to get in, and the snow scoured the siding. It would be full-dark soon.

"Should we light the lamps?" Savannah asked, as if reading his mind. Between each window there were kerosene lamps with reflectors. They were seldom used, only when there was a nighttime activity at the school.

"How much kerosene is there?" He counted four lamps.

"They're practically full."

"Good. Give me a hand, will you?" He waited until she'd passed Ingrid to one of the other girls, and then reached down to help Savannah up. She staggered a bit, stumbling into him. His arms went around her to steady her, and she looked up at him. Her eyes were dark blue and wide in the dusky room.

"I'm sorry. I got stiff sitting there, even in such a short time."

He nodded, letting go of her reluctantly. "Can you help me light two of the lamps? I'd like to put one in a window on each side of the building. If anybody is out there lost, the light might help them find shelter."

After pulling one of the desks up under a window on the west wall, she took a lamp down and went to the box on the back wall behind the stove for a match. Elias did the same at a window on the east wall.

Savannah set her lamp on the desk, the flame outlining her silhouette. His heart clenched, and his shoulders bowed under the responsibility of keeping her and the children safe. He wanted to open his coat, take her into his arms and shelter her from the cold and the hunger and the worry. How had she slipped under his guard? When he knew better than to fall for an outsider, one who made no secret of her intention of leaving at the end of the school year?

She looked up and he blinked, afraid his feelings were all too evident. Motioning her over, he lowered his voice. "What did you find for food?"

Biting her lip, she shook her head. "There wasn't much left from the lunches. Lars and Rut and I had potatoes in our coat pockets." This time she smiled softly. "I told Agneta it was too nice a day to need hot potatoes to keep our hands warm, but she insisted. I'm glad now she did. We have six potatoes, two dried apple tarts and—" Savannah stood on tiptoe to whisper in his ear "—I brought the rest of my Christmas pralines. They're in my desk. I was thinking tomorrow to teach a lesson on North Carolina in geography, and I thought sharing the pralines would be fun."

Her breath brushed against his cheek, and he caught a whiff of her perfume. Even through the layers of winter clothing, her hand on his arm felt warm. "That's generous of you. Maybe we should save those as a nice surprise. Things are going to get tougher before they get better, I have a feeling."

"You don't think the storm will abate in the night?"

He shook his head. "This has all the earmarks of a

three-day blizzard. We're going to have to go sparingly with food and fuel."

They rejoined the children.

"Sheriff?" Peder asked. "Do you think our families are safe? It is chore time, and my pa will need to go to the barn."

"Your pa is a smart man, Peder. He understands storms like this. All of your pas are winter-smart. If they have to go out, they'll rig ropes so they don't get lost. I know that's what my pa is doing right now." Elias prayed he was speaking the truth. The timing of the storm was bad, just when lots of kids across this part of the state would be leaving school, and when a lot of farmers would be heading out to check their livestock. He prayed Tyler and his students down in Kettinger were safe.

Astrid, Peder's sister, sniffed and gulped, swiping at her eyes with her mittened hands.

Savannah straightened. "I think we need some singing to cheer us up. Who has a favorite song?"

Johann pulled a harmonica from his pocket, tugged off his gloves and tapped the instrument against his palm. "I can play 'A Mighty Fortress'." He began the hymn, and the children sang in Norwegian.

Elias grinned when he realized Savannah was singing in Norwegian, too. Her language skills had really come along in the last four months. Though she would probably always have a Southern drawl mixed in, she spoke—and sang—Norwegian passably.

When everyone had had a turn at choosing a song, Elias pushed himself up. His feet were numb and his legs stiff. "All right, folks. We need to get some blood moving. Everybody on your feet."

"It's too cold to move." Nils Rambek shook his head and stayed put while several of the students staggered up.

"That's why you have to move. C'mon." Elias helped him rise. "Johann, give us a sprightly tune on that little blow harp. We're going to dance. Grab a partner."

They stared at him as if he'd lost his wits.

"You do know how to dance, don't you?"

They shook their heads. The boys looked like they'd rather run out into the snowstorm.

"Savannah, help me out here."

She shivered, and seemed as if she was having a hard time concentrating. "What can I do?"

"Teach us a new dance, something you do down South."

"You mean like a reel?"

"Sure. Something to get us moving, and something to occupy our minds." He swung his arms, clapping them across his chest, and stamped his boots. Staring hard, he willed Savannah to join in and chirk the kids up.

"Johann, can you play this?" She hummed a simple tune.

He copied it perfectly.

"I had no idea you were so talented at music, Johann."

The boy ducked his head and blew on his bare hands before repeating the tune.

"Children, line up here, boys on one side, girls on the other. Elias and I will be what's called the 'top couple.' You follow what we do, all right?"

Before long, they'd caught on to the simple steps and pattern, and they were ducking around and under and marching through. Cheeks pinked and smiles emerged. Captain barked and wriggled. Savannah laughed as

Elias deliberately messed up and collided with Rut, picking her up and swinging her around. Cap joined the fray, and laughter filled the room, drowning out the sound of the storm. Soon they were all warm, getting silly and collapsing into a heap on the floor.

"I'm hungry." Ingrid was the first one to voice it, and several of the kids nodded.

"I know you are, *elsker*, but we should hold off on food for a while yet. Best if we eat right before it's time to sleep." Elias chucked her under the chin. "That way you'll sleep better."

The thought of spending the night in the school sobered everyone, and they made their way back into the circle of benches around the stove.

"How about if we put the potatoes on to roast?" he suggested. "While they're cooking, maybe Miss Cox will read to us."

"I want to go home." Margrethe looked up at him, big brown eyes ready to weep. "I don't want to stay here."

"I know you do, sweetheart. We all do."

Hakon shifted his weight. "I am thinking of my pa. He will try to milk the cows and clean the barn without me. Maybe I should be trying to get home."

Elias shook his head. Hakon's father was a frail man who had heart troubles. He relied on his husky son to do most of the chores. But as much as Elias could sympathize with the boy, he had to be firm.

"Nobody is leaving, understood? Hakon, your father would have me flayed if I let you go tonight, and you know it." Elias put his hands on his hips and used his best lawman voice. "We're staying. All night. Best if we just brace ourselves for it and face it head-on. Miss Cox and I are here to look after you. We'll get food going, and we'll listen to some fine literature, then we'll sleep. Now, let's get to work."

He hoped he sounded more in control than he felt. Any way he looked at it, it was going to be a long, cold night.

Chapter Fifteen

It seemed to take ages to get everyone settled for the night. They each had a piece of potato and a bite of tart for supper. Savannah was proud of her older students, who gave the bigger pieces to the youngest kids and made sure they had sleeping places closest to the stove.

"How much longer will the coal last?" she whispered to Elias when all was quiet in the schoolroom.

"At the rate we're burning it, we'll run out sometime around dawn, maybe a little later. I've got the dampers as closed as I can without smothering the fire." He stepped over sleeping children and opened the door to the stove. Quietly, he tossed in a couple more chunks and came back to sit beside her.

In the flickering lamplight, she checked the children. They all lay like spoons, huddled close to share warmth while they slept. Wrapped as they were in coats and hats and gloves and mufflers, it was difficult to tell one from another. Elias had spread three of the saddle blankets out on the floor and covered the youngest students with the fourth. Captain lay among them, raising his head from time to time to check that everyone was all right.

"What will we do then?"

Their shoulders brushed, and Elias's arm came around her shoulder, snugging her up to his side. "We'll have to burn benches and desks. No help for it."

She sighed, feeling so tired her muscles ached. "I suppose not."

"You should get some sleep. It's going to be a long night. I'll stay awake."

Savannah shook her head. "No, I can't sleep. I have to watch out for the children. Anyway, I'm too cold to sleep."

"Just as well the children aren't. They're better off sleeping for a while. We'll keep the fire going and make sure they stay covered up."

Drawing her knees up, she leaned into him, gripping her hands together, wriggling her fingers inside her gloves. Her hands ached, but not for worlds would she say so. Elias had enough to worry about.

"You must be wishing you were back in balmy Raleigh right about now."

His statement caught her off guard. Did she wish to be in North Carolina? Did *he* wish she was there?

"I wouldn't mind some milder temperatures, but I'm not sorry I came." She shifted her position, wrapping her arms around her waist. Elias's arm and the bench behind her supported her, and somehow, in the dark and cold, it was easy to unburden her heart.

"I was very unhappy when I first arrived. Everything was so strange, and you were antagonistic. I was sure I'd made a mistake." She remembered his doubts about her abilities and her staying power—doubts he still seemed to feel. "I left Raleigh under a bit of a cloud. Nothing illegal or immoral, but it was humiliating all the same. I was jilted at the altar. There I was in my wedding gown, with the attendants, the flowers, the veil, the church full of friends and family, and no groom to be found."

Elias's arm tightened around her.

"His name was Girard Brandeis. He was from New Orleans, in Raleigh to visit family. We met at the Christmas Eve ball at my home, and I was swept off my feet by his charm. He courted me so persistently. It was hardly any time at all before we were engaged. I was sure he loved me and that we would be happy forever."

"Girard of the bookmark and the letter?"

"I'd forgotten I even had that bookmark with our names on it. The violets were the first flowers Girard ever gave me. I pressed them and glued them to that pasteboard and wrote our names on it. Silly now, I suppose. When I got home from church that day, I threw it in the fire." A gesture that had given her much satisfaction, even while it made her sad.

"What happened to Girard?"

She closed her eyes, waiting for the pain and humiliation to wash over her. But she waited in vain. Where sharp pain and a lingering ache had once been, she felt gratitude now. If Girard hadn't run out on her, if he had gone through with the wedding, she wouldn't have flown from home. She wouldn't have found herself capable of so much more than she'd thought. She wouldn't have met Elias.

And she would've been married to a man who loved another. Intolerable.

"At first I thought something terrible must've befallen him, that he'd met with some accident on the way to the church. But when Girard's best man went to his lodgings, the landlord said he'd packed everything up the night before and left on the late train." She summarized the facts she'd learned about Girard's first love.

"Aunt Carolina forwarded his letter. In it he explained about the other woman and asked for his ring back."

"I'd like the chance to teach him some manners." The hard edge to Elias's voice made Savannah smile in the dark.

"If Aunt Carolina is to be believed, she sorted him out quite thoroughly when he came to the house to get his ring."

"I think I'd like your aunt Carolina."

"You know, I realize now I was more in love with the idea of Girard than with Girard himself. He represented so many things I'd been told were expected of me. Marry well, run a household, have children." She sighed. "It's the loss of those things that hurt more than the loss of Girard himself after a while. Now I look at sweet little Ingrid and mourn the loss of those children I'd hoped to have."

"What makes you think you won't have children someday? Or your own house and husband?"

Savannah shrugged, growing drowsy. "I couldn't even tell that my own fiancé didn't love me. Getting jilted smashes a girl's confidence. In Raleigh, folks were wondering what was wrong with me that my groom would run out on me like that." She yawned, fighting the waves of sleep rolling over her. "A girl starts to wonder herself."

"You're not in Raleigh now, and there's nothing wrong with you. That Girard fellow needs his head examined. He missed out when he jilted you."

Elias's voice rumbled against her cheek, and his gruff confidence wrapped around her like a warm blanket.

Her eyelids drooped, but before sleep claimed her, she savored his words. A bit of hope trickled into her chest. Maybe he was right, and she did have a future that might include a husband and children someday.

Funny though, how when she tried to picture a husband, it was Elias's face she saw.

A jilted bride.

Elias blinked hard and jerked his head to keep himself awake. Savannah slumbered in his arms, and from time to time he took off his glove to touch her cheek, testing for cold. She'd been asleep for about an hour, and all the while he'd rolled her story around in his head.

Her broken engagement explained the remoteness in her demeanor when she'd first arrived in Snowflake. She'd been hurting and trying not to let it show.

Elias knew plenty about that. After Britta left, he'd been pretty jaded. She'd led him a merry dance, and he'd fallen hard. At least he hadn't proposed to her, though he'd been planning on it. He understood what Savannah meant about losing not just the person but the future you'd built up in your mind with them.

Cap got up and shook his coat, then clicked across the floor, stepping over sleeping children until he came to Elias. Elias used his free hand and ruffled the dog's ears. The collie sniffed Savannah's hair where it peeped out from the edge of her hat, and then made a tour of the room. Finally, he threaded his way between the small bodies around the stove and lay down again, his nose resting on Rut's sleeve.

The storm raged outside, howling and shaking the building. Elias prayed the snow was piling up along the outside walls. If they got buried in a few feet of fluff, the room would be much easier to heat.

Easing Savannah down onto her side, he forced himself to get up and move. Cap raised his head, but Elias signaled him to stay put. Walking as quietly as he could, he went to the window. He couldn't feel his toes inside his boots. His stomach rumbled, reminding him that two bites of an overdone potato weren't enough to fill a grown man's stomach.

Quietly, he put more coal on the fire, banking it a bit higher as the cold crept farther into the room. He worried about the children's feet and hands. Though they all wore heavy socks and mittens and boots, their blood would slow while they slept. Maybe he should wake them all up for some more dancing and get their blood moving?

The clock said half past one. The coal was going quicker than he'd hoped. But he could see his breath anywhere in the room more than about five feet from the stove. How he wished he had a couple buffalo robes or horsehide blankets to wrap these children up.

"Lord," he whispered, "keep us safe, and help me know what to do and when to do it. Thank you for this shelter, and for bringing me here to help Savannah. She's been through so much. Help me know the right thing to do about her, too. My head says to be sensible and wait, and my heart says snatch her up before she gets away."

He grimaced. He'd been full of himself and his own opinions when Savannah first stepped off that stagecoach. Talking big, talking out of his own hurt, aware that if he didn't he was in danger of falling in love with another teacher who would decamp as soon as things got difficult.

But Savannah had proved him wrong. She'd stayed, in spite of the accommodations, the lack of school supplies, the language barrier. In spite of the responsibilities and the cold and the snow.

And in spite of his best efforts, he'd fallen in love with the schoolteacher, anyway. What was he going to do if she decided to leave after the school year and didn't come back?

The long hours of the night stretched out, giving him plenty of time to think. And all the while, the snow continued to fall, the wind continued to blow and the temperatures remained low. At three, feeling cold and lethargic himself, he turned up the lamps and roused everyone.

"Come on. You have to get up and get moving. It's too cold in here for you to sleep all night. You'll freeze." He shook shoulders and patted hands. "Johann, wake up. We need some marching music."

Savannah shook her head, eyelids heavy. "Just let us sleep. It's too cold to move."

"Which is why we have to." He reached for her hands, pulling her up. "The children will freeze if we don't get their blood pumping."

The children's needs brought her wider awake, and she began helping him rouse them. "Ingrid, Rut, Margrethe, wake up."

Hakon stumbled to his feet, yawning and shivering. "What is it? What's wrong?" His nose and cheeks were red in the lamplight.

"We're going to dance and get warmed up."

Johann dug his harmonica out of an inner pocket with his eyes closed. Once all the kids were on their feet, Elias realized they were too stupefied by sleep and cold to follow more than basic orders.

"No music for now. Kids, line up." He tugged and guided and prodded them into a smallest-to-tallest line. "Put your hands on the shoulders of the person in front of you." He had to help some of them. Chastising himself, wishing he'd roused them an hour before, he got them lined up.

"Now, march. Stomp your feet. Ingrid, follow me." He held her mittened hand and started around the small open space in a circle, his boots pounding the floorboards.

"I can't feel my feet," Lars complained.

"All the more reason to get moving. Stomp hard."

Round and round they went. The older children revived first, letting go of their classmates and marching around on their own. Hakon and Peder began swinging their arms, crossing them and slapping them. Savannah perked up enough to take the littlest girls in tow. When everyone was wide awake and panting with exertion, Johann began to play his harmonica.

"I can't believe how you've all caught on to dancing the Virginia reel." Savannah crossed her hands and clasped Elias's, letting him swing her down the row.

The song ended, and everyone stilled, breathing fast. The noise inside the school quieted and the storm outside caught their attention. Icy pellets of snow scraped against the siding, and the glass rattled in the panes as gust after gust assaulted the building.

Eyes grew round and teeth gnawed lips. Ingrid sniffed and blinked hard.

"Savannah, I think it's time for that surprise."

Rut tugged on Elias's sleeve. "What surprise?"

"Wait and see," he said. "Everyone find your places around the fire. Hakon, help me over here, will you?"

The young man came to him right away, while the children scrambled over the bench barrier and huddled beside the stove. The fire was a bed of low embers.

"There is no coal left, *ja?*" Hakon's shock of almost white hair pressed against his forehead under his knit cap.

"Yes, which is why I need help breaking up some of these benches. We'll burn the leg supports first, then find a way to cut or break the longer pieces for the stove."

Savannah went to her desk and dug in one of the drawers, sliding out the candy box. She brought it to him. "These are going to be frozen solid. I'll need to warm them up by the fire."

"Let us get some of these benches broken up." He flipped one of the long seats and, while Hakon held it down, kicked against the stringer, knocking it out from between the end supports with a thwack. "Go ahead and kick off that end, Hakon."

The boy kicked and then twisted the broken board off the nails. Elias did the same with his end, and soon they had a few pieces of wood that would fit into the stove box.

"Elias, would it be easier to break up the desk drawers?" Savannah asked. "I could empty them out easily enough. And when the storm is over, I'm sure one of the men could make new ones. I've never seen so many talented woodworkers as in this settlement."

"Good idea."

While she emptied the desk, Elias fed the fire. The wood caught quickly, and it would burn quickly, too, faster than the coal. He'd have to be even more sparing with the fuel.

"What's the surprise?" Margrethe asked.

Savannah brought several empty drawers and piled them near the stove. "I have a treat for you. I was going to give it to you tomorrow." She glanced at the clock. "Actually, it *is* tomorrow."

"What is it?" Ingrid asked. Elias nodded, glad that she was alert and warm enough to both care and ask.

"It's called a praline. And it's just the best bite of candy anywhere."

"Candy?" Lars asked.

"Everyone get settled in, and I'll give you each a piece. It's frozen, but you can gnaw on it." Savannah tugged her mitten off with her teeth and opened the box. "It's chocolate and caramel and pecan."

With round eyes that shone in the flickering firelight, the students accepted the morsels. "While you eat, I'll tell you about where these came from."

Elias settled in, leaning against one of the benches. When she got to him, there was only one candy left in the box. He glanced up at her. "Have you kept one back for yourself?"

She shook her head. "No, this one's for you."

"Let's go halves." Tugging her hand, he brought her down beside him. Around them, the kids warmed their chocolates with their breath, licked them, gnawed off bits, and looked at one another with smiles in their eyes as the flavor of the treat hit their tongues.

Savannah pushed the box near the stove to thaw the last praline.

"Miss Cox, tell us about where you lived before here." Ingrid pillowed her head in Savannah's lap, sucking on her chocolate, her voice already drowsy.

As Savannah described her life in North Carolina, the cotton fields, the textile mills, one by one the students finished their chocolate and dropped into sleep.

Waves of tiredness washed over Elias, and he fought to keep his eyes open. Somebody had to stay awake and feed the fire. It was the last thing he remembered as he nodded off.

Chapter Sixteen

For hours Savannah paced between the windows, silently swinging her arms when her hands grew too cold, keeping watch over the sleeping students and poking broken bits of wood into the fire from time to time.

The windows were black squares, and the light from the lamps, which she'd turned down to conserve kerosene, penetrated only far enough into the night to show the vicious swirl of deadly snow fighting to get inside.

Would this nightmare ever end? And when it did, what then?

At last, pale gray light began to filter through the glass. One could hardly call it daylight, more like "less dark." Maybe it was the optimism that comes with morning, but she thought the wind might be dying down a bit. Between gusts, she could make out the dark form of the animal shed to the west of the school.

She started when Elias put his hands on her shoulders, standing behind her. "You should've woken me. I shouldn't have fallen asleep."

Savannah wanted to turn her cheek and rest it against the back of his glove, to draw strength from his presence and comfort from his touch. What would she have done if he hadn't shown up yesterday? Right now she and the children would be lost on the prairie.

"You needed your sleep. The storm seems to be waning."

He kept his hands on her shoulders as he looked out over her head. "Or it's in a lull. Now might be a good time to go check on the horses."

"I'll go with you."

"No, I'll take Hakon. I don't want the children left in here with no adult if something should delay us."

She grabbed his hand. "You will be careful?"

"I will." For a moment, he rested his cheek against her hair, then he was gone, quietly rousing Hakon and slipping out into the foyer.

Savannah stayed by the window, watching their dark forms struggle through the drifts, losing sight of them when gusts of snow blew up.

The rest of the kids still slept, and she prayed they would for a good long time. The longer they slept, the less time they would have to be hungry and fearful. She fed the last broken drawer into the stove and held her hands to the warmth, flexing her aching fingers. Elias's father had told her she would probably always be more sensitive to the cold since the frostbite incident, and so far, he was proving all too depressingly right. All night her hands had ached and tingled. Still, she had much for which to be thankful. Everyone had survived the night.

She prayed the same could be said for the citizens of Snowflake.

Her heart was on tenterhooks until she heard Elias and Hakon in the entry, kicking the snow from their boots as quietly as possible. When they came in, they were shivering and caked in snow, with only their eyes showing between their hats and mufflers.

"Come to the fire," she whispered. "Give me your wraps, and I'll go shake them out while you thaw." After helping them unbutton coats and unwrap scarves, she ushered them to the stove and opened its door to let out billows of heat. She slipped into the entryway with their heavy garments, the icy cold of the unheated room slicing through her, making her gasp.

When she returned, some of the children were pushing themselves upright, rubbing their eyes and yawning. The clock showed it was a little after eight. She gave the coats and gloves to Elias and Hakon and went to blow out the lamps.

When Elias was warmed enough to speak, he shrugged back into his coat and drew Savannah toward the front of the schoolroom. "It's bitter out there, and the wind is kicking up again. All the horses are fine. Cold and hungry, but we managed to drag more hay into the shed for them. There's a huge drift in front of the opening that is blocking the wind, but it made it a challenge to get the feed inside. I couldn't have done it without Hakon. That kid has no idea how strong he is."

"So there's no sign of the storm letting up?"

"Not so far." Elias scrubbed his hands down his face, his palms rasping on his beard. "We'll have to keep the kids busy and warm without overexerting them and making them even hungrier than they need to be. Is there anything left to eat?"

She shook her head, and her stomach grumbled. "Just the one praline. You fell asleep before it thawed."

"Save it for now."

They passed the longest day Savannah could ever remember. For a while they sang and played games, but eventually the cold and hunger got to everyone and they wound up sitting on the floor around the fire, doing and saying nothing.

All the bench supports were gone, and every scrap of easily burnable wood consumed. Elias had brought the ice breaker inside and used it to splinter the long bench boards. Though Savannah knew it was necessary for their survival, when he had to start in on the desks, a lump formed in her throat and tears stung her eyes.

Late in the afternoon, the howling outside diminished, then ceased. At first, Savannah, who sat on the floor with Ingrid on her lap and Margrethe tucked up at her side, didn't realize what had happened. She was so used to the banshee wail of the storm that when it stopped, her ears rang and felt empty.

Elias, hands hanging limp between his upraised knees, lifted his head. His dull, tired eyes brightened, and he pushed himself up to go to the window. "I think it stopped."

Savannah was too tired to get up. Her bones ached from sitting on the hard floor, and her head felt heavy. Some of the boys stood and joined Elias.

"Can we go home now?" Rut asked, propping her head on her hand.

"The sun is breaking through the clouds." Peder pointed.

Savannah shook her head to clear it and noted that the room was lighter than it had been all day. The longing for sunshine was enough to impel her to rise. "Come on, Ingrid, let's go look."

Snow scudded along the tops of sculpted drifts, frozen waves and eddies carved by the wind. The back edge of the storm formed a hard line of clouds that raced away to the southeast, and behind them the sun emerged.

"Sun dogs," Hakon said. "It must be very cold."

"Sun dogs?" Savannah asked.

"See the rainbows on either side of the sun?" Elias pointed. "It's the light shining through ice crystals in the air. It has to be very cold for those to appear."

"We can leave though, right? Now that the storm is over?" The thought of escaping the schoolroom lightened her heart.

"We can and should. The sooner the better, if we want to make it to shelter before dark." Elias gathered the boys. "I want you to break a path to the corral. Don't bother with saddles for the horses. We'll all be warmer riding without. Don't use bridles, either. The bits will be too cold for the horses' mouths. Halters and ropes will be fine."

When Elias opened the outside door, a wall of snow as high as ten-year-old Nils greeted them. "Hakon, you go first, boys follow close. There will be some deep drifts out there, so be careful, help each other along."

Savannah banked the small fire and made sure all the girls had their coats buttoned, hats and scarves secure, and their mittens on tight. Elias climbed up to the cupola, using the slats nailed to the wall in the foyer, and shoved hard against the trap door, letting in an avalanche of snow. He was gone for a few minutes, then the bell rope snaked down through the hole in the ceiling, falling stiffly to the floor.

"We'll take the rope along. I want all the horses strung together so nobody gets lost," Elias said, climbing back down.

"How will some of the children make it? They live so far."

"We'll strike out for Halvorsons' first. Those that live more than a mile away can stay there until their parents come for them. Write a note on the blackboard so if any parents come here first, they'll know where we went."

She hurried to comply, glancing out the window and seeing the horses struggling through the drifts.

The ride across the prairie was as miserable a trip as any Savannah had ever had. They put the youngest students up on the horses and ponies, while Elias, Savannah, Hakon, Peder and Johann battled through the thigh-deep snow. Savannah's skirts hampered her, and snow made its way into every wrinkle and seam of her stockings and boots. The wind, much quieter now that the storm had passed, still kicked snow into their faces, and she had to keep her chin down as she labored to keep up.

Smoke rose from the chimney at the Halvorson house, and as they neared, Savannah wanted to cry with thankfulness. The cold lacerated her lungs, and weariness and hunger made her weak, but they were almost home.

Elias had to scoop snow away from the cabin door. He pounded on it, and Agneta answered, her face alight with relief. When she saw who it was, the smile dimmed a bit, but she welcomed them inside.

"I need to leave some of the kids here. The Pederson and Rosedahl kids live close enough that I can get them home, but the rest will need to stay here. They're pretty cold and hungry."

"No, do not go." Agneta clung to his snow-covered arm as the children slid from the horses and crowded inside.

"We can't all stay here, and parents will be getting worried."

"No, it is Per. He has not come home all night. I have been alone in the storm, praying and worrying."

Elias stood still. "When did you last see him?"

"Before the storm hit. He was checking on some cattle near the creek. At least that is what he said he was going to do."

Savannah stopped unwrapping children and ushering them to the corner fireplace. "What should we do?"

"Stay here with the children," Elias responded. "Hakon, Johann, grab something quick to eat. Lars, I know you want to go, but you need to get the horses to the barn and get them fed and watered. Once that's done, see to the rest of the barn chores. Take Nils and Peder with you to help, and then haul more fuel into the house for the fire. We'll be back when we find your pa." He took the boy by the shoulders, stooping to his eye level. "Under no circumstances are you to follow us, understood? You stay here and protect the girls."

Agneta had gone to her larder and returned with bread and sliced meat, slapping sandwiches together. She handed one to Elias. "Per's buffalo coat is on the door. Take it with you."

Savannah remembered that it had been warm before the storm broke. Per wouldn't have needed his heaviest coat. Was he wearing even a jacket?

Elias bolted his sandwich, as did the older boys, and slipped into the big coat. He rested his hand on Agneta's shoulder. "We'll find him."

Wanting to tell him to be careful, to make him promise to return unharmed, Savannah laced her fingers under her chin, unable to say anything. He reached for the doorknob, but before he pulled on it, he looked back over his shoulder and winked.

She nodded, knowing he understood what she wanted to say but couldn't.

* * *

The last thing Elias wanted to do was return to the frozen landscape outside, but he had no choice. If Per had somehow managed to survive the storm, every minute would count. Elias felt as if he had anvils strapped to his feet as he pushed through the drifts. Behind him, Buck floundered on the lead rope.

Elias's breath froze on his muffler, rubbing against his lips and cheeks, making them chapped and raw. Snow drove through his clothes and caked in the long hair of the buffalo coat, weighing him down, but he was grateful for the enormous garment.

Behind him Hakon and Johann trudged in the path he and Buck broke for them. Sunshine sparkled in a million crystalline lights on the snow, and forced them to squint against the glare.

The creek lay a quarter mile northeast of the homestead, and Elias could make out the stunted trees that clung to the creek bank, their skeletal arms, coated with snow, reaching for the white-blue sky. Chances were the cattle Per had gone to check on were sheltered there along the frozen stream.

But where was he?

They topped a small rise, and several hillocks of snow stood at intervals.

Haystacks. They were on the edge of Per's hayfield.

Elias stopped to rest, putting his hands on his knees and leaning over to catch his breath. He unwound his muffler, planning to rewind it to a dry place, and found he'd run out of those. Every inch of the knitted scarf was coated with ice and crackled when he shook it out.

Hakon stomped his feet. "Where do we look?"

"We're going to hope and pray he's in one of the haystacks. That's the only shelter between the creek and the homestead. Make your way to the nearest one and start digging. I'll take the next. If you find something, holler."

They found him in the fourth haystack, curled deep inside, hugging himself. Johann's shout brought Elias as quickly as he could manage, postholing through the snow, dragging Buck in his wake.

"He's here! He's alive, but barely!"

Elias shrugged out of the buffalo robe as he ran, folding it to preserve his body heat. Hakon and Johann dug furiously, sending cascades of snow and hay out of the drift.

Per was unresponsive. They bundled the burly farmer in the buffalo coat, and among the three of them, managed to get him on the horse. Elias boosted Hakon up to ride behind him and hold him on.

By the time they got back to the house, several horses and sleighs stood in the yard and a search party of fathers was streaming toward them. Hands grabbed Per, sliding him off the horse and carrying him to the house. Someone took Buck's reins from Elias and someone else took his arm.

When they arrived inside, Elias could barely stand. His muscles burned from the exertion, and his head hurt from the cold. He sagged onto a bench.

They'd laid Per on the bed in the corner, and with all the men and children in the tiny house, there was barely room to stand. Agneta bent over her husband, and Savannah threaded her way through the crowd to Elias's side.

"You found him."

He nodded. Was it too late, though?

Mr. Rosedahl took charge of the room. "All you with sleighs, bundle up the children and take them home.

Give Agneta room to work. Elias, we thank you for what you did for the children and for Per. You need to rest now. I am sure you will find a bed here. When I pass by your parents' place, I will tell them you are here and fine."

Elias shook his head. "I have to get to town. I'm the sheriff. Need to see if anyone else needs help."

"No, Bjorn will see to all that. You need to rest." Mr. Rosedahl pressed Elias back down onto the bench. "Anyway, the ladies here might need your help."

The room emptied, leaving just the Halvorsons, Savannah and Elias.

Savannah put her arm around Rut. "Lars, you and Rut eat something more. Then I want you to both go to bed."

"But our papa…" Rut's tired eyes filled with tears.

"Your papa will sleep now. I will help your mama tend him. He would want you to rest."

The children were too worn-out to do much more than nibble on some bread before they trudged upstairs. Elias eased out of his coat. Savannah took it and hung it on the back of the door. She went to a trunk under the stairs and pulled out an extra blanket, while Agneta filled a kettle and placed it over the fire.

Savannah wrapped the blanket around Elias's shoulders and tugged him to the rocking chair beside the fire. "Soup will be ready soon. You sit still and get warm."

"You should rest, too. You've been awake longer." Even as he said it, he could feel himself drooping toward sleep.

"I have to help Agneta with Per. I'll be fine." She knelt and tugged on Elias's boots. Soon she had his socks off. "Can you feel your feet? Do I need to bring in some snow?"

"No, they're not frozen." She'd learned well through her own experience.

Soon she had his bare feet soaking in a basin of lukewarm water.

He wanted to tell her what a good job she'd done during the storm. He wanted to tell her how proud he was of her. He wanted— His thoughts stopped on the one overwhelming thing he couldn't ignore. He wanted *her.*

Chapter Seventeen

Before Savannah could dish up a bowl of broth, Elias was asleep in the chair. Agneta tended to Per, wrapping him in blankets and spooning first warm water and then warm broth between his lips.

"What can I do?" Savannah asked.

Agneta shook her head and a tear plopped onto her dress. "Pray."

Pray. She'd been praying, praying hard for what seemed like hours. Her heart was as exhausted as her body.

Darkness fell, and she lit both glass lamps, setting one on the bedside table and one on the kitchen table. Elias slept through her removing his feet from the water, drying them and slipping on a thick pair of Per's knitted socks.

Agneta sat beside the bed, stroking Per's head, giving him sips of water, applying salve to his chapped lips. As he'd warmed, she had placed hot bricks wrapped in towels onto the bedding along his sides. "We must warm his body before we worry about his hands and feet." She spoke to herself, stroking Per's hair off his forehead.

Savannah dragged the stool from beside the spinning wheel and sat on it next to Elias's chair. Her head drooped to rest on his knee.

Her conscience was so heavy she couldn't get her mind to rest. Seeing Per nearly frozen to death had shocked her. Every one of the children she'd been entrusted with as a teacher would've met a similar or worse fate if Elias hadn't come and stopped her from sending them out into the storm.

What had she been thinking, coming here? Acting as if she could handle the climate and hardships, as if everyone, especially Elias, was exaggerating the difficulties just to scare her. She had no business having children in her care. She had no business being here, no business forcing people to risk their lives because of her ignorance. Her shortcomings rose up to mock her.

You didn't speak up when the coal store got low.

You didn't have any emergency supplies to feed the children if they got snowed in.

You didn't know enough not to send them out in a blizzard.

You could've killed those children.

You don't belong here.

The desire to go home, to throw herself into Aunt Carolina's arms and weep, overwhelmed her.

A dry sob escaped her throat.

In his sleep, Elias's hand came out and stroked her hair, coming to rest on her shoulder as he sighed and slipped deeper into slumber.

You don't belong here.

You can't stay. No matter how much you might want to.

Per Halvorson developed pneumonia, school was canceled until new furnishings and more coal could be procured, and Savannah had nothing to do but carry around her guilt and her resolve to leave as soon as possible.

The nights were the worst. Nightmares plagued her sleep, hours where she struggled in a blizzard, trudging through the snow, lost, calling for the children she'd turned out into the storm. She would wake up gasping, tangled in the bedclothes, cheeks wet with tears. The darkness and cold seemed to press in on her, and it would be hours before she could sleep again.

A doctor came from the next town over to see Per, giving Agneta detailed instructions and medicines. He carefully examined Per's extremities and decided that the big farmer would be able to keep all his digits. The news should've made them happy, but the fear over his pneumonia kept everyone tense and pensive.

A week after the storm, Savannah and Lars hitched up the sleigh and headed to town, he to do his mother's shopping and Savannah to send a wire home.

At the telegraph office, she struggled to find the right words, torn between guilt and grief. Guilt at the way she'd endangered her students and grief at the thought of leaving them. In the end, she kept the telegram as brief as possible, set her coins on the counter and walked out. She had one more thing to do before heading back to the Halvorsons'.

The mercantile hummed with news. Someone had brought newspapers from the area towns, and the residents of Snowflake pored over them, sharing snippets of the aftermath of the storm. Lives lost, lives saved, the toll on livestock. When she stepped up to the post office counter to mail her letter, the conversations ceased.

Mr. Svenby stepped forward. "Miss Cox, it's so good to see you. We can't thank you enough for your bravery. You saved the schoolchildren, you and the sheriff.

Look." He held up a newspaper. "You made it into the *Tracy Gazette.*"

The headline read As If They Were Her Own.

Scanning the lines, Savannah felt her cheeks heat, and she wanted to run outside into the cold. They thought she was a heroine. They thought she had saved the children from the storm, when it had been Elias all along. They were lauding her when they should be packing her into the first eastbound stage.

She laid the paper down, unsure what to say.

People crowded around her, people she'd come to think of as her friends. Congratulations and thanks poured out. The knot in her stomach tightened. "Mr. Svenby, I need to mail a letter."

"Sending another epistle home? Your family must like how often you write. Wish I had a letter for you, but the stage hasn't come in yet."

"Not home, just to the other end of the county." Savannah set the envelope on the counter.

"Ah, reporting in to the boss down in Kettinger, *ja?*"

"Yes." She couldn't look him in the eye. Tyler deserved to know about her resignation before anyone else.

"And how is Per doing? Is there anything we can do?"

Grateful for the change of subject, she shook her head. "He's very ill. Agneta won't let anyone help tend him, and she's about worn-out. The doctor says he's got a good chance if the strain on his heart wasn't too much when he was out in the cold. Lars has taken over the barn chores, and Rut and I are pitching in where we can." Savannah searched the store for Lars and found him near the back, where the patent medicines and herbs were shelved. "Agneta gave us a list of ingredients for an elixir. I hope you had everything on hand?"

"Sure did. And I threw in a couple of extra things for her to try, plus some candy for the kids." Karl Svenby took the pencil from behind his ear and marked a few lines in his ledger.

"Thank you." Savannah tightened the strings on her cloak and pulled on her gloves. "I'm sure Agneta appreciates it and will thank you when she can."

"You stopping in to the sheriff's office on the way home?" He gave her a teasing look. "The two of you are garnering plenty of attention in the paper and over the checkerboard." Jerking his thumb toward where two old men sat beside the stove, moving the red-and-black pieces around on the board, he laughed. "Some folks are even matchmaking, scheming to make sure you stay in Snowflake permanently."

Her blush deepened, heating her cheeks even more, which made those around her laugh.

Lars hefted the basket and headed her way. "Ready, Teacher? We need to get home."

Making her escape, she wondered what they would all say when the news of her departure hit. They wouldn't be singing her praises then.

She walked to the sleigh and got in, not looking at the sheriff's office, trying to hold together the pieces of her breaking heart.

"What did you do?" Tyler didn't say hello or mince words. He stalked into the jail and tossed a folded piece of paper down on Elias's desk. "What on earth happened up here? She was fine enough at Christmastime. Now I get this?"

"What are you talking about, and close the door."

Elias let his boots drop off the corner of the desk and picked up the paper. He stifled a yawn. The past two weeks had been some of the most grueling of his life. Today was the first day he'd had where someone wasn't in need of his help. "Didn't expect to see you in town. You want some coffee? I just made a pot."

Captain sat up from his place on the rug beside the stove, yawning and shaking his head.

"I want to know what you did or said to Savannah." Tyler yanked off his gloves and shoved them into his coat pocket. He stalked to the stove and poured himself a steaming cup of the brown liquid. "I don't get mail regularly down in Kettinger, especially not with all this snow. When I finally made it in to the post office, I found out that letter had been sitting there for two weeks. What did you do to Savannah?"

"I didn't do anything to Savannah. What's got you in such a lather?" Tyler could fuss and worry with the best of them, but this was a whole new level. Puzzled, Elias unfolded the paper, immediately recognizing Savannah's precise penmanship.

Mr. Parker,
It is with great regret that I must submit my resignation, effective as soon as you confirm reception of this note. I apologize for not finishing the term, but for me to do so would be folly. I appreciate all I have learned while I have been here, and I will remember you all with great fondness.
Sincerely,
Miss Savannah Cox.

Elias read it twice. "Resigning?" He couldn't grasp the notion. "What's going on here?"

"You didn't know about this?" Tyler set his cup down without taking a drink.

"Of course not." Panic and a sense of déjà vu swept over Elias. He found himself standing without realizing he'd gotten to his feet. His hands gripped the paper, creasing it badly.

"Then you didn't say something or do something to once again remind her that she's a greenhorn outsider who shouldn't have come here?" Hands on hips, his older brother skewered him with a look.

Elias squirmed. "Not for a long time." He smoothed out the letter and read it again. "I know I thought that early on, and I said as much, but I changed my mind a while ago."

"Where is she now? Is she already gone?"

"No, we had to postpone school for a week or so until we could get things squared away, new benches and desks and things, but she's been there every day since it reopened." Elias cast through his memory of the past two weeks. She'd been quiet the few times they'd met, but he'd been busy and distracted. She couldn't have escaped Snowflake, anyway, since the stage hadn't been able to run until three days ago, when Keenan had finally gotten through.

"Have you seen her?" Tyler's accusatory stare did little to calm Elias.

"Not much. What with the big storm and all, I've been busy." He heard the defensive tone in his voice, angry that he should feel guilty for not keeping better tabs on Savannah. "Things haven't exactly been normal around here. I had to ride out to all the farms and make sure folks were all right, and there were repairs to do on houses and barns, not to mention making sure the schoolhouse furnishings got replaced. I've been working flat out seeing to the whole township. I had no idea she was thinking about leaving." Elias ran through what might've happened and how she'd looked the last time he'd seen her.

"I stopped at the Halvorsons'…when was it? Thursday afternoon? I'd been at the Rambeks' helping repair the lean-to that got blown off the back of his house during the storm. It was getting dark, so I couldn't stay long, but I wanted to check on Per. Savannah met me at the door. She looked serious, sober, but that seemed appropriate given that Per is so sick. She didn't say a word about leaving."

A spark of anger lit in Elias's chest. A spark that grew into a flame. She was leaving. Without telling him. He wanted to wad up the paper and throw it as hard as he could. This was what he got for hoping. For letting himself fall for another woman who had no more business being here than the Queen of Sheba. What a fool he'd been. He'd almost made the same mistake twice.

"Fine, if she wants to go, let her. At least this one had the decency to tell you before she lit out." Elias shoved down the hurt and buried it in bitterness.

Tyler groaned, ramming his hands into his hair and sending his bowler toppling to the floor. "You know what this means for my job and my future political career, don't you? If she resigns, I'm sunk."

"She is *not* resigning." A woman's voice pierced the room.

Elias whirled toward the door. A tall woman filled the opening, silhouetted against the snow outside.

He didn't want to be bothered now, not when he was mad enough to spit hot rivets. How could he have been so stupid? Scraping together some manners, he asked, "Can I help you, ma'am?"

"Are you the sheriff?"

"Yes, ma'am." He removed his hat as she stepped farther into the room. The woman had a Southern accent, a commanding presence and travel-worn garments. In a flash, he knew her, though they'd never met.

"Miss Carolina Cox?" He'd almost said "Aunt Carolina" and barely caught himself in time.

"Mr. Elias Parker?" She held out her gloved hand. Only a shade shorter than his own six feet, she looked him in the eye, her gaze appraising.

"That's me." He shook her hand, surprised at the strength of her grip. "I've heard a lot about you, ma'am."

"And I you. I'm here to see Savannah, Snowflake and the sheriff who has been filling up so much space in her letters."

Her grim tone set a pit of dread into his gut. Savannah had been writing home about him? From the look on her aunt's face, whatever Savannah had said couldn't have been good. The woman gave him a long, steady stare and then transferred her attention to Tyler, raising her eyebrow.

Elias remembered his manners. "Pardon me, ma'am. This is my brother, Tyler."

"The superintendent."

Tyler nodded, looking as stunned as Elias felt.

"Would you care for a chair?" Elias whisked a halter he'd been mending and a stack of old newspapers off the ladder-back chair beside his desk.

"Thank you, no. I've been jounced and jostled in that butter churn you call a stagecoach for far too many miles. I'd rather stand at the moment."

Elias edged around her to close the door. He shot Tyler a what-do-we-do-now look and received a shrug in reply. Aunt Carolina surveyed the room, and Elias winced at the disarray. His deputy was supposed to keep the place swept out, but Bjorn wasn't much of one for housekeeping.

"Now, you were speaking of Savannah's resignation when I arrived?" Aunt Carolina asked. She picked up the letter Elias had tossed onto the desk, smoothed it out and scanned it. "Her telegram to me was even more cryptic. After months of letters extolling the virtues of this place..." she paused and glanced once more around the room and out the grimy window, as if wondering about Savannah's sanity "...I get a two-line telegram telling me she's coming home as soon as she can manage it."

"We had no idea, ma'am." Tyler picked up his hat. "This is hitting us out of the blue."

"You aren't the only one. I've been worrying for hundreds of dreadful miles, and then I discover *this* at my hotel last night." She dug in the capacious handbag she carried and withdrew a newspaper, snapping it open. "Did you two really survive a terrible storm by sheltering with the children in the schoolhouse?" She held the paper under Elias's nose. "This says you spent a night and most of a day trapped in the school with little food, little fuel and nearly a dozen children and a dog?" Her eyes sliced toward Cap, who had risen to his feet but hadn't advanced.

Smart dog.

"Yes, ma'am, we did. We had no choice." Elias put his hands in his pockets. Who did this lady think she was, crashing in here, looking down her long nose at him, treating him like a kid caught sneaking *krumkake* before dinner?

"Do you think the two things, the storm and her resignation, are somehow tied together?"

"I don't know. I haven't had much time to think about either." Elias shifted his weight. Why was she grilling him? Why not ask Tyler? His brother was Savannah's boss, after all.

Miss Cox tapped the floor with her toe. "Savannah's a complex girl, always has been. Feels things deeply. She's taken something to heart, that's what." She picked up the paper and closed it into her bag with a snap of the clasp. "Now, young man." She pointed to Elias. "I require you to deliver me to wherever Savannah is at the moment so we can sort this whole thing out."

He glanced at the clock. "She'll be at the schoolhouse this time of day."

"Then that's where we'll go." The woman brooked no argument, speaking with total confidence that they would fall in with her plans.

Elias reached for his coat. He had no beef about taking the lady to her niece. Fact was, he wanted to have a word or two with Savannah himself. "This way, ma'am. I'll get a sleigh from the livery. Do you have bags over at the stage depot?"

"I do." Her stern, mannish face softened a touch. "And I'll thank you not to comment on either the amount or the contents."

He stuffed his hands into his gloves. Savannah must've written home about their first meeting. "No, ma'am, I've learned my lesson there." Too bad the one he'd learned over Britta didn't stick.

The sunshine nearly blinded them on the trip out to the schoolhouse, and Aunt Carolina said not a word. Through the loading of her baggage, which like her niece's was considerable, she sat on the front seat of the sleigh as if she had a stair rod for a backbone.

Tyler wedged himself into the backseat between

bandboxes and valises without comment, and Captain wriggled in beside him.

Miss Cox sucked in a breath when they started off and the wind cut around them like icy knives. Much like Savannah, this Southern lady was not prepared for the climate. Her hat sat high on her upswept hair but offered nothing in the way of protection for her face or ears. Elias unwound his muffler and passed it to her, raising his coat collar to protect his own neck and cheeks.

She nodded, quickly wrapping the scarf around her face.

The schoolhouse rose before them, the cupola piercing the sky. Elias made a mental note to replace the bell rope, something he'd forgotten about in the busyness of the past three weeks. Smoke emerged from the chimney, quickly blown sideways and disappearing against the brilliant sky. Someone was there.

As they pulled to a stop before the door, Tyler broke free of the baggage and dropped to the snow. "I'll take care of the horses. You two go on inside." He took the reins from Elias.

"Coward," Elias muttered under his breath.

"Just a quicker thinker." His brother grinned.

Miss Cox stood and waited for Elias to help her from the sleigh. Captain jumped down and trotted up the steps ahead of them.

"Where is that animal going?" Her voice might've been muffled by the woolen scarf, but it was every bit as assured and disapproving as it had been since the moment she arrived.

"Inside." Elias kicked snow off the steps. "This way."

Time for a reckoning with Miss Savannah Cox.

Chapter Eighteen

Savannah wrote simple equations on the blackboard for her oldest students, but her arm felt leaden and her mind dull. Since the storm, since seeing Per fight for his life, since hearing about the damage to the region, she hadn't been able to shake her quiet despair.

And she watched out the north windows constantly, afraid of seeing that wall of gray clouds advancing like an avenging army. Afraid of another storm that would endanger the children.

A movement caught her eye. Peder, raising his hand.

"Yes?"

"May I put more coal in the fire?" He spoke slowly, in English. "We are cold."

Savannah nodded. "But just a little."

Her new constant struggle, the desire to keep the children warm, but to guard and ration the fuel so they wouldn't run out ever again. Mr. Rosedahl had seen to it that the coal shed was full to bursting now, but Savannah couldn't help herself in rationing each bucketful.

The children were different, too, since the storm, less carefree, more watchful. But perhaps they were only picking up on her mood.

Almost all the students were in attendance, seeming none the worse for their ordeal. Lars and Rut were taking turns staying home to help their mother care for their father, and today it was Lars's turn at home.

Savannah checked the western horizon, the clock and the calendar. Almost the first of February. Why hadn't Tyler contacted her? She'd mailed her resignation two weeks ago.

Heads swiveled at the sound of heavy footsteps on the stairs, and the door opening. The familiar click of nails on the hardwood had her heart leaping and then crashing down in her chest.

If Captain was here, Elias wasn't far behind. She braced herself to see the sheriff again. Surely he would know soon about her resignation, and she dreaded his reaction. Would he be angry or relieved? Hurt or smug? She'd envisioned every scenario.

But it wasn't Elias who entered.

Savannah's legs went weak, and she sank into her chair, mouth agape. Even bundled in what she was certain was Elias's scarf, the visitor was unmistakable. Savannah would know those eyes and that commanding presence anywhere.

While the children stroked Captain as he passed them on his way to her side, she tried to find a thought to hold on to. The collie rested his head in her lap, nudging her limp hand until she absently rubbed his ear. His tongue came out and swiped at her wrist, and his tail swished across the floor.

"Well, I can't say this is much of a greeting after the long trip I've had." Aunt Carolina pulled off the muffler and handed it to Elias, who had come through the doorway behind her.

"Aunt Carolina!" Savannah found her voice. "What

are you doing here?" The question ended in a squeak
of disbelief. She glanced at Elias. His eyes burned hotly
and his jaw muscles were tense. He knew.

Aunt Carolina surveyed the room like a general sizing up a barracks. If Savannah hadn't been so shocked,
she would've laughed at the way the children straightened and stared. After her initial surprise, it was all Savannah could do not to race down the aisle and throw
herself into Aunt Carolina's comforting embrace. All
her homesickness and despair rose up and tried to crowd
into her throat, eventually leaking out her eyes as two
tears plummeted down her cheeks.

Her aunt's eyebrows canted. "Obviously, I've come
to see you. I've just arrived in town. This gentleman
and his brother were kind enough to drive me the rest
of the way."

Elias flipped the scarf over his head to lie on his
neck and down his coat lapels. "Kids, I think school is
dismissed for the day. Bundle up. It's brisk out there."

The children moved slowly, not at all as they normally would when being given early release. Johann
sent Savannah a troubled look, and she tried to pull herself together. Drawing a handkerchief from her sleeve,
she wiped her cheeks.

"It's all right. Children, this is my aunt, Miss Carolina Cox, and she's come all the way from Raleigh to
see me. I didn't realize how much I had missed her until
I saw her again, and that is why I'm crying—because
I'm happy. Do as Sheriff Parker says and head home.
Hakon and Astrid, you make sure everyone is properly buttoned up, hats and gloves for everyone." She
stopped herself when she almost said that she would
see them tomorrow.

She wouldn't see them tomorrow. Most of them she

might never see again. If Tyler was here, he must have come to talk about her resignation. Her heart felt like a bag of sand with a hole in the bottom. Perhaps she would come in the morning, just to say goodbye to them. She owed them that, didn't she?

When the last student had filed out, Aunt Carolina unbuttoned her coat—much too thin and light for this place and time—and stood before the stove, holding her hands to the heat. "I thought I knew what cold was, but I see I was mistaken."

Tyler came in, stomping the snow from his boots and blowing on his hands. "I blanketed the horse. It's almost as cold inside as out."

Elias opened the stove door and shoveled in more coal. "Why *is it* so cold in here? Haven't you been watching the fire?"

He sounded angry, and his movements were quick and jerky. Savannah couldn't meet his eyes. Why did he have to be here while she rehashed her failure in front of her boss?

Tyler drew a paper out of his breast pocket, and she knew it was her letter. "I have to say, this is most disconcerting. I only this morning received your resignation, and it disturbs me very much."

Savannah nodded, her chest aching.

"Is anyone else aware of this? The school board? The Halvorsons?"

She shook her head. "I thought you should know first."

Elias grunted and crossed his arms. He backed up to lean against a windowsill, and his face could've been carved from stone.

Tyler sat in the front row where Ingrid usually sat, and put his elbows on his knees. "I'm glad of that, because there's still time to turn this thing around. It's not too late to forget all about this letter. Perhaps you were merely overwrought after your ordeal? Or did someone say something to you to make you feel you need to resign? Frankly, I'm baffled."

Faced with his questions, with the disappointment and puzzlement in Tyler's eyes, Savannah froze. Elias already knew the reason. Hadn't he told his brother what had happened? How she'd endangered the children? He had to agree with her decision to resign. After all, he'd been the one to tell her in the first place that she wasn't equipped to live here, to be in charge of the students.

She studied her hands. "I am not overwrought. No one said anything. I just need to go."

"But why? What changed? The children love you, the community admires you. You've made friends and fit in so nicely, if all the reports are to be believed. I don't understand it." Tyler beseeched her.

Elias slammed the stove door. "I don't know why we're even asking. Be glad she had the grace to at least tell you she's leaving, and call it done." He glared, making Savannah feel small and incapable. "You can't hold her against her will. If she wants to go, let her. I told you in the beginning it was a mistake to hire someone from so far away. I told you she wouldn't stick."

His words pierced deep, and Savannah gasped. She'd known this would be difficult, but his anger rolled off him in waves. He had to be furious with her for being so ignorant about blizzards. When they'd been trapped, he'd hidden his anger well after the first outburst, no doubt to keep the children from being frightened, but now he could let it have free rein. He was probably thinking *good riddance*.

Aunt Carolina rolled her eyes and sailed up the aisle.

"Gentlemen, I suggest you give Savannah and me some privacy. I'll get to the bottom of things, and we'll have a resolution one way or another. Perhaps you could take my belongings to Savannah's lodging place while we sort this out?"

"There's no room at the Halvorsons', and there's sickness in the house." Elias picked up his hat. "I'll take your things over to my folks' place. You can stay there for the next couple of days until the stage comes back. It will take me an hour or so, but I'll pick you up then."

Tyler rose, but hesitated.

"Go ahead." Aunt Carolina flicked her hand toward the door. "I'm sure we can get along better on our own. We will see you in one hour."

When the door closed, Savannah flew down the aisle and into Aunt Carolina's arms. The smell of the lavender water she always used surrounded Savannah, and she couldn't hold back the tears.

After a few moments, Aunt Carolina took her by the shoulders. "Now, now. Brace up, child. I'm glad to see you, too, but this sobbing needs to stop so we can get to the root of the problem. Where is your handkerchief?"

Savannah allowed her aunt to direct her to a chair, comforted at having someone else in charge. She mopped her cheeks and sniffed. "I never expected you to come all this way."

"I never expected to need to," Aunt Carolina said, as drily as ever. "Your telegram was much too cryptic for my peace of mind. After all, week by week, we've received glowing letters, praising the people, the freedom, the fresh air of Snowflake, then suddenly a telegram saying you have to leave and will be home as soon as you can make arrangements? I packed my bags and was on the train that very night."

Gratitude welled up, along with more tears, and Savannah swallowed. "Thank you."

"After all, I feel responsible for all of this."

"What? Why?"

"I'm the one who let you come here in the first place. The one who let you run away from your troubles. I was of two minds about it at the time, and now I wish I'd put my foot down and forced you to stay." Aunt Carolina sat on the front bench, crossing her arms and shaking her head. "You ran then, and you're running now."

"I'm not running." It wasn't running when it was for everyone's good, was it?

"Suppose you tell me what happened, and I will judge for myself."

Haltingly, Savannah started with her arrival here and how Elias had been doubtful of her suitability. "And I was proving him wrong. I loved it here. Even though I had some adjusting to do, and a few hiccups." Not speaking the language, the skunk, the frozen pump handle. "I was succeeding. Until the storm hit. I didn't realize it was a blizzard. I didn't know how dangerous it would be to let the children go. If Elias hadn't come when he did, they all would've perished, and I would've caused it."

"It isn't your fault. You'd never seen a storm like that before. Next time, you'll know better."

"It was my fault that we ran out of coal. It was my fault that I was ready to send children out into the teeth of a blizzard. I wouldn't have known what to do, even if I had kept the children in the school. I would've let them all sleep through the night, and they might've frozen. Elias knew to wake them up and get them moving. I have nightmares nearly every night that the children are lost and I can't find them in the storm. Don't you see? Elias was right. I had no business coming here to teach, being in charge of these students. He's so angry at me for my stupidity that he can barely be in the same room with me. After all, who's to say that, next time, my lack of knowledge won't get someone hurt or killed?"

Aunt Carolina frowned. "What about your contract? What about your obligation?"

"You don't understand. I can't stay. I'm jeopardizing the children if I do. When the school board finds out, they'll be only too glad to see me go. I'm surprised Tyler's resisting at all. The children's welfare has to come first."

"Are you sure it is the children you're thinking of, or is it your pride?"

Savannah's chin came up. "My pride? I'm as humbled as I can possibly be. My pride got killed the day Girard walked out on me on our wedding day." How could Aunt Carolina say such a thing? She had stood there in the church vestibule as all Savannah's dreams crumbled to dust. She knew how humiliated Savannah had been.

"Are you sure it got killed, or was it just wounded? You ran from Raleigh because you couldn't stand the pity and the whispers. If your pride was dead, you wouldn't have cared. Now you're afraid someone might find out that something you'd never encountered before almost got the better of you, that perhaps you're not as capable and self-sufficient as you've been pretending to be. And there's one major point that you've not mentioned at all."

Stung, Savannah asked, "What?"

"What about the young man who has been filling up so many pages of your letters? The sheriff, who, if I might say, seemed quite put out and startled at the idea of your resignation. Are you sure you're not running from him?"

Fisting her hands, Savannah rose. "I am not running from Elias. I've explained why I'm unsuited to teach here. The safety of the children is all I am concerned about. Elias is only angry that all his predictions about me have proved true."

Aunt Carolina sized her up and shook her head. "You sound as if you truly believe that. You're clearly distraught. We'll let the matter rest for now. Tell me something about the family I'm to stay with."

Glad to be on safer ground, Savannah told her about the Parkers' comfortable farmhouse and how delightful Ian and Tova were. By the end of the hour, she'd spoken of nearly everyone in the settlement that she knew. Aunt Carolina asked pointed questions, and Savannah answered faithfully.

"You've come to know people quite well here. From complete outsider to one of their own, by the sounds of things."

"Not really. They've been very kind, but it was always supposed to be a temporary position. They'll do much better with someone else. I'll find another teaching position."

"In Raleigh?"

"No, but somewhere in the South, no doubt." Somewhere she knew the culture, the pitfalls, the dangers.

"I hear your young man coming." Aunt Carolina rose and began buttoning her coat. "We're not finished discussing this, Savannah. At the very least, I believe you owe it to the people of Snowflake to finish out your contract."

"And I am just as certain that I should not."

It wasn't Elias who opened the door, but Tyler. "Have you changed her mind?"

"She remains adamant at this time." Aunt Carolina turned to him, leaning on her walking stick. "I shall try again tomorrow. Are your parents prepared to take me in as a guest?"

"Yes, ma'am. My ma is looking forward to getting to know some of Savannah's family. Savannah, can we give you a ride to the Halvorsons'?"

"You go ahead. I have some things to finish up here."

As Tyler ushered Aunt Carolina out, Savannah overheard him asking, "Do you think you'll be able to convince her to stay?"

"It's too soon to tell. She can be quite headstrong when she latches hold of an idea."

Savannah shook her head, firming her resolve as she banked the fire and cleaned the blackboard. Aunt Carolina had it all wrong. It wasn't her pride or her heart that made her have to leave.

It was fear. Fear that Elias had been right all along.

Elias stayed in the barn until after dark, currying horses, cleaning tack, killing time. He'd seen Savannah arrive to visit her aunt, and the sight of her twisted his muscles. How had he been so wrong?

Were all women fickle? Leading a man to believe he had a chance at winning her heart, at making a life with her, then ripping those hopes to shreds and walking away as if he didn't matter?

He thrust the pitchfork into the pile of hay and swung down the ladder from the haymow. His stomach rumbled, but he ignored it. Time enough to return to the house when Savannah had gone and their guest was in bed.

He took up a broom and began sweeping the center aisle, clearing stray bits of straw and dirt. The latch lifted on the small door set into the larger rolling one, and Elias looked over his shoulder, expecting his father or brother.

Ma held her lantern high and eased inside the barn, shutting the door behind her to keep out the cold.

Elias stacked his hands on the top of the broom handle and rested his chin on his wrists.

"You did not come in for dinner." She spoke Norwegian.

"I wasn't hungry."

"I think it is something more. Your brother tells me Savannah is leaving?" Ma hung the lantern from a peg and folded her hands at her waist. She wore a scarf over her head, and her heavy coat and mittens. And her most concerned expression.

"That's what she says." He flicked the broom, raising a puff of dust.

"Why?"

He shrugged. "She didn't tell me. She didn't tell Tyler, either. But it doesn't matter. She's just one in a long string of teachers who couldn't stick it out. I think we'll be better off to send one of the older girls from here to school somewhere else, and bring her back to teach when she's trained."

"You did not have a fight, you two?"

"Nope. Far as I know everything's the same as it has always been between us. Which isn't saying much." He flipped the broom around and hung it in its place among the barn tools. "I told Tyler from the beginning it was a mistake to hire her. She's a good teacher. And she seemed to fit in fine in Snowflake, but it was all a sham. First time it gets hard, she's a puff of smoke on the horizon."

Tova stepped close, taking his face between her hands and staring up into his eyes. "You are lying. To me, yes, but mostly to yourself. I know my son. You care about her, and if she leaves, it will break your heart."

He swallowed, wanting to jerk his head from her grasp, but not wanting to hurt his mother that way.

"Elias, you fought it for a very long time. Longer than made sense, until I remembered Britta. You thought you were falling in love with her when she left you. Now you are afraid Savannah will do the same thing, only this time, the love is real. Are you going to let her leave without telling her how you feel? Maybe she would stay if she knew the truth."

"And maybe she wouldn't." He covered his mother's hands with his and drew them down. "If she wants to leave, we can't make her stay. If she would cut and run without explaining herself, would I really want her to stay at all?"

"You are afraid. You are afraid to tell her how you feel."

It stuck in his craw, but he had to admit he was. But it was much easier to hide behind anger and pretended indifference.

"Maybe she is also afraid of something? The storm frightened her very much. And Per Halvorson's illness." Ma gripped Elias's hands. "Maybe she is afraid to be here alone without someone to help her, someone to love her and care for her and make her brave."

And maybe she just wanted out. "Her aunt's here to take her home. They'll leave on the Saturday stage, and we'll never see them again."

"Only if you let that happen, son."

Chapter Nineteen

"I can't help thinking you're making a mistake." Aunt Carolina supervised the piling of their bags in the stage office. "Be careful with that harp, young man."

Savannah sighed, her heart heavy. Yesterday at school had been so hard. The children hadn't understood, and she couldn't explain it to them. Every face asked *why?*

Ingrid had cried. "Do you not like us anymore, Teacher?"

She loved them so much, she had to go.

Even now, waiting for the stage, her throat burned and her eyes welled.

Lars brought in the last bag and added it to the stack. Savannah patted his shoulder. "Thank you, Lars. Remember to keep reading and learning. And tell Rut the same for me."

"Why should we read and learn? Nobody cares if we have school. The next teacher will not stay. Nobody stays." He shrugged off her hand.

Savannah sucked in a deep, painful breath. Before she could answer Lars, the door opened again, and a man's silhouette filled the doorway.

Her heart jammed in her throat.

Elias.

She'd hoped to avoid facing him one last time. And yet she'd longed to see him. She braced herself for whatever he'd come to say.

He didn't say a word, striding into the room and taking her hand. With a tug, he turned and headed back outside.

"What are you doing?"

Keeping her hand firmly in his, he strode across the street to the jail. Saturday shoppers stopped and gawked on the sidewalks. Savannah looked over her shoulder to where Aunt Carolina stood on the steps, hands on hips, mouth agape.

Savannah tugged against Elias's grip, but he didn't loosen his hold. "What are you doing? Let me go." She wasn't afraid of him...this was Elias, after all. But his actions puzzled her.

Elias nudged the jailhouse door open and marched straight to the first cell. With a little push, he had her inside, then swung the door shut and locked it. With a clatter, the keys landed on his desk.

So he was upset with her. That was to be expected, but locking her in a jail cell? In view of the entire town? Outrage burned through her, and she gripped the bars. "Would you kindly tell me what it is you think you're doing?"

"I'm arresting you."

She gasped. "On what charge?"

"Breach of contract."

"Breach of... That's preposterous."

He held up a bundle of papers. "I have your signature right here, a signature I witnessed, by the way. You are contracted to teach at the Snowflake School until the end of May."

She shook her head. "But nowhere does it say that failure to do so results in incarceration."

"Savannah." He threw the papers down on a chair and plunked his hat next to them. Raking his fingers through his hair, he paced the small area in front of the cell. "I'm not letting you go until you tell me why you're leaving. You owe me at least that much after all we've been through."

She shook her head. "You know why I'm leaving. You're the only one who does. I'm surprised you haven't broadcast it to all and sundry, since it completely proves your point."

He stopped, his brows lowered, questions in his eyes. "If I knew, I wouldn't be this frustrated. Savannah, what went wrong? I thought, during the storm, that we'd come to an understanding of sorts."

All her fear and guilt rose up like a monster and enveloped her with strong arms. "We did come to an understanding. I finally admitted that you were right all along. I don't belong here. It was a mistake coming here at all."

"Savannah, make sense. How could it be a mistake? People here love you…" He swallowed. "We don't want to lose you. You're the best teacher we've ever had."

"How can you say that? You've held all along that hiring me was a mistake. And you were right. You were there. I almost killed my students. I was too stupid to know the dangers of a blizzard. You've read the newspaper reports, seen the damage the storm did, the lives lost. If you hadn't arrived when you did, those losses would've included the entire Snowflake school. Who is to say that I won't endanger them further if I stay?"

Fear and guilt clogged her throat, and she couldn't look at him.

"I don't belong here. You've maintained it all along, and I've proved it." The bitterness of her words coated her tongue. She hung her head, feeling small and broken. "Just let me go."

"I can't." He stepped close, close enough for her to see the torment in his gray eyes. "If I let you go, I'll be losing something too precious to me to bear." His voice got husky, and his hands covered hers.

"Savannah, I was wrong from the outset. I was so wrong I don't know why you didn't hit me over the head with one of those many bags of yours. You coming here was the best thing to ever happen to me. Stop blaming yourself for something that didn't happen. It's not a crime to be a greenhorn, though I'll admit I made it sound like one." He squeezed her fingers.

"Savannah, I love you. I want to marry you and walk beside you the rest of my life. You've taught me so much already about being brave and taking on new things. You've brought your Southern culture up here and melded it with these hardy Norwegians, and we're better for it. You've embraced your students and their families with an open heart. Can't you open it a little further and embrace me, too?"

She lifted her eyes to his, doubt squeezing her chest. He loved her? He didn't think her coming here a mistake? He thought she had value?

"But what about everything you said? What about my unsuitability?" She had to make sure. "You were so angry when you found us ready to head out into the blizzard. You said…" She stopped.

"I was an idiot of the first water. I take it all back. Hiring you was the best thing Tyler ever did. From the first minute I saw you, I was a goner, and I was fighting it because I didn't want to be hurt again. But every time I turned around you were doing something sweet and thoughtful and brave."

She felt as if she were stepping out onto a frozen lake, testing the ice to see if it would hold her. "You're serious?"

"I've never been more serious. When I think of all the ways you were proving me wrong every day you were here... The way you worked the trade of school supplies for winter clothes so you wouldn't hurt anyone's feelings, the way you rode Elsker across the prairie with your hair flying free, the way you're willing to try out everything in Norwegian culture. Even that first Sunday, when you worshipped openly even though you didn't understand a word of the service or the songs, I couldn't help but admire you. It all adds up to the fact that you're the perfect woman for Snowflake. The perfect woman for me." He pressed his forehead against the cell bars, closing his eyes as if bracing himself for bad news.

Hope and happiness had her standing on tiptoe, clinging to the bars. "Are you sure?"

He raised his head, eyes snapping open. "More sure than anything." His chest heaved as he drew a huge breath. "Savannah Cox, will you marry me?"

She'd just opened her mouth to answer when the door banged open and Aunt Carolina barged in, followed by Elias's parents and brother. "Savannah, what are you doing in that cell?" her aunt demanded.

"I've arrested her for breach of contract, and I'm holding her until she agrees to stay in Snowflake." Elias spoke without breaking his gaze from Savannah's. A teasing light glowed there, and she bit her lower lip, unable to believe what was happening. Love shone in his eyes, and all she wanted was for everyone else to leave and for there to be no more bars between them, metaphorically or physically.

Tyler stepped forward. "Elias, as much as I appreciate the gesture, I don't think throwing her in jail is the answer. It might cost me my job and my political aspirations, but I think you should let her go."

"Nope, not until she agrees to marry me."

Savannah tried to smother her smile, but couldn't. She blinked back happy tears.

Aunt Carolina laughed and clapped. "Finally, you've both come to your senses. I thought he was really going to let her leave." She put her arm around Tova and hugged her. "All our late night talking and worrying was for nothing."

Elias shook his head. "You two have been conspiring? I'm not even surprised."

"Not conspiring. Praying." Aunt Carolina raised her eyebrow at Elias's mother, who nodded.

"And maybe a little conspiring." Tova giggled. "I am so happy for you both."

"Let her out, son." Ian Parker tossed him the keys.

"I can't."

"Why not?"

"Because she hasn't given me an answer. You all barged in at the crucial moment." He put his hands on his hips. "Well, Savannah, what's it going to be?"

Savannah's lips trembled as she looked from one dear face to another. She had rocketed from despair to delight, and all because Elias loved her.

"It's going to be yes. Yes. Yes. Yes."

The keys rattled in the lock, and he swung the door wide.

Elias gathered her in a hug that lifted her feet from

the floor. He glanced at the onlookers and shrugged. "I hadn't counted on an audience for this, but right now, I don't care."

She wound her arms around his neck, knocking his hat off, and raised her face to his. "Me, either. Oh, Elias, I love you so much. I think I've been waiting for this all my life."

"Me, too."

His kiss sent shivers through her, and she had to hang on tight lest she spin off into space. His hold tightened, and his whiskers rasped on her cheek. Dizzy, near to bursting with happiness, she tunneled her fingers in his hair and kissed him back, trying to show him how much she loved him.

"Tyler," Ian said. "I think we're going to need a special dispensation from the school board. Looks like the teacher will be getting married before too long."

Elias broke the kiss with a laugh, and Savannah tucked her head under his chin, clutching his lapels. Her cheeks were flushed, she knew, and all she wanted was to be alone with him. His arms stayed around her, and his heart thundered under her ear, twin to her own racing pulse.

"Guess I'll have to take it up with the school board, but I don't think anyone will mind as long as she's staying in Snowflake for good."

Epilogue

Savannah stepped down from the sleigh, turning back to make sure Charlotte and Virginia were following. Her sisters shivered and hurried toward the church. Lars drove the horses around to the leeward side of the building, grinning and red-cheeked.

Someone had swept the steps free of snow from the night before, but huge flakes drifted down from the clouds, dotting Savannah's dark cloak with bits of frozen lace.

"I can't believe you want to live here. You'll turn into a block of ice." Charlotte's teeth chattered. "All this snow and it's only February. You still have weeks of winter left. I'd be surprised if you see the ground before June."

Savannah stepped into the vestibule, her heart knocking against her ribs. She couldn't help but compare this day to her supposed wedding day last summer. Her arrival this time was much more subdued, her dress simpler, the flowers made of silk instead of coming from Aunt Georgette's garden. The guest list was much smaller, but it contained everyone she loved.

Butterflies attacked her stomach, and her heart

skipped and hopped, making it difficult to breathe as she battled her nerves and her memories.

"We were about to send out a search party." Father, immaculate in a black frock coat, checked his watch. He'd arrived last night, spoken at length privately with Elias and given his blessing. "You look suspiciously happy."

She gave him an unsteady smile. "Were you this nervous on your wedding day?"

"Probably worse." He shot his cuffs. "Until I saw your mother walking down the aisle. Then I was fine."

If only Savannah could see Elias right now, perhaps she wouldn't feel so wobbly.

"Here, let me help you." Charlotte reached for Savannah's hood. "I hope you didn't crush your dress."

She couldn't answer, as her thoughts tumbled with the questions that had plagued her in the middle of the night—silly questions, but ones she couldn't seem to quash. What if Elias wasn't there when she walked up the aisle? What if, like Girard, he abandoned her at the last minute? It all felt so foreign and yet familiar.

"You look beautiful." Charlotte stepped back, and Virginia handed Savannah a bouquet of white silk roses.

Savannah smoothed her gown, not the elaborate satin and lace she'd worn in Raleigh, but an ivory woolen dress with pale blue lace trim. Her hair fell in waves and curls to her waist. So strange to have her hair down during the day, but it was the Norwegian custom.

Tova peeked around the vestibule doorway, cradling a square carved box in her arms. "You are ready?" she whispered.

"Almost." Savannah swallowed hard. "There's just the one thing."

"Here, I will help." Tova opened the box. "You are

a beautiful bride. My son is very blessed, and so is our whole family." She lifted the silver crown from the box.

"You're so generous to lend me your wedding crown." Savannah bent her head, and Tova put the small, gleaming circlet on her hair, her eyes misting.

"I did not have a daughter to pass it down to. You make my heart happy by wearing it."

Virginia helped pin the veil in the back. Savannah checked her reflection in the small mirror by the door. "Now I feel like a Norwegian bride." All around the top of the crown, tiny silver snowflakes stood up on each of the points.

Tova hugged Savannah one more time and left them, giving the signal for the music to start. Aunt Carolina had vetoed the *psalmodikon* as the only form of music and hired a string quartet from Saint Paul to play. It was amazing, all that she'd accomplished in two short weeks. Everything from the dress to the music to the flowers, to getting the rest of the family here.

Aunt Carolina had hit Snowflake like a blizzard.

Charlotte and Virginia began their slow walk up the aisle, and Savannah took her father's offered elbow.

"It's not too late to change your mind, you know," he said, covering her hand with his. "Are you going to be happy so far from home?"

They rounded the corner and entered the sanctuary, and all her fears and nerves slipped away. She raised her chin and took a deep breath. Elias stood at the front of the church, handsome and manly in a dark suit. His eyes locked with hers, and she could see the pride and love shining there. In that instant she knew that wherever he was would always be home for her.

"I am home. And I'm very happy."

When she reached Elias's side, he took her hand, squeezing her fingers gently. "You look beautiful."

She remembered little of the service beyond the certainty in Elias's voice when he said, "I do."

"You may now kiss your bride."

The kiss was a promise, and when he finally took his lips from hers, he rested his forehead against hers and whispered, "I love you, my little Snowflake bride."

Applause burst out around them. Savannah laughed, looking from one familiar face to another, filled with joy.

"Get ready," Elias whispered in her ear, sending a shiver down her spine. "Norwegians love a good party."

They were swept outside and into a sleigh, the first in a cavalcade of wedding guests headed toward the schoolhouse. Elias kept his arm around her and piled on the lap robes as Lars drove.

Savannah and her sisters had spent the previous day, with the help of her students and under Aunt Carolina and Aunt Georgette's direction, decorating the schoolhouse for the reception. The women of Snowflake had brought out their best hardanger tablecloths and silver and rosemaled serving dishes.

Elias helped her from the sleigh, taking her hand and guiding her up the steps. "So much seems to have happened to us in this little schoolhouse. And here we are, set to make some more memories."

Wedding guests flowed around them in the foyer, laughing, talking. Savannah found herself tugged away from Elias and into a crowd of ladies who removed her cloak and fussed over her. Tova beamed, Ian chatted with her father and people found places at the long tables they'd set up. Agneta and Per entered, Per looking thin and drawn from his illness, but on the mend. Savannah's students took people's coats and passed around glasses of punch.

Savannah leaned to the side to see around Aunt Carolina, only to find her new husband's eyes on her. He winked and grinned, then excused himself from the knot of men surrounding him and threaded his way toward her.

"That's enough monopolizing my bride." His hand reached through the ladies and clasped hers. "Ma'am, the sheriff wants a word with you."

The women giggled and gave them indulgent smiles as Savannah went into his embrace. Heat swirled in her cheeks as Elias put his arm around her waist and guided her to the head table, where her teacher's desk normally stood. "Your chair, Mrs. Parker."

Like the ceremony, much of the reception passed in a blur for Savannah. The food, the speeches, even the dancing. The only element in focus, the only thing that stood out for her, was Elias. Holding her hand, touching her shoulder, brushing her curls off her face. He was the pivot point of her world, and she suspected it would be that way for the rest of her life.

Finally, he stood and held her chair, tucking her hand into his elbow and working his way toward the door. Laughter and teasing followed them through the room and into the foyer, where Elias took her navy cloak and wrapped it around her shoulders. He eased her hair out from under the collar, lingering over the task.

"I've wanted to touch your hair since the moment I met you." He threaded his fingers through her curls. "You have beautiful hair, Mrs. Parker."

Her breath caught in her throat, and she had to try twice before any words would come out. "I don't think I'll ever tire of you calling me Mrs. Parker."

He brushed a quick kiss across her lips. "You ready to go home?"

Savannah followed him out into the cold. The snow had stopped, and overhead, an indigo sky strewn with diamond-point stars reached from horizon to horizon. Lars drew the sleigh up to the door, and Elias handed Savannah into the backseat.

Once they were on their way, with Elias's arm firmly around her, tucking her into his side, she stiffened. "Elias, where *is* home?" She couldn't believe she hadn't thought to ask earlier.

He laughed, hugging her. "I wondered when you'd get around to that. Actually, I have a house. I started building it a couple years ago and never finished it. It's about a half a mile from my folks' place, on the farm property. This past two weeks, while you were getting ready for the wedding, I was working on it. I had a lot of help, too. Nearly every man and boy in the township showed up to plaster and paint and build furniture. Ma and Agneta brought your trunks and harp over this morning while you were sequestered with your aunts and sisters, getting all gussied up." He took advantage of her astonishment to kiss her again. "And I have to say, they did a first-rate job. You are the most beautiful bride I ever saw. When you rounded the corner at the church and started up the aisle, I almost had to sit down to catch my breath."

"I was so nervous, remembering last time, afraid maybe you wouldn't be there. Then I saw you and everything was fine." She laid her head on his shoulder, relishing the strength and security of his embrace.

They drew up before a pretty little white house. A furry mass rose from the front porch and shook his coat, sending snow flying. With an eager bark, Captain flew down the stairs to cavort in the drifts alongside the sleigh.

Lars dropped them off and pulled away, and Elias turned to Savannah, sweeping her up into his arms and striding up the steps. Savannah let out a shriek and flung her arms around his neck, laughing.

He opened the door and stepped across the threshold, easing her to her feet, but keeping his arms around her. Using his boot, he shut the door, leaned down and whispered, "Welcome home, Mrs. Parker. Welcome home."

* * * * *

Dear Reader,

Thank you so much for coming along on this journey with Savannah and Elias. In their story I got to combine so many of my special loves: history, romance, Minnesota, pioneers and storytelling. I admire the brave and hardy souls who left everything familiar to come to a new land where they hoped to accomplish their dreams, not only for themselves, but also for their children. I wonder if I would have their bravery and fortitude in a similar situation.

Another thing I love is connecting with readers who enjoy the same things I do, and I hope you come find me at my online home at www.ericavetsch.com. There you can find links to my Facebook page, learn about my writing and sign up for my newsletter.

Warmly,
Erica Vetsch

COMING NEXT MONTH FROM
Love Inspired® Historical
Available June 7, 2016

PONY EXPRESS HERO
Saddles and Spurs
by Rhonda Gibson

Pony Express rider Jacob Young sets out to search for his birth mother, but instead he discovers his orphaned five-year-old half sister and her pretty guardian, Lilly Johnson. And when he figures out that someone's trying to hurt them, he vows to be their protector.

BRIDE BY ARRANGEMENT
Cowboy Creek
by Karen Kirst

On the run from a dangerous man, widow Grace Longstreet is determined to protect her twin daughters—even if it means pretending she's the mail-order bride Sheriff Noah Burgess's friends secretly arranged for him. But can their blossoming relationship survive her deception?

ONCE MORE A FAMILY
by Lily George

In order to bring his young daughter home, Texas rancher Jack Burnett needs a wife—but he won't marry for love again. And an arranged marriage to penniless socialite Ada Westmore will benefit them both...if she can survive life on the prairie.

A NANNY FOR KEEPS
Boardinghouse Betrothals
by Janet Lee Barton

After widowed Sir Tyler Walker's daughters run off their latest nanny, he hires the schoolteacher next door as a short-term replacement. But when Sir Tyler and his two little girls fall for Georgia Marshall, will the temporary arrangement become permanent?

SPECIAL EXCERPT FROM

Love Inspired **HISTORICAL**

A mail-order bride seeks a fresh start for herself and her twin daughters with a small-town Kansas sheriff— but will she lose it all when her secret is revealed?

Read on for a sneak preview of
BRIDE BY ARRANGEMENT,
the exciting conclusion to the series
***COWBOY CREEK**.*

"Make another move, and I'll shoot you where you stand…" He trailed off, jaw sagging. Had he entered the wrong house?

"Don't shoot! I can explain! I—I have a letter. From Will Canfield." A petite dark-haired woman standing on the other side of his table lifted an envelope in silent entreaty.

At the mention of his friend's name, he slowly lowered his weapon. But his defensive instincts still surged through him. When he didn't speak, she gestured limply to the ornate leather trunks stacked on either side of his bedroom door. "Mr. Canfield was supposed to meet us at the station. His porter arrived in his stead… Simon was his name. He said something about a posse and outlaws." A delicate shudder shook her frame. "He said you wouldn't mind if we brought these inside. I do apologize for invading your home like this, but I had no idea when you would return, and it is June out there."

Her gaze roamed his face, her light brown eyes widening ever so slightly as they encountered his scars. It was like this every time. He braced himself for the inevitable disgust. Pity. Revulsion. Told himself again it didn't matter.

When her expression reflected nothing more than curiosity, irrational anger flooded him.

"What are you doing in my home?" he snapped. "How do you know Will?"

"I'm Constance Miller. I'm the bride Mr. Canfield sent for."

"Will's already got a wife."

Pink kissed her cheekbones. "Not for him. For you."

His throat closed. He wouldn't have.

"I was summoned to Cowboy Creek to be your bride. Your friend didn't tell you." A sharp crease brought her brows together.

"I'm afraid not." Slipping off his worn Stetson, Noah hooked it on the chair and dipped his head toward the crumpled parchment. "May I?"

Miss Miller didn't appear inclined to approach him, so he laid his gun on the mantel and crossed to the square table. He took the envelope she extended across to him and slipped the letter free. The handwriting was unmistakable. Heat climbed up his neck as he read the description of himself. He stuffed it back inside and tossed it onto the tabletop. "I'm afraid you've come all the way out here for nothing. The trip was a waste, Miss Miller. I am not, nor will I ever be, in the market for a bride."

Don't miss
BRIDE BY ARRANGEMENT
by Karen Kirst, available June 2016 wherever
Love Inspired® Historical books and ebooks are sold.

www.LoveInspired.com

LIHEXP0516

Reading Has Its Rewards

Earn **FREE BOOKS!**

Register at **Harlequin My Rewards** and submit your Harlequin purchases from wherever you shop to earn points for free books and other exclusive rewards.

Plus submit your purchases from now till May 30th for a chance to win a $500 Visa Card*.

Visit **HarlequinMyRewards.com** today

Earn
FREE
REWARDS
Join Today!
HarlequinMyRewards.com

MYR16R1